That Is ALL Wrong!

An Anthology of Offbeat Horror: Vol III

Edited by Jan-Andrew Henderson

A Black Hart Publication

Scotland. Australia.

Published by Black Hart. Copyright © 2022.
www.blackhartentertainment.com

Black Hart Publishing. Brisbane, Australia. Edinburgh, Scotland.

Book Layout © 2019 BookDesignTemplates.com

Edited by Jan-Andrew Henderson
Cover design by Jan-Andrew Henderson and Book Design Stars

That is ALL Wrong!
ISBN: 978-0-6452722-5-3
ISBN: 978-0-6452722-6-0 eBook

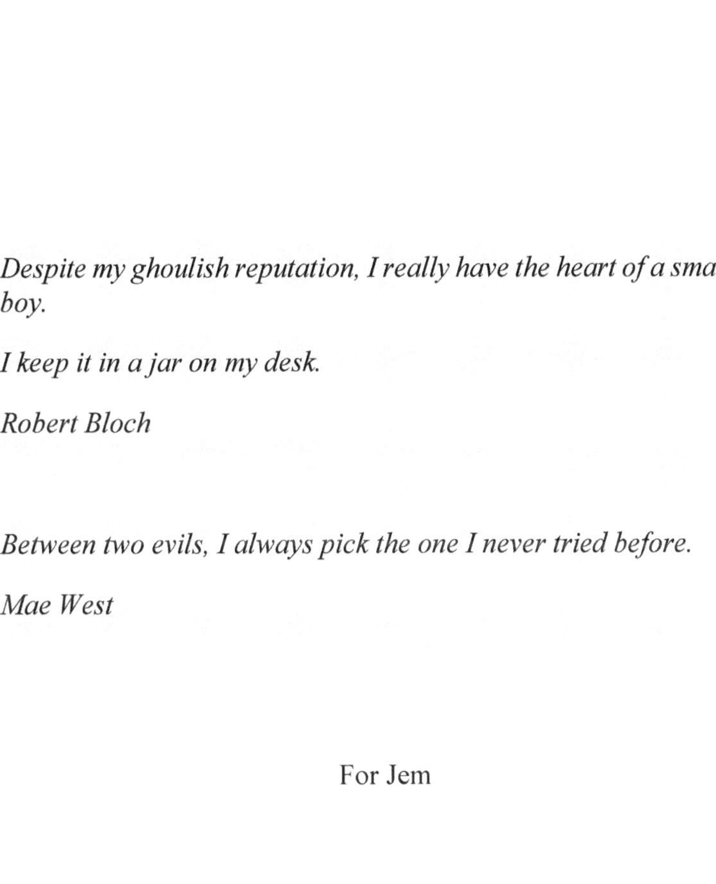

Despite my ghoulish reputation, I really have the heart of a small boy.

I keep it in a jar on my desk.

Robert Bloch

Between two evils, I always pick the one I never tried before.

Mae West

For Jem

Introduction

Welcome to the third and final volume of the *That is Wrong* anthology series of offbeat horror, subtly titled *That is ALL Wrong!*

Here you will find the usual collection of award-winning writers and talented newcomers - but this volume is a slight departure from what came before. The last two instalments tended to shun zombies, werewolves, ghosts, vampires and teens in the woods in favour of something a little more… offbeat. But I received too many excellent submissions featuring horror fan favourites to miss them all out.

I've allowed a few vampires, though they're not the normal sort (a trio called Pork, Shark and Boner and another who attacks postmen). One story throws in every kind of legendary monster you can think of and there are traditional staples like alien invaders, Satanists and even a werewolf - though none are portrayed quite the way you might expect. To up the weirdness quotient, there's also a talking martini, a bathroom guide that ends in tragedy and a woman covered in vaginas.

People sometimes say things like this to me:

Why would you want to dwell on nasty stuff? Isn't there enough horror in the world? Wouldn't you rather read about fairies? Who wants to be more scared, for goodness sakes?

All valid points, apart from the question about fairies - nasty little buggers who will steal your children and replace them with a sinister changeling. Seriously. It obviously happened to my own kids.

So, I've chosen carefully. Some tales are humorous. Some are about mythical creatures or impossible situations which bear no relation to the distressing things we encounter in everyday life. As such, I consider them a pleasant distraction. Or an unpleasant distraction, depending on how you look at it. Others lean right into what is, for me, the most frightening aspect of horror. Being human and all that it entails.

One of the most disturbing stories in this volume is simply about the mundane terror of life in hospital. A shocking twist at the end is merely icing on the cake. Another conjures up dread by exploring the effects of peer pressure on moral decisions. A third explores how females become willing accomplices in the subjugation of their own sex. It is upsetting and may well offend but the theme is certainly prescient. And it was written by a woman, so I have no right to judge.

Besides, we *should* be confronted by the vulgar, weak and tragic side of humanity - not just malign supernatural influences. Edmund Burke famously said *The only thing necessary for the triumph of evil is for good men to do nothing*.

Only he didn't. What he actually wrote was this.

When bad men combine, the good must associate; else they will fall, one by one, an unpitied sacrifice in a contemptible struggle.

No mention of evil at all. He attributes the struggles of the world to the mettle of mortals, not an abstract concept or objective force. Doesn't make for such a good soundbite but it's vastly more accurate. It would be neglectful if some of the stories in this trilogy didn't reflect that.

Words are important. So, I've also included a couple of strange and unique tales that suck you in simply by being so beautifully written.

Words are important. So are the ideas they express. Good horror, like every other genre, should be a vehicle for the best of both. Offbeat horror thinks outside the box we often feel trapped in. This is never a bad thing.

It has been my privilege to sift through thousands of exceptional words and hundreds of wonderful ideas. To collect the ones that struck a real chord with me in this trilogy - *That is SO Wrong!*, *That is TOO Wrong!* and *That is ALL Wrong!*

Or, perhaps, the devil made me do it.

Jan-Andrew Henderson

Contents

The Friendship Machine

Jan-Andrew Henderson

All was quiet in the little town of Sewageboom. The only sound was the patter of raindrops, a cat wailing, the whistling of projectiles in flight, a grinding smash, several loud thumps, a dog barking, the rattle of machine gun fire and a sound like a giant elastic band hitting a trash can.

Harlan McFarlan glanced to the right and left and then above. Satisfied he was alone, he relaxed his karate stance and stood properly upright. He was wearing his usual gangster-style raincoat and had a plastic carrier bag on his head.

He stepped out of the shadows and into the menacing glare of the one unbroken streetlight. A wry smile touched his lips as he realised he had managed to walk all the way through Sewageboom without getting his hair wet. Or mugged. Or shot.

He halted at the doorway of *The Nipple Washers Arms* and ran his fingers fondly over teeth marks on the window sill. Then he stepped inside to find his client.

A few seconds later, he was back on the street, trying to untangle the door handle from his pocket. It came off in his hand, so he dropped it and continued indoors.

Memories flooded back. This was where his mother had met his father. Harlan Senior was employed as a living slot machine, while mum was president of the local biker chapter - *Satan's Chicken Slippers.*

Harlan had spent a happy childhood here. D ad would plonk him in the spittoon, out of harm's way, while his mum amused the boy by dropping her glass eye in his milk. Now it was a sports bar with all the personality of Donald Trump's answering machine.

"Heh," Harlan grumped. "In my day, the dudes in here were so real they could fart the blues."

He spotted Fats, skulking in a dark corner, nursing a pint of Guinness.

Harlan flicked a cigarette into his friend's drink to get his attention and waved to a group of scantily clad females, who completely ignored him. He plonked himself down opposite his companion with an odd sounding crunch.

"Don't sit on my pork crackles," Fats scowled.

"No sweat. Where did you put them?"

"Forget it."

"Don't just slouch about like a massive lounge lizard on a smooth jazz rock." Harlan glanced around. "You're supposed to give me the lowdown on the joint. That's what I'd be paying you for. If I was paying you."

"I came in an hour ago and asked a few subtle questions. But nobody had seen any strange faces."

"Except yours, of course," Harlan chuckled.

"Don't add to my self-esteem issues," Fats protested. "I hung around near the ladies' toilets for a while and even tried pumping the barman. He certainly seemed to like it."

"No clue as to who our client might be?" Harlan asked.

"I think the correct term is *whom*. That's an odd word, isn't it?"

"Get on with it, Fats."

"I did spot Louis the Tomahawk and Eddie the Beagle. They were having a dingo tickling contest in the back room."

"Louis and Eddie?" A look of alarm flashed across Harlan's face.

"I saw your girlfriend as well."

"Candy-Anne? I thought she'd moved away!" The look of alarm turned to one of panic and Harlan slid under the table.

"It's OK." Fats pulled him up by the ears. "I think she's unconscious."

"She's not my girlfriend anymore, buddy. She ditched me, remember?"

"And beat you senseless."

"Yeah. Let's not go there."

"Anyway, she came past, balancing four vodkas in each hand. She's a lovely girl, so I asked if you two were ever going to be an item again."

"What did she say?"

"She smashed a chair over my head."

"Wasn't in too bad a mood, then."

"Her eyes were crossed, so it was hard to tell." Fats pointed an accusing finger at him. "You broke her heart."

"And she broke my nose," Harlan sighed. "I swear she's not the girl I used to know."

"Oh, she is. I recognised her." Fats took a sip of his drink. "She told me if she saw you, she'd remove your unmentionables with a claw hammer."

"My unmentionables?"

"Yeah. So, I better not mention them. I think she's still mad about you always lying to her."

"I don't lie," Harlan huffed. "I just find truth a relative thing."

"True. And you can't pick your relatives. That's why friendship is so important."

Harlan stared at him in disbelief.

"Then she staggered off," Fats continued unperturbed. "Left me alone with my thoughts."

"That must have terrified them."

"When you're on your own in a bar, you get to thinking about metaphysical things. Like, what was the name of Kelly Maree's second single? Cause everyone remembers the first one, right?"

"Only if they're over 50 with a penchant for shit disco."

"Suddenly, Louis the Tomahawk was standing next to me, looking like a camel crapped in his window box." Fats twiddled his thumbs. "Then he reached down and grabbed hold of it."

"He *did*?"

"My Guinness. He picked the glass up, looked at it, put it down and walked away without a word. Why would he do that?"

"Perhaps he was trying to out-stare it."

"He's certainly not a man to be tinkled with but I decided to follow him anyway. He and Eddie the Beagle were going from table to table peering into the drinks.

"That's rather unhygienic."

"No. Peering. I stopped to take your girlfriend's head out of the ashtray. Hope I did right."

"Ex-girlfriend," Harlan repeated. "What happened next?"

"It just fell back in again."

"No! Louis and Eddie! What happened next?"

"Well, a really good song came on. It was one of my favourites… and this pretty little red-headed girl was smiling at me."

"Stop being so slap-happy and haberdash!" Harlan snapped. "Who and where is our client?"

"I don't know."

"Come on, mate. You talked to him on the phone!"

"But he didn't say anything except he'd be in here tonight wearing a pink orchid."

"How could you miss *that*?"

"Maybe he took it off. Would you wear a pink orchid in a rough joint like this?"

"It's not really my colour." Harlan tapped his friend's forehead. "Think, Fats. Isn't there anything else?"

"He did sound kind of foreign."

"Great. That means we're looking for someone who can dance in time to the music. Let's just keep our eyes open for something out of the ordinary."

"Candy-Anne is sitting upright and looking around. That count?"

Harlan slid under the table again.

"So she is." His muffled voice drifted up. "Something doesn't smell right, bud."

"That's probably my pork crackling, which you were squashing with your big hot ass."

"*Never* describe my ass as big and hot again." Seeing he was fairly safe in the shadowy booth, Harlan struggled back into his seat. "You know, I miss Candy-Anne, especially when she's wearing a skirt that short."

"It's a skirt?" Fats raised an eyebrow. "I thought it was a belt. You sure know a lot about women, Harlan."

"You've just got to see them as people." He leant over conspiratorially. "You see, Fats, girls are like cars."

"How so?"

"They weigh a lot."

He took off his coat and licked his lips.

"God, I need a drink. I'll go steal us some."

"Can't you just buy one?"

"I'm broke. Back in a mo."

He took off, keeping a wary eye out for Candy-Anne. Soon, sounds of violence erupted from the other side of the bar. Harlan returned carrying a tray of various beverages, including a large cocktail in a hurricane glass, a gaudy flower jostling with a paper umbrella for space on top.

"What an ordeal!" he panted. "I spotted one table where some hoons had just got up to dance. So I helped myself to their drinks. Then I noticed this interesting looking thing on top of the one-armed bandit."

He indicated the cocktail

"Anyhoo, I'd just picked it up and was about to return, mange tout, when Louis the Tomahawk and Eddie the Beagle appeared. Demanded I hand over the tray."

"What a nerve!" Fats was outraged. "They could have stolen their own. I hope you didn't stand for it."

"No. I was going to run. Then I decided to use my head instead."

"You nutted them?"

"I handed them the tray." Harlan looked smug. "See, I noticed a Nick Cave song had just come on.

"So everyone stopped dancing?"

"Correctamundo. The pisshounds returned to find Eddie and Louis holding their booze."

"Nice one! I take it a small fracas ensued."

"Medium rare. I obligingly took the tray back from Louis, as he needed both hands to hold on to his gonads."

"And you got out unscathed?"

"Absolutely. I smacked one bugger in the fist with my face and gave another several thumps in the knee with my nose." He wiped some blood from his lip. "They'll have a few scuff marks on their Nikes they won't forget in a hurry."

He slid a drink towards Fats.

"This one's yours. Half pint of Guinness, one Sambuca with pineapple and two Pickled Tinks. I put them all in the same glass for easy carrying."

"I don't normally mix my drinks," Fats admitted. "But it is Tuesday afternoon."

"This one's for me." Harlan reached for the cocktail. "I think it's a quadruple martini. You could use the umbrella in it to shelter from a typhoon."

He raised the drink to his lips.

"Get your hands *off* me!"

"Who said that?" Harlan looked around, puzzled.

"Listen, friend. Put your tongue near me again and you'll be wearing your tonsils on a string."

Harlan slammed the cocktail down and stared at it in horror. He reached out his hand experimentally.

"I'm warning you!"

"Oh my GOD!

"Sorry to be rude," the cocktail said. "I get a bit abusive when someone tries to swallow me.

"Fats!" Harlan whispered. "My martini is talking to me!"

"I didn't know you'd had a falling out."

"Ha! Ha!" The cocktail gave a snort. "I like that. Nice going, pal."

"It's really talking to me." Harlan's eyes were on stalks. "I can't believe it."

"You *are* pretty anti-social."

"Dislikeable, even," the martini chipped in.

"I'm going to give up drinking."

"Now, that *is* hard to swallow," Fats sniggered.

"Well, I'm not, so paws off." The martini revolved on the table. "You must be Fats."

"Pleased to meet you." He shook the proffered straw. "And you are?"

"Call me Alan. Which one of you is Harlan?"

"I am, of course. The who isn't Fats."

"Of course," Alan gave a hiccup. "It's a bit hard to focus."

"I suppose you haven't got eyes, have you?" Fats said sympathetically.

"It's not that," the cocktail replied. "I'm permanently pissed. Stands to reason, really."

"All right! All right." Harlan ran a hand down his face. "Let's stay calm about this."

"I'm calm as a newt."

"Me too." Fats took a huge gulp of his own concoction. "Drunk as well."

"Let me just check I'm not having a nightmare." Harlan began pinching his cheeks. "Wait a minute… How do you know our names?"

"I ought to," Alan scoffed. "I hired you."

"I knew I recognised your voice from somewhere," Fats slurred.

"God, I need a drink." Harlan reached out.

"Arghhhhhhhhhhhhhhhhhhh!" the martini screamed.

"Arghhhhhhhhhhhhhhhhhhh!" Harlan quickly withdrew his hand. "I'm sorry!"

"I just hope you don't make a habit of drinking your clients, is all."

"We don't know," Fats said. "Haven't had any for years."

"So, you've hired us, eh?" Harlan's shock was quickly replaced by a natural instinct to make money. "All right then, martini. Let's discuss payments."

"Oh, money's no object. I'll pay whatever you want."

"Good, that's exactly what we charge. Who do you want us to kill?"

"Nobody." Alan objected. "I want you to get me out of this place, first of all. There's a girl here and I don't like the way she keeps staring at me."

"Which one?

"Beats me. All human females look the same in the dark."

"Funny," Fats smiled. "That's what Harlan always says."

"I remember she kept falling off her stool and had her skirt on back to front."

"Candy-Anne!" Harlan looked nervously around

"I'm not surprised she was staring at you," Fats commented. "She's an alcoholic."

"Aaaaaaaaaaaaaaargh! Don't let her get me."

"Shhhh, shhhh," Harlan pulled Alan into an embrace. "She isn't an alcoholic. She just drinks more than most people."

"She drinks more than most neighbourhoods," Fats corrected.

"Harlan, I can't breathe."

"Apologies." He let the drink go.

"It's OK. I can't breathe any of the time."

"Let's continue this conversation somewhere else." Harlan shoved the martini towards his companion. "Fats? Put Alan under your coat and we'll blow the joint."

He gave a wry chuckle.

"I haven't sneaked a drink out of this bar since I was eight."

"You're not. I'm sneaking it out." Fats slid the martini into his jacket and weaved towards the door.

"We'll meet around the back," Harlan called. "Don't let the barman catch you."

"No worries, bud. Watch out for those hoons."

"What?" Harlan turned to find a dozen of Sewageboom's finest hard men advancing on him. "Ow! Ooyah, Ouch… Bloody hell… Oooh!"

Fats and Alan sat on upturned milk crates in a smelly side street, singing to each other.

Walk on. Walk on.

With hope in your hearts.

And you'll never walk alooooooooooooooooone!

"You'll never walk at all, I guess." Fats gave his new friend a nudge.

"At least I can sing."

"Listen, do you know this one? *That's me in the spotliiiight…*"

The back door flew open and Harlan was catapulted into the alley. He pulled a pink blob from his mouth and threw it on the ground.

"Ha! You're not getting your nose back, neither."

He turned round and spotted his companions.

"There'll be a few higher pitched voices in Sewageboom tonight," he rasped, collapsing in a heap.

Fats ambled across and poured a drink over his partner's face.

"Come on, mate. Don't be a wimp."

Harlan put a hand to his face. Feeling wetness, he leapt to his feet, screaming.

"Get it off me! My God, it's eating my eyes!"

"Harlan, it's only Guinness."

"I'm over here," Alan waved his straw.

"Right, right." Harlan dusted himself off. "I think you better tell us why you hired Fats and me."

"I'm beginning to wonder that myself."

Before he could continue, Louis the Tomahawk and Eddie the Beagle appeared at the entrance to the alley, both carrying pool cues and a bag of tinnies.

"I think we'd like to hear that story too," Louis advanced on Alan. "You didn't tell me you knew Harlan."

"Me and him go back a long way, Louis," Alan grunted. "Several feet, at least."

"And you didn't tell us you knew Louis and Eddie," Harlan growled. "How *do* you know them?"

"That's simple enough," Eddie broke in. "We work for him."

"He hired us too," Harlan grunted. "What are you playing at, you jumped up Cinzano?"

"Cinzano?" Alan turned purple. "How dare you insult me!

"Great," Harlan groaned. "Our client is a racist."

"And if you got any dumber," Alan seethed. "You'd be an amoeba."

He spotted Eddie's puzzled look

"That too big a word for you, Ed?"

"Amoeba is a *word*?"

"You don't have any reason to insult my pal," Louis warned.

"I know. I'm doing it for fun. Eddie the Beagle. What kind of stupid name is that?".

"About as stupid as a martini called Alan."

"Right!" the cocktail stammered. "You're fired."

"A belligerent drunk too." Harlan blew on his nails.

"You're fired as well! Go on. Beat it."

"Steady on, Alan," Fats cajoled. "Be reasonable."

"Bugger off. I don't need any of you."

"Suit yourself." They began to walk away.

"Waaaaaaaaaaaaaaah!" Alan burst into tears. "It's all right for you lot! You don't have to sit on a bar all day listening to the same Karaoke songs. You can walk down the street or scratch your nose when it gets itchy. I haven't even *got* a nose."

They trooped sheepishly back again.

"Don't cry," Louis pleaded. "I've got a nose you can have. I found it lying over there on the ground."

He stuck the pink lump on the side of the glass using a wad of chewing gum.

"You don't know what it's like," Alan sniffed, trying out his new shnozz. "Always looking at the world through the bottom of a glass."

"Can't you see through the sides?"

"I guess I'd better explain why we're all here," Alan pulled himself together. "Hadn't I?"

"Yes, you better."

"I hired Harlan and Fats to do something for me."

"Fix you up with a nice little lime?"

"I wanted them to get me off this planet."

"That's understandable." Harlan shrugged. "Fats, how high can you throw?"

"I'm serious!" Alan shouted. "Surely it occurred to you that I'm not actually a talking fucking drink?"

They all looked at each other.

"Nope."

"I'm an alien, you morons. I just happen to look like a martini."

"That's the most ridiculous thing I ever heard," Louis snorted.

"I thought if I hired Harlan and Fats, they could help me get off earth. They came highly recommended."

"OK. *That's* the most ridiculous thing I ever heard."

"Don't rule us out because we're incompetent." Harlan frowned. "If you employed us to get you off the planet, Alan, what did you hire *those* goons for?"

"Bodyguards."

"Bodyguards? I wouldn't use them as mudguards."

"Hey!" Eddie protested. "We may hate violence, but we're good at it. That's why we tried to jump you earlier. We were alarmed about you abducting Alan."

"Nice bit of alliteration, Ed." Louis nodded appreciatively.

"I don't think that's a word either, but thanks."

"I understand." Fats stroked the cocktail's dewy side soothingly. "Half of that bar would kill their own granny for a drink."

His eyes widened.

"Hello, Candy-Anne. How long have you been listening?"

"Long enough." The woman stepped out of the shadows. "Louis, Eddie, Fats. How's it hanging?"

"Hey, doll," Louis replied nervously. "Good to see you standing."

"Harlan." Her eyes narrowed.

"Hi, babe." He shuffled around on the spot until Candy-Anne turned her attention to Alan.

"You must be the talking drink, huh?"

"No, I'm Ron De Santos."

"Sorry for staring earlier but you certainly are well proportioned."

"Hands off, Betty. Got my homies protecting me."

Candy-Anne moved toward the martini. Louis blocked her path. She kneed him in the groin and he sank to his knees.

"Don't worry, Lou." Eddie patted his head. "You never needed your knacks much, anyway."

"Relax, Al." She winked. "Cocktails are for pussies. I like shots."

"That lot aren't going to be able to help me, are they?" Alan heaved a huge sigh

"I seriously doubt it," Candy-Anne admitted. "Harlan's the smartest one and he's still an idiot."

"I'm not standing round here just to be insulted," Harlan huffed.

"Where do you usually go?" Alan gave a guffaw. "Sorry. That's a bar joke. I hear a lot of them."

He adopted a cajoling tone.

"Since you're all here, let's party a little. There's lots of booze, though I hate to say it. Shame to waste good liquor, eh?"

"That's true," Harlan relented. "What about it, Louis?"

"My swollen gonads say no." Louis struggled into a sitting position. "But my tongue says yes."

"I've used that line!" Harlan grinned.

"*Seriously*?" Candy-Anne glared at him and Harlan winced.

"This is what I like about earth," Alan chuckled. "It's got atmosphere. That's another bar joke."

"What the hell." Candy-Anne emptied out the bag of tinnies and everyone helped themselves. For a while, they drank in silence, eyeing each other suspiciously.

"Well, this is pleasant." Fats raised his can in salute. "It's the first time in years we've all been together without arguing."

"We've done nothing but argue," Harlan pointed out.

"Not at this precise moment, though."

"We are now."

"We're not. We're discussing."

"All right! I don't want to argue with you."

"Guys, guys!" Alan interrupted. "Stop it. Looks like you used to be friends. So, what happened?"

"Nothing. Time passed.

"Come on. I wasn't uncorked yesterday. What is it with you lot?"

"I don't want to bore you," Harlan grunted.

"Yes, he does. It's his specialty."

"I won't be bored," Alan insisted.

"Yes, you will." Eddie stroked his exceedingly large chin. "But here goes. I guess the natural inhibitions of small-town society, mixed with a clash of Alpha male egos, worked as a repressing agent and created a pushing away effect which turned to resentment."

"That and the fact Harlan stole my car," Louis added.

"Tell him the truth, guys," Candy-Anne threatened.

The former companions looked at each other.

"At one time, we ran a detective agency together," Harlan said. "The Sewageboom Panthers. Candy-Anne was our secretary."

"Despite being more competent than the rest of them put together."

"We were young, enthusiastic and absolute bastards, so reckoned we could go far. We had a modest little office in Eddie's toilet."

"Embarrassed even."

"Our leader was a bloke called Big Dick McShane."

"Truly unfortunate handle," Alan whistled. "Where is *he*?"

"That's the sad part." Fats took up the story. "One day, we were approached by a bunch of bedraggled villagers. Their hamlet was being terrorised by a gang of vicious bikers, so the town scraped together their possessions and asked for our help. Said we were their last hope."

"Why didn't they go to the police?" Alan inquired.

The others burst out laughing

"Fair enough. What did you do?"

"We told them to get lost."

"All except Big Dick," Harlan sipped his drink sadly. "He persuaded us to go and protect them."

"Just the five of you?"

"He was counting on recruiting some villagers when we got there. But there was a flaw in that plan."

"Yeah. If they'd intended to fight, they wouldn't have hired us in the first place."

"The women were all called Calum," Eddie complained.

"Anyway, we taught them the meagre defence techniques we knew, like screaming and hiding. Built some adobe walls. Then we settled down to wait."

"For three months," Louis recalled bitterly. "I've never been so bored."

"Yet they still took you by surprise," Candy-Anne snorted.

"They came on a Sunday afternoon!"

"They were bikers, not Jehovah's Witnesses."

"Next thing anyone knew, we were locked in mortal combat," Fats continued. "Many a villager was injured running into lampposts or tripping over crisp packets."

"Still, we fought nobly for at least 8 minutes," Eddie said proudly. "Except Harlan."

"I was under Louis' car, considering the best course of action."

"Which turned out to be driving off in it."

"*You* jumped into a passing truck carrying nuclear waste." Harlan jerked a thumb at Louis. "They finally dumped him in the Coral Sea. He still glows in the dark."

"I spent two years in a cave," Louis shuddered. "Hiding from men with Geiger counters."

"Eddie surrendered and joined the bikers as a navigator," Fats said. "They ended up in the Coral Sea as well."

"I saved the village, didn't I? And where were you?"

"In the toilet," Fats replied sheepishly. "I've got a weak bladder."

"There you have it. We all betrayed each other and haven't been pals since."

"What about Big Dick?" Alan was certainly an attentive listener.

"He buggered off too. We didn't expect that."

"He didn't run out," Candy-Anne corrected. "How many times do I have to tell you? A huge flying saucer appeared on top of the hill and sucked him up."

"Do you honestly expect us to believe Dick was sucked off by aliens?"

"Sucked *up*."

"By aliens!" Louis scoffed. "A likely st..."

His voice trailed off and he slowly turned to look at the martini.

"Ehhh. Alan? Why exactly *did* you hire us?"

"Some bloke in a bar had one of your business cards. Suggested you'd be the very people to help me out."

"Where was this?"

"Cirrus 5. In the Horseshoe Nebula."

"Was it *Dick*?"

Alan thought for a moment.

"Did he have four arms?"

"Don't think so. He always had the right number of sleeves."

"That was him, then. Everyone else in the pub was a double quadruped."

"Do you know what this means?" Fats was the first to catch on. "Big Dick is up there somewhere, still running a detective agency."

"I believe we owe you an apology, Candy-Anne," Louis said contritely.

"And six months back pay." She shrugged. "Still, I think it's time we let bygones be bygones. Group hug?"

"Nope."

"Not a chance."

"When hell freezes over."

"C'mon guys," Candy-Anne pleaded. "Would it really hurt that much?"

"Hmmm. I suppose not."

As they moved together, arms outstretched, Harlan kneed Louis in the groin.

"That's for being a big beardy bumhole."

"Ooooh," Louis wheezed. "It hurt after all."

"You ok?" Eddie helped him to his feet.

"Not in the slightest."

"Good." Eddie kneed him in the balls as well. "I love this game."

Louis straightened up and punched both of them in the mouth.

"I am going to fucking kill you and then shit in your cremation urns."

They rolled across the dirty alley floor, slapping and kicking each other. While they were distracted, Candy-Anne shuffled closer to Fats and slid something into his pocket. Then she quickly dropped a pill into Alan's glass.

There was a loud parping from the tangle of bodies.

"Oh no! Someone did a fluffy!"

"Christ! That fart stinks of sweaty, rancid bum crack."

They broke apart, still swiping at each other.

"Can we get back to the business at hand?" Alan interrupted. "I need you to build me a matter transmitter ASAP so I can get out of this hellhole."

"Sounds pretty technical," Harlan straightened his collar. "I have trouble with Lego."

"I'm serious. You get me the materials and I'll show you how to make it."

"It might not be easy getting parts," Fats said. "Sewageboom only has Foodworks, a post office and 24 pubs."

"The main component is spaghetti."

"I could handle that. Short or long cut?"

"Doesn't matter. You could ditch those losers and come with me if you wanted. Have you ever seen the seven moons of Cagliostro?"

"I don't go to the movies much."

"You might find Big Dick there."

"You could have phrased that a little better," Fats blanched. "But it's a tempting offer."

"I think this cruel practical joke has gone on long enough." Candy-Anne leaned over and pulled a book from Fats' pocket.

"I thought so." She held up the cover for them to see. *"Advanced Ventriloquism."*

The others stared at him.

"Fats? Are you making that martini talk?"

"It's not my book! Alan… say something!"

There was no sound from the cocktail.

"Eddie?" Louis held out his hand. "Pool cue, please."

"Shit!" Fats turned and ran with Louis and Eddie in hot pursuit.

"Aw, Fats," Harlan sighed. "I never figured you'd do something so underhand. That's my role."

"He runs fast for a ventriloquist." Louis and Eddie trotted back. "Well, we better head. Give us your number, Harlan. We'll have a catch-up sometime."

"2556452131." Harlan lied. Neither wrote it down.

"Nice to see you again, Candy-Anne." Eddie bent to kiss her hand and she poked him in the eye.

"Too soon. Got it."

He and Lois backed away and vanished.

Harlan hung around for a moment before plucking up the courage to speak.

"I best be off too, Candy-Anne. You… eh… want to go for a drink sometime?"

"No."

"OK. Yup. Take care."

He shuffled into the night.

Candy-Anne took a tubular object from her bag and pointed it at Alan. It bleeped twice.

"Oooh. What happened? Did you just *roofie* me?"

"I'm here to take you back. Hope you don't intend putting up a fight."

"What am I going to do? Fire straws at you?"

"We both know you're capable of much more than that. You can't hurt me, though."

She didn't notice Fats sneak back into the alley.

"*I* can." He pointed a gun at her through his coat pocket. "So, I better get some explanations fast."

"*I'll* tell you the whole story," Alan urged. "Kill her first."

"You both better spill. I'm out of breath, fucked off my tits and everyone hates me. I'm starting to get pretty ratty."

"The truth is a bit implausible," Alan warned.

"Says the talking martini." Fats sat on an upturned crate. "Candy-Anne? What's going on?"

"There are huge similarities in all the races across the galaxy." The girl took a deep breath and sat down next to him. "Everyone has the same problems and worries."

"You mean there's a whole universe full of depressed people out there?"

"Pretty much."

"*That's* depressing."

"This… object is supposed to help." She indicated Alan. "He's a Mass Anxiety Reversal Therapy Internal Negation Integer. MARTINI for short."

"I'm getting a bad feeling," Fats sighed.

"Martinis are designed to sit in pubs and listen to people's struggles," Candy-Anne continued. "That's why Alan looks the way he does. All inhabited planets have bars, you see."

"Thank God for that."

"The setup is much the same as here. Except women can go in on their own without getting harassed."

"Just tell the story."

"Martinis are programmed to cheer them up. Get everyone talking to each other. Friendship machines, if you like. Except, it doesn't always work."

"And then?"

"If they can't fix the problems, they scoot out some euphoric gas to make everyone forget their troubles for a while."

Fats gave Alan a nudge

"So, your job is to make any world a better place?"

"That's right."

"Doesn't sound so bad, CA."

"Problem is, this one went rogue. Alan would show the customers how to make a matter transmitter, promising guaranteed happiness in return. Then he'd transport himself to another planet. But not before he overdosed them, leaving behind a bar full of zombies with their minds completely wiped."

"Why would you do that, buddy?" Fats frowned.

"People fuck me off. They wander in, get pissed and talk about the things they're going to do and how their lives are going to be different. I listen. I encourage them. Off they go. Next night, they're back and I have to do the same thing all over again. Six months of that nonsense almost sobered me up."

"Sounds a bit like the *Nipple Washers Arms*." Fats stroked his chin. "Where did you learn *how* to make something like that? I meant to ask."

"You pick up a lot hanging around bars."

"True. That's where Harlan picked up Candy-Anne.

"When it was done," Alan said. "I'd transport myself somewhere else, sure. But I always kept my side of the bargain."

"You zombify whole pubs," Candy-Anne snarled.

"I only gas people if I can't make them satisfied any other way. And, you have to admit, they're blissfully happy. Don't even drink anymore."

"Plus, it was pretty handy for covering your trail."

"Got any left?" Fats inquired.

"Fats!"

"Sorry." He prodded his human companion. "What's this all got to do with you, CA?"

"Big Dick McShane was hired to hunt Alan down. But, instead of arresting him, he suggested *The Nipple Washers Arms* as a great next destination and recommended the Sewageboom Panthers as the perfect people to help him."

"We've never been recommended before," Fats blushed. "Though I *was* once followed home by a flasher."

"Dick contacted me and offered to split the reward money. All I had to do was wait around in the pub for Alan to appear."

"I guess it wasn't much fun for you."

"Not until I discovered pineapple vodka."

"Hah," Alan interrupted. "She wouldn't know how to have fun if she was on fire. I still think you should shoot her."

"Why didn't Big Dick apprehend Alan right away?" Fats stuck out his lip. "Why didn't you grab him the moment you saw him? Why go through this charade and make me look like a liar?"

"Despite all appearances, I got to quite like Louis and Eddie. Even Harlan. And Dick was their mentor. He hated the way they all turned on each other."

"I don't get it."

"The martini is programmed to help people. Bring them together." Candy-Anne shrugged. "We wanted to give Alan a chance to actually make you friends again."

"But you sabotaged that!"

"They were kicking seven bells out of each other! In another minute Alan was going to start gassing the place. He wouldn't be able to help himself."

"True dat," Alan agreed. "If only to cover up that smelly fart."

"I had no choice but to get rid of you lot and neutralize him." Candy-Anne squared her shoulders. "You still gonna shoot me?"

"This isn't a gun." Fats lowered his hand. "It's door handle."

"Looks like the party's over," Alan said sadly.

"Don't be mad at me, buddy."

"You did what you had to do. I'm an illegal alien."

"I'll kind of miss you, Alan."

"Let's go, martini." Candy-Anne waved the cylinder in the air and a glowing blue portal appeared.

"OK. Remember you're driving."

"Shaken but not stirred, eh? Don't worry, I've had four coffees."

"Fair enough. Bye Fats. You can have my umbrella."

"It's not raining."

"Good job. It's made of paper."

Candy-Anne picked up the martini and stepped through the portal. It closed with a small raspberry sound.

Fats sat on the ground and lit a cigarette. Picking up Alan's discarded nose, he stared at it miserably.

"Hey buddy." A voice whispered behind him. "You can pick your friends but you can't pick your friend's nose."

"Harlan!" Fats spun round. "You came back!"

"Once I thought about it, I realised you'd never pull a fast one like that. You're too decent a guy." Harlan ruffled his companion's hair. Fancy a drink?"

"I think I'll stick to coke from now on."

"*Really?*"

"Yeah," Fats grinned. "But put a bit of rum in it."

The March of the Monsters

Cliff McNish

We children all came out to watch the slow march of the old monsters.

We were made to feel like it was our duty. Every year the pageant replayed, only with a few more of the monsters missing – dead. In my father's youth the procession had lasted for hours, the packed line of monsters throwing up a dusty miasma that clogged the skies for weeks. These days the 'march' was a smaller, meaner affair. More an apology than a pageant. We were encouraged to see it that way. Nothing to be feared here, folks. Buy your ice creams and souvenirs. Just a troupe of geriatric aberrations passing through town; we're in charge now, not them.

As tradition dictated, the two timeworn female shamblers led the way. Spogny, with her once-terrifying insect children that now only nagged her, followed by Tandoulia, the Porcelain Princess. To meet her cold blue gaze had once meant instant death. Now she just looked badly in need of soothing eye ointment. They were amusing, if you were encouraged to see them that way – which we were.

Farduk-Ma slouched past next, looking appallingly weary. His celebrated 'murder-crush' was more of a grandad's fond embrace these days. A little girl, egged on by her parents, pushed forward to be 'hugged to death' by him. While Farduk-Ma squeezed and squeezed her inside his now puny arms, the girl nibbled nonchalantly on her lemon cupcake.

It was tragic to see the monsters so miserably humbled, but at least they weren't being pelted with rocks these days. When they were finally captured all those years ago and made to march in shame in front of us for their misconduct, folk were encouraged to rip into them. Citizens brought clubs, cattle bullwhips, even bottles of acid.

That kind of crude behaviour is officially frowned upon now, but not on compassionate grounds. It's a practical matter. The district authorities still make a pretty buck from the annual monster march. The revenue comes mainly from out-of-towners visiting the concession stands these days, but it's still enough to incentivise the town council to preserve our shrinking cluster of monster oldies. Not many remain alive. Neglect in the past was rife. Wounds left to fester. Revenge slayings. Beatings administered in private.

My dad brought me along to the march for the same reason he celebrated Christmas or his marriage – you were supposed to. Monster Procession Day was also a compulsory attendance event on our school syllabus. Students lost end-of-year marks if they didn't turn up. Parents could be fined.

Most of my schoolmates despised the old monsters. They'd groan as the creatures shuffled past us, holding their noses at the smell (or pretending to, it wasn't that bad).

For me it was the best day of the year. I loved the monsters, hated seeing them paraded so degradingly. These senile creatures had once been vaunted foes. They'd been our nemeses, our night-haunts, our killers. What I saw lumbering towards me today – released from their south section enclosure/prison – looked more like a slouching herd of outsized, exhausted sheep.

No surprise, really. They were meant to look that way. Humbled. Broken. We were the masters now. To screw that point home, the monsters were ordered to keep their heads (if they had them) down. An attitude of guilt. Atonement for past misdeeds. Punishments were swift if they disobeyed. The town leaders wanted to make sure we children saw only tamed freaks, horror reduced to entertainment.

After Farduk-Ma, but minus her wand (the authorities didn't dare give her that back, we'd be up shit creek if they did, and they knew it) came Magda the Witch. With her bristling sideburns and licking her translucent frogs, she still looked scary enough. But every tongueful of her spellcraft fell on dead air these days. The biggest insult the town elders had heaped on her (as if drowning her familiars was not enough) was to force her to carry a toy wand during the procession – a plain wooden stick topped with a tacky silver foil star. It was difficult to tell if Magda was shaking the wand's tinsel tassels at us or some kind of palsy was animating her ancient hand.

Behind Madga, however, came power you could not entirely tame.

Katanka.

The giant wolf's sheer size alone made her awesome. Bigger than a barn.

Her legs were chained together, of course, as was her mouth - stuck inside some kind of steel mesh. Couldn't take any chances, could we? As she trudged past, I noticed how patchy her pelt was this year. Dad told me they'd softened her up decades ago by covertly introducing industrial levels of drugs into her feed. As she slogged along the dusty road, Katanka certainly looked more snoozy than tyrannical. I watched with dismay as a teen boy leaned against her tail and posed long enough for his girlfriend to take a snapshot. There were cheers, and Katanka dutifully waited for the couple to get another pic before trudging on. Then she wheezed, her once-haunting howl reduced to a phlegmy cough.

All this indignity. All this humiliation. So many once-wondrous creatures reduced by Father Time, but mainly by us, to this withered, enfeebled state.

Argon came next, and I could have cried. Was this travesty of sagging flesh really the lizard whose great jaws had once reduced skyscrapers to rubble? Nowadays, according to the brochure, Argon was on constipation medication and only allowed to chew well-rounded pebbles. You could buy a bag of them to throw into his mouth at any stall. The cost was less than an order of fries. A notice on the bag stated that all the pebbles had been checked for size and pre-smoothed for Argon's protection.

"Gum disease," Dad told me with satisfaction. "Takes a toll."

The monsters trailed past us. They came limply: on dragged wings, on flaccid claws, on drooping, flailing barbs. All of them looked heavily sedated. The few that could still run had metal braces preventing them. Lothar the Spider managed a brief skitter even so but, afterwards, looked exhausted. Mandy the Doomsnake somehow got caught up in her own tail and had to be helped by the human ground crew staff. From the bored, efficient way they untwisted her it had happened many times before.

Even so, some of the monsters were still impressive.

Chupacabra the Giant Rat could be heard from over a mile away, her feet scampering unevenly over the ground despite the crippling chains muzzling every stitch of her flesh. She had her own group of minders, this monster. They'd been trained to strew cheese biscuits in front of Chupacabra's sensitive nose to encourage her forward. I noticed she ignored the bribes until she was covertly whipped. I saw her minders do it, the bastards, hiding the whip behind smiles and a faded poster of Chupacabra in her heyday.

Then Dad, beside me, took an involuntary step back.

The really dangerous monsters had arrived.

Roger, everyone's favourite uncle, always sweetly calling the children (still dangerous that one; I would definitely have followed his strangely high, siren voice). Followed by Toops. Toops of the vast biceps, sagging these days, his flint knives replaced by papier-mâché versions (just in case). But still somehow an imposing presence as he sliced the air over his head.

Then a lot of the men alongside me nodded with a different kind of interest.

The Marcello Sisters were here.

Dad definitely found them sexy, though he'd never have admitted it. Bats from the waist down, but above that all femme fatale and slinky curves, their dark silk dresses shiny as oil in moonlight. As their carriage rolled past on its rickety wheels, the sisters kept flashing their eyes at us youngsters and telling us to be bad. Winking, they handed out candy drops – child-friendly versions of the poison droppings they were once infamous for. Encouraged by parents and grandparents to take the candied sweets, infants pretended to choke as they chewed them. The entire thing was farcical, but the well-coached Marcello sisters grinned throughout, like they were supposed to.

All these humiliations were a clever tactic on the authority's part. Pity is a not a deep emotion; its longer-lasting brother is contempt. And I could see that contempt already settling in on the faces of some of the younger children witnessing the spectacle for the first time –children who might otherwise have been awed.

A wraith drifted past. Vaunted Whisper.

"Hear me and die!" was the tacky catchphrase someone had come up with for her. In her original incarnation, Vaunted Whisper's voice could blind you from greater distances than this. Medics had operated in some way on her throat to stop all that. The younger children, coached by their teachers, only pretended to lose their sight as Vaunted Whisper slipped past on the wind. Slamming little fingers over their eyes, the toddlers screamed happily. Then – without even giving Vaunted Whisper enough respect to wait for her trailing dress to seep past them – they were giggling and pointing at the next monster.

Varm!

The Mountain Troll thumped cloddishly past. As usual, he was tossing his 'mace'. Only now his weapon was merely a slender willow branch and, even then, he was so old he could barely cast it beyond his sunken oatmeal chest. But he was no-one's fool. To be sure he was fed later, Varm played his part. He let the youngsters treat him like a climbing frame. Let them wander at will through the labyrinth of his beard. He even stopped from time to time to allow the more courageous kids to shove open his nostrils to count the huge sprouting hairs. Every year there were more of them, and a raffle prize was offered for whomever's guess was closest.

Behind Varm came true villainy, Pádraig the Tricksy Leprechaun. All nimble diving Irish fingers, he had once employed his pianistically dexterous hands on screeching flesh. But in his dotage? Well, he still had his wooden piccolo, at least. I watched him use it now, mock-threatening those mothers holding the cutest babies with minor chords.

There's a short gap before the last of the procession passes through. During it I grab some chocolate cake from a stall and a bottle of lemonade. It's so fizzy that I get lost in its bubbles for a while and almost miss the procession re-start.

Jadis leads the way, the White Witch of Narnia. Fading but still imperious in her fur wrap and spiky heels. She's accosted, as she strides past, by a pre-schooler. Part-hidden inside a home-made Aslan costume, he leaps clumsily in front of her. Jadis indulges the child. Makes a pretend moue of fear at his high-pitched roar.

"Boring! Boring!" another boy chants, candyfloss stuck to his lip. He licks it off messily.

"Which school do you go to?" Jadis asks him.

"Kramer Kindergarten!" he pipes back proudly.

"How delightful!" Jadis says, patting his head with her long restless fingernails.

"Hey, look! It's Boney!" a mother calls out, trying to liven up the kids closest to her.

And it surely is. Boney! My all-time favourite monster. All bone except for that single lush arm, that hideously fat and loose-skinned limb; the way it still draws us when we catch sight of it, the way it unfolds! Even now, in his wheelchair, with his oxygen mask flapping, and festooned with more medical tubes than I can count, Boney looks stunning. Last year he couldn't make the procession - a prostate issue, apparently. There'd been real doubt we'd ever see him again.

The old eviscerator is back! proclaims a placard hung around his neck. Be nice to Mr Boney. He's been sick.

It's interesting to study the younger children's faces as they read that, as they try to come to terms with feeling sorry for Boney. In later years they'll mostly scorn the monsters but, right now, their hearts are still naturally tender and most look mightily confused.

Boney is a sight like no other, however: no ears left, no hair, no memory, they say. No name he can remember; no lips to say that name with even if he could. He hasn't got a face at all really, just leftovers. A blackened, decaying jaw, a single piece of sinew attached to it linking his nose and eyes; the entire unlikely balancing act bobbing atop a skeletal neck. Inside Boney's jaw one single tooth remains, and it's shaking, you can see that, literally shaking to bite something. Magnificent Boney! Despite all the sedatives poured into his veins, despite the holes drilled into his bone marrow to weaken him, despite the multitude of straps manacling him to his wheelchair, you can just tell he still has an insatiable desire to kill!

"Boney!" I shout out. I can't help myself. And, surprisingly, he turns towards me.

"Is that him?" he whispers to Tandoulia, and the Porcelain Princess nods.

"Good, good," he mutters, making a scissoring motion with one of his hands. His other hand still lofts Boney's legendary scimitar. A fake scimitar now, of course, smothered in fake blood, being twiddled back and forth. Or is that one of Boney's minders subtly moving it for him? Tandoulia winks at me as she pushes Boney's wheelchair along.

The procession is almost over now, but not quite. Close to last comes Loose Child. Not a child at all, but a demon elf, his left arm holding up Wom, his Toad Bride of Yesteryear. You only have to look into their eyes to see how hopelessly in love the couple are. Some say Loose Child is the oldest of the monsters. People, uncertain about him, especially that suspiciously angelic face of his, attempt to reduce him to the status of a dull mute boy or a senile old man. A fool. A fool, moreover, now gentled by us, wearing his cardboard crown for the procession, thinking he's a real king. But I watch the way Loose Child wipes his nose, which is really a covert salute to Wom. Her reciprocating amphibious moan of sheer pride in him makes me tingle inside.

Wom flicks her tongue at me as she passes. She could have grabbed me with it; could have lassoed my thin neck, eaten me in a flash. She does not. A tiny part of me is not relieved but disappointed.

Finally, behind them all, picking up the rear as tradition dictates, comes true monster royalty.

Pit-Face!

What a sight! A monster's monster: sexless, holding his boneless fish and dribbling on his hot aching feet while, above him, the Stench of Hades reeks!

Glorious, magnificent Pit-Face! Few of the monsters, tethered and restrained as they are, scare the kids any longer, but this one is different. Maggots still spill out on each of his ancient, panted exhalations and as for his shriek... I can't even begin to describe its shredded, polyglot menace. Even hanging as he is from a neck rope, nailed to a platform and partially decapitated (they have to do it afresh each time he leaves his enclosure, or he bites through his ropes) Pit-Face somehow looks like he's the free spirit out here, us the ones in chains. Even the cockiest teenagers fall silent as Pit-Face's guillotine platform rumbles past. The town council have voted to euthanize him innumerable times, but the act is never carried out. Again, it's not pity that stays their hand. Pit-Face is simply so primordial a monster that no-one's quite sure how to kill him. Plus they're worried that, if they do so, he'll only return – but younger, stronger, and basically unstoppable.

Partly to blunt his influence on the children (we're meant to despise the monsters, not fear them) the town elders always stick Pit-Face beside Carla the Vampire. The original Carla died a few years back. She was moved during daylight hours so the council didn't have to pay overtime rates. A stray beam of light across a crack in her ill-maintained coffin was all it took.

The new Carla is a ripe fake. Wearing the company logo of the procession's sponsoring sports company across her prominent chest, she throws incisor-shaped sweets at the children, winks at the men and hisses at the women. That last part's a nice touch; the men like it, anyway.

Last of all, always hanging close to Pit-Face, and erratically banging human (now imitation) heads, is Little Impy. Impy is the monsters' ceremonial spoon. He's their cheeky mascot, his provenance and means of locomotion a total mystery. But it's all I can do not to moan with misery as he passes by. The bastards have emasculated Impy this year even more than last. He's not even bashing fake skulls. They've reduced him to plastic buckets painted with comic smiling faces.

Then - breaking though my anger, I didn't expect this, how wondrous! - the procession organisers give us a final surprise.

It's Bint!

Bint's come!

He was rumoured to be a no-show this year due to haemorrhoids, but they've trundled him out. All scaffolding and bike wheels, Bint is, but where are his eyes? You think it doesn't matter. Who cares where his eyes are? But suddenly you do care because his sidekick, Crowdboy - no his life partner, Mum corrected me recently, deciding I'd reached an age when I could be introduced to that idea - Crowdboy, the consummate persuader, calls for you as he passes.

"Come on, young fella, what do you think? Where are his eyes?" And not me but another boy, unwary, has a guess.

"First guess is free!" Crowdboy cries, and the boy doesn't know he's being suckered in. It's practically a given every year one child will fall for the act. In fact, it's allowed. It's part of the cleaned-up fun.

"Guess where Bint's eyes are and win a prize!" Crowdboy bellows. And this year's stupid boy, licking his lips, is smitten by the voice. But, pretty soon, his free go is over and he's paying – or rather his dad is paying – for extra guesses. Not with his life, as in the old days, but with real coin, and everyone smiles good-naturedly and applauds our great monsters. This is entertainment, this is what we want. A fun note to end on. Meantime, the stupid boy is still crawling all over Bint, still looking for his eyes. He can't stop.

And that's when I get my first real inkling there's more to our geriatric monsters than they're letting on. I see it in Bint's self-restraint. It would be so easy for him to eat this child.

But no. he spits the boy back out. And Carla the Vampire, well-trained employee that she is, knows to quickly push Bint's livid black tongue back inside before he changes his mind.

Finally, as custom demands, Murgh's Darkness brings the event to a close.

Murgh arises from every direction at once, a shapeless extravagant soul, all anti-Christian shadow. Once that shadow was the deep grey of Satan's open palm. Now, though children put down their snacks to clap politely, Murgh's umbra is more symbol than shade. We youngsters still all look up, though. We've been taught to do so by our parents and teachers. Paying proper respect, our mouths fall open in imitation trepidation at Murgh's once-awesome shadow.

Wrapping matters up comes the usual tired announcement. Carla the Vampire delivers it because, even in their decrepit state, none of the real monsters will.

"Today." Carla bares her white prosthetics, swishes her black cape. "We will spare you! Just for today, mind! Bye bye now!"

She waves at the children.

"Try to stay alive until next year!"

"No chance!" we trot out in unison, the customary ending to the ceremony.

Even before those words are done with, Dad is grumbling about the time and heading to the park exit. Mum and my sister haven't even bothered to come this year.

With kiosks and stalls being efficiently folded up around me, I look at the line of monsters gradually disappearing up the road, and my heart sinks. I have a terrible feeling in the pit of my stomach that this is the last time we will see these remarkable creatures. Too few of them remain alive. By next year, or the year after at most, there won't be enough left to make the march viable.

With that sickening thought lodged in my gut, I can't bear the idea of going back home. I just want to stay with the monsters, watch them until they're completely out of sight. I give Dad an excuse that I'm going over to a friend's house, and he's fine with that.

The entire crowd melts away. And it was only a small one this year. Every year it gets smaller, another reason they'll cancel future processions. People head back to their homes to whatever they've decided is a better use of their time than being here.

I'm still small for my twelve years. To follow the monsters, I stand tall and then taller still, on tiptoes. I watch Katanka, the biggest wolf ever to walk this earth, easing her broad grey back into the pit where she's chained up every single fucking day of her life. I cry a bit after that, keeping the remaining monsters in sight for as long as I can. They're caged on the eastern part of town and the council never lets them out unsupervised. I can understand that, I suppose. At night the monsters get some of their old vigour back. I've sneaked out occasionally after midnight to watch their shadows behind the shutters of their cages. They're always pacing.

Here's the truth: we have loads of kids in our town. Loads of kids and hardly any monsters. Some of those kids are ignorant and mean. If they vanished no-one would care. We wouldn't even miss them.

"You'd like that, huh?"

My eyes spring open at the voice and I realise I've been dozing by the side of the road. It's night, so I must have been here for hours. The wind is up. So is the moon. I'm surprised Mum and Dad haven't come looking for me.

I am surrounded by monsters.

"Shush," the Marcello Sisters whisper together in each of my ears. "We came back for you."

My heart thrums.

"To kill me?"

"No, dear child." Smiles warm their faces. "To speak to you. To ask you something."

I stumble upright and gaze around me. Monsters of every jag and hue throng the road. Toops is back, and Spogny, with her suddenly well-behaved insect children. And Madga the Witch, skirts hitched across her broomstick. And look! - there's Lothar the Spider, no longer stumbling. He's freed himself of his bindings, as have all the others.

"Well, well!" Pit-Face chortles, his neck kinked to one side from the hanging rope. Boney, his jaw awhirl with insanity, steadies him. Boney, I realise, is standing upright. He's no longer in his wheelchair!

"No, no, yes, yes!" Pit-Face bellows, looking at me - a willing, keen, insatiable glare.

Monsters! They stretch away into the distance and into the darkness, which is always where monsters make their choices. I'm being allowed to see them, to be amongst them! Why?

"Because there's a decision to make," Spogny informs me.

"Can you guess what we're offering?" Bint asks. And, staring up at him, I can only humbly shake my head.

"Don't you wish to join us? Did we misunderstand?" It's Vanquished Whisper. She strokes my cheek. "You want to become a monster, don't you?"

Her grave white face offers me a chance to change my mind. I blink, expecting to go blind, and she smiles.

"We don't blind our own."

Tandoulia the Porcelain Princess steps forward from the darkness then. She's glowing. I've never seen her look like this, so beautiful. Her eyes are clearer than the stars. Beside her the Marcello Sisters' ears flap with rhythmical grace, all bat, all convivial chitter.

"What will it be then, boy?" Madga grunts, combing her sideburns with Little Impy.

The other monsters wait to hear my answer. They creep forward under Murgh's shadow.

"That shadow is formed from Hell's own rippling darkness, eclipsing Heaven," exclaims Pit-Face with a laugh. I have no idea if he is joking.

The monsters regard me critically. They speak amongst themselves. They thrash. They rasp.

And suddenly I realise I am not worthy. I have not earned the right to join this ineffable horde, this protean family of evil - so dire yet, at the same time, curiously affable. The possibility I might join their ranks is so far beyond anything in my wildest dreams that I'm tongue-tied. My head drops. I bow. I bow so low my chin strikes the grass.

"I've done nothing to deserve you," I whisper. 'Nothing.'

A statement of innocence and modesty that pierces their hearts. Those that have hearts. Those without them just twirl their limbs and knives. Boney bends down to anoint me with, well, I never do discover what it is. Crowdboy kisses Bint, snaps his fingers.

"The real question, boy," he says. "Is whether you wish to be a lone monster or companioned?"

At first I don't understand the question. But then I look around and see how many of the monsters are paired. The Marcello sisters. Loose Child with his beloved Wom. Crowdboy and Bint.

On reflection, a companion sounds like fun.

For a moment I have true power. Power over monsters. Because they wait. For me. For my answer.

"A companion," I murmur.

There's a roar of approval.

"He is a small one, he needs a mount," Chupacabra chitters, her twitchy rat-feet shuddering through the soil. "He needs an underneath creature."

"Yes," Bint agrees. "Something big and solid and unpretentious. We must raise him high."

Tandoulia, whom I now see they look to for final decisions - Pit-Face is their King, but she their Empress - nods her neat shiny glazed chin and, next moment, a huge lump of granite-grey rock sets off. Until now it has been bashfully hiding between Katanka's giant haunches. Spraying dust, it freely tumbles towards me.

"Name her!" thunders Murgh, and I realise he's talking to me. I am being asked to name this huge rock-thing thudding my way. The rock – she – I don't know how I know it's a her, I just do – hurtles forward, all stiff uneven edges, and I sense her wildness. But she is unsure of herself yet, unsure of me as well, unsure because she is still unnamed. I must name her and she is almost upon me now, arriving end over crashing end, the size of a small truck.

"Pancake!" I shout, the only word in my head, it's too late to come up with anything cooler, and as she arrives she names me back.

"Doogg!"

"Thus it will be always!" Boney slavers. "Pancake and Doogg!"

There's a huge cheer, and Pancake and I find we are ready for each other. Sensing her scrunching down, I automatically leap up as she approaches. I could never leap that high before, but I'm a monster now, a young one too. I sense there's not much I won't be able to do if I put my mind to it, and anything my mind cannot figure out Pancake can grind into dust if needs be - if things just have to be settled.

Farduk-Ma's eyes are blackly repellent and cold, the way they should be. He takes me and Pancake in his willowy arms and embraces us half to death with his crush.

Then - abruptly - Pancake and I are underway. We're off! We are running with the horde! My new companion rumbles gleefully beneath me, all stone power and attitude, but she's not the only monster anticipating a wild evening. There'll be no going back to the enclosure tonight.

In fact, there never has been, Boney tells me, trotting at my side. Vanquished Whisper always lays a forgetfulness veil over the town. Folk remember nothing of the mayhem the monsters bring. Procession Day is for the monsters' benefit only, to help them choose from amongst us. Choose the most promising youngsters. Those that do not pity them. Those that see in them, instead, a vision of glory.

I gaze across at Magda. Cutting through the sky, she hands me her toy wand.

"A true witch needs not any form of this," she whispers playfully in my ear. "Puissance lies in the intent. It's all in the blood, in the womb, in the twitch of fingers. No? Yes? Do you understand?"

And no, I don't. I haven't a fucking clue what she's talking about, but I go with it. And now we're really flying, now we're speeding up, now we're deep into the darkness, and there's a hungrier look about the monsters. Pancake pulverises the ground beneath us as if she hates it. She's practising. I realise. Ahead of us, all is chaos. Varm the troll's pewter mace smites the sky. Mandy the Doomsnake uncoils with abandon. Crowdboy is so excited he farts. Boney's fattened arm is like a bouncy castle as he propels himself along. Bint lets out tiny girlish shrieks. Encouraging us, Little Impy the spoon can hardly contain himself. Sitting up straight on Pit-Face's lap, he's banging away on real skulls. They look like fresh parental ones to me.

"If any child is called Peter or Edmund or Lucy or Susan, they are mine!" Jadis warns us. No one dares argue with her as, together, we run. We run, we rumble, we flaff and flap, we wail and wobble, and we smile maniacally at one other, mostly we smile. Ahead, the lights of an outbuilding are just being switched on. Pancake shivers with anticipation under me as she makes out the sign.

Kramer's Evening Kindergarten Club.

The Queer

G r a h a m   J .   D a r l i n g

It all came out in gym class.

Mister Poynter, in his ratty tracksuit, was dishing out one of his 'serious talks'. While he ran on, we and the rest sat around pretending to listen - we trading looks and nods on who to beat up in shower today, and the rest trying hard to f-a-a-ade out, natch.

When, just like that, the goat voice cuts out in mid-bleat, the mole eyes go wide, and the guy makes like he's reaching for the next word in a place it usually was but isn't now and'll never be again. Then this weirdo kid jumps up and catches him before he hits the floor, and starts hilariously humping his chest and yelling, "Call 911! Oh God, call 911!"

This looked like a good time to step out behind the school for a smoke. But we checked back in when the fire engine showed up -Brad the Rad got to hook a helmet that later made us a cool ashtray.

While those dudes were jump-starting old Poynter - and asking each other who'd taken the call, or had they really all just piled into the truck without knowing why? - 911 kid flops against the wall bars like a spaz. Even after the ambulance came and left, he was still all sweaty and shaky, like he'd just run a mile away and two miles back. The whole dumb class was gawking at him. Then he looked up and around.

"I saw... saw his heart stop," he said. "Suddenly, I could see inside him, inside every one of you..."

And he touched the shoulder of Mitch the Twitch, who went all still, straightened up, and never copped crank from us again.

He'd never given us grief, this kid, about forking over his milk money; or he'd take his licks when we found him broke, usually from paying some other chump's tab. Scrawnier than most, otherwise every-one-in-a-blender average; no homies, spent his spare time mumbling on his knees in a corner. The quiet type, and we like 'em quiet.

But now he'd pulled some Respect his way and so away from us. And then we started to get some lip from the sheep, especially those who'd begun following him around, listening to his stupid stories. Time to cut him down to size.

But when we hid his lunchbox, a crow brought him a sandwich through an open window. When we dinged him with dirt clods on the way home, bears came out of an alley and chased us away. When we stuffed him into a locker, someone let him out behind our backs without the key. When we dunked his head in the can, the toilet water turned into *eau de toilette*. When we tried to give him a wedgie, the waistband kept reeling out till it made a pile on the floor. When we dog-piled him on the playing field, he got up from under and walked away like we weren't there.

His hat, tossed back and forth with him in the middle, would fall short and land back on his head. Tacks on his chair turned to rubber, gum in his hair melted away, tied shoelaces came undone, spitballs missed, towel snaps backfired painfully, 'Kick Me' signs wouldn't stick, hate mail got lost, whisper campaigns went nowhere. And, even though we could corner him anytime and bring him to tears, we got no satisfaction from it, because you could tell they were for something about us and not for himself at all. And the pics turned out blank.

We couldn't use any of this. Though he never did either, from what we could see. When he wasn't wasting our time, he was wasting his own, with kid stuff.

Every morning, he'd walk in through that homeroom door, take his seat and write down the teacher's ramblings like the rest (we don't have to, since we already know the only thing worth knowing). Math gave him trouble, though he helped other suckers with their history homework - except he wouldn't do our essays. And he paid no mind to the pecking order but would talk to every doofus who'd talk to him. He'd listen to their prawwwblems, and, in their own home jabbers, tell 'em what he told us - that someday they'd get away to a world we didn't rulez - as if.

Day by day, we smelled the rising stink of hope, heard more mutterings behind our backs, saw more eyes meeting ours. It got so bad we even offered to cut him in, if he'd just shut up and get with the program. No deal.

The last straw came when we tried to mess up his act by siccing the school slut on him. Instead, the day after they 'accidentally' got locked together in the supply room, she started a 'No Nookie' club and got all her friends to join. That made us madder than ever.

So, after the last bell, we carried him over to the old quarry, stripped him down and pitched him in. When we fished him out he still had this goofy face on, so we climbed back up and did it again - only this time, he somehow managed to miss the water.

Swimming accident. Kids fooling around. Happens every day. We got time off class for grief counseling.

Funny thing, though. When we let go of him then – it was like everything turned upside-down and bass-ackwards. All at once, it was him up in mid-air, holding still, gazing sadly down on us. And it was us along the edge who were falling headfirst with the whole world away from him, into a dark sky crawling with twisty clouds glowing red in the sunset. It seemed to welcome us, like a wide-open mouth filled with flames.

But, finally, it was him who went splat, and we're still here.

The stream that sprang up from the rock where he hit, we stuffed with dirt till it stopped flowing. The flowers that people left, we threw away till they stopped coming.

Things soon got back to normal, pretty much.

Life is good again.

Vampires On Vacation

Mandy Chandler

Ker-thunk.

A large silver casket landed heavily in the attic of Mrs Wilson's house. She didn't go up there anymore, not since she'd broken her hip a few years before. Though the noise caused her to stir in her sleep, it didn't wake her.

Inside the coffin, Pork opened one bloodshot eye. Something large and smelly pressed against his beak-like nose. Pork jerked his head away from the disgusting object, smacking it hard against the lid of the port-a-coffin.

"For Christ's sakes, Shark. Get your grubby toes off my face."

"Sorry Pork. It's a bit cramped in here. I've had Boner's balls on my chin all day."

"Too much information, buddy. Let's get the heck out of here. It's time for a feed."

"Damn right it is. I can't wait to sink my teeth into something juicy." Shark flung the coffin lid open and the three stepped out into the darkness.

Stretching his back and cracking his long neck, Pork took in the surroundings.

"Wow, these Scare BnB accommodations may be budget-friendly, but they don't offer much in the way of creature comforts."

The room was bare, except for a closet and a tatty old rug, on which their port-a-coffin squatted like a silver slug.

Shark did a kind of hula move that made the rolls of his ample waist and buttocks jiggle.

"Aroof," barked Boner. He ambled around the room, nose to the floor, bushy tail in the air. Finding a corner that suited him, he cocked a leg and peed. A long stream of pungent urine stained the faded floral wallpaper and dribbled between the floorboards.

"Faw, Boner. Not in the room, mate. We've talked about this."

Boner gave Pork an indignant look, farted, and swaggered over to the window.

Moonlight streamed through the gable and Boner whined a little.

"Cheer up, we're on vacay now. Think of all the juicy meals we're going to enjoy, here in Furso - with a whopping 17 hours of darkness each night to spend as we please."

"Awoooh," Boner agreed.

"Shut up and let's get going," Shark opened the window and swooped out into the star-studded sky.

An elderly gent, taking the air on his back porch, was startled to see three winged forms emerging from Mrs Wilson's attic.

"Always knew she had bats in her belfry." He was so amused by his sharp wit he failed to notice the three shapes landing in a tangled heap on Mrs Fletcher down the road.

They decided to walk the rest of the way to the centre of town. A group of late-night revelers passed them, singing about getting knocked down but getting back up again.

"Humans are weird," observed Shark.

Pork had to agree. They *were* weird. And tasty.

"Hey," he nudged his companion. "There's the pair for us."

Two plump girls in their mid-twenties were walking arm-in-arm down the deserted street towards a kids' playground. They were what Pork's mum, in another life, had called 'two sheets to the wind'. Both were whooping and giggling and one of them made a grunting sound when she laughed that made Pork horny as well as hungry. They smelled delicious, even from far away. Seeing the wicked leer on Shark's pock-marked face, Pork pulled him closer.

"Remember, keep a cool head. We want to be gentlemen. We do *not* want to leave a bloody mess that will give the game away on our first day of hols."

"Yar." Shark slid a white-coated tongue across his thick rubbery lips in anticipation. His yellow fangs gleamed in the streetlight.

"Put those away for now! Remember we're playing the long game. Just a few sips tonight. Got it?"

Pork grabbed Shark by the shoulders, resisting the urge to shake him. His mate was lost in bloodlust already. Dammit. Shark's appetite was ferocious. Pork had hoped the couple of pints they'd packed in the port-a-coffin would have kept him calm for a few more hours but he was already revved up and ready to rip the females apart.

"Tell me you've got it, Shark?"

"Yeah, yeah. Long game or something."

They sidled up to the girls, doing their best to look attractive and non-threatening.

"Good evening, ladies," said Pork in his most seductive voice. This sent the girls into effusive fits of giggles.

"Cor, did ya hear that Luce? He called us ladies."

More giggles ensued and a lot of saliva sprayed about. Pork brushed some off the front of his Pink Floyd T-shirt, frowning. It wasn't like you had a hell of a lot of clothes to choose from, being a vampire. You were pretty much stuck with the set you were wearing when you changed. In Pork's opinion, you had to pay special attention to them.

Shark didn't care about things like that. His polo neck was covered in old blood stains and had a hole under one arm. Pork wondered what it would look like a hundred years from now.

A shout brought him back from his reverie. The tubbier of the two girls was lying flat on her back on the grass. Shark gave Pork a wink and held out his hand to help her up. The cunning bastard had tripped her just so he could play the hero. He wasn't without a certain charm, Pork had to admit.

"Oooh, thank ye," she gushed, getting to her feet.

"Enchanté la gras." Shark kissed her dimpled knuckles.

"O.M.G. Suze," Luce turned to her friend. "He speaks Spanish. Innit romantic?"

Suze gave her friend an emphatic nod and Pork rolled his eyes. Things might turn out alright after all.

"Nice pooch." Suze pointed at Boner. The scabby brown mongrel came waddling over, tongue lolling, begging for a pat. Suze got to work, rubbing him behind the ears, making Boner go all gaga.

"You must really like dogs," Pork remarked. "No one ever says that about Boner."

"As a matter of fact, I do." From the depths or her enormous handbag, she dragged out what Pork assumed was some kind of mutant rat. He took a step backwards.

"What's that, then?"

"This is Bruiser. He's a pure bred Shitpoo."

"Oh. You don't see too many of those around, do ya?"

"Designer dogs, they are. Very spensive."

"Hmm, you don't say." Pork wondered what it would taste like.

"Boner's an odd name for a dog, why'd you call him that?"

Pork, pointed to where Boner and Bruiser were getting better acquainted.

"Oh, my Gawd, that's disgusting." Suze screwed up her face. "Does he always behave like that?"

"Boner by name, boner by nature."

"But Bruiser's a boy."

"Makes no diffs to Boner."

Suze grabbed Bruiser and stashed him back into her giant bag.

Boner winked cheekily at Pork. Bruiser'd be back for more. Once they'd had a taste of Boner, they always came back. Lucky bastard.

The two couples settled side-by-side on a nearby park bench and Pork and Shark turned on the charm. The girls were quite tipsy and happy to take part in a little tête-à-tête.

Suze tucked her straggly hair behind one ear and glanced up at Pork from beneath the world's biggest false eyelashes.

Why do girls always do that? Pork wondered. *It makes them look like they have spiders attached to their faces.*

"What's your name?" Suze asked.

"Pork." He braced himself for what inevitably followed such an introduction. He'd learned to live with it, the way you have to put up with a wart or a big hairy mole.

"You don't hear that name too often, now do ya?" Suze wistfully curled a strand of bleached blonde hair around her index finger "Where'd you get a handle like Pork?"

"He slept with a pig," Shark piped up.

The girls exchanged a look.

"I absolutely did not."

"Did too. I'm the one that found ya. All cosy, side by side, in the pen."

"Okay. I did lie down in the pig stall. But all we did was sleep. Scouts honour. Besides, pigs are actually very clean animals if kept in the right conditions. And this pig had fresh straw…"

Suze's eyes were stretched wide as saucers.

"It was an honest mistake, really. I was drunk and, well, the pig looked like my girlfriend at the time. Same little eyes, fat cheeks, pinkish hirsute skin. Large snub nose. Gorgeous, really, and such a gentle soul…"

He trailed off, realising he was only making things worse.

"Your girl didn't see things that way," Shark commented. "She dumped you."

"Dammit Shark, it was years ago. Why do you have to drag this all up now? You're scaring the ladies."

The girls did, indeed, look horrified.

"Erhem, just our little joke. As I was saying, I'm Pork, and my friend over there is called Shark."

"Why are you called Sh…" Lucy began.

"Oh, shut up, Luce. After what we've just heard, do you really want to know?"

"You make a fair point."

"Anyway," Suze continued. "Who cares about names and pigs and such? Like Will Smith once said: *Human beings are not creatures of logic; we are creatures of emotion. And we do not care what's true. We care how it feels.*"

The others stared at her.

"I think what she's trying to say," Lucy explained. "Is, let's stop wasting time and get down to it."

She grabbed Shark around the neck and pulled his face to hers.

Next thing, Pork felt Suze's luscious fish lips smacking up against his own. They were big and soft and full, and her passionate kissing was so ardent, Pork worried she might suck his face right off.

"Ouch," Lucy pulled away from Shark and put her hand to her neck. "That stung, you beast."

She mock slapped him on his barrel chest.

"Not so rough now."

Shark grinned and licked a drop of blood off the tip of one long yellow fang.

"Sweet. Oh, so sweet," he muttered. "This is going to be the best holiday ever."

Taking his friend's cue, Pork gently kissed Suze's white throat.

"Ooh, it tickles," she grunted between giggles as Pork slipped his needle-sharp white fangs into her soft skin. She would hardly feel a thing. He drank long and deep, stopping before he'd taken anywhere near as much as he wanted. He'd have blue tonsils tomorrow for sure.

But that was the price you paid for playing the long game.

Initial rush of passion sated, the foursome caught their collective breath for a moment.

Time to take the next step, thought Pork.

"You ladies live around here?"

"We've got a share house just over there." Suze pointed to a grimy two-up, two-down at the end of the street. The place was ablaze with light, even at this late hour.

"Whatcha doing?" Shark hissed in his ear. "Let's just finish them off here."

"Shut up and trust me," Pork whispered back, before turning to their dates.

"Got any booze at your place? My friend Shark here is a tad thirsty."

"We're skint but our housemates are having a party tonight, so there'll be plenty to go round. Would you like to come over, then?"

"How lovely of you to invite us." Shark bowed. "Merci beaucoup."

"Ooh. He speaks Italian too." Lucy elbowed her friend.

Pork looked up at the blue velvet sky and sighed. The things he did for a drink.

They made their way to the house.

Meanwhile, Boner had been having his own bit of vacation fun with a family of squirrels who lived in one of the nearby spruces. Seeing his mates head off down the road, he licked a few stray clots of blood from his chops and followed. The squirrels had certainly hit the spot. They were so tame that catching them had been like shooting fish in a barrel. Except that he'd never shot fish in a barrel, or anywhere else for that matter. Damn his lack of opposable thumbs.

The house was pumping, folk spilling out of the crowded lounge and into a tiny front garden. They squeezed past couples necking in the

hallway and into a brightly lit kitchen. The girls headed to the refriger-
ator, leaving Pork and Shark standing by the doorway.

Pork eyed Shark warily. His pal had the look of a hungry lion in the
midst of a herd of gazelle.

"Easy does it, Shark old boy." He laid a hand on his companion's
arm. "We don't want to spook them."

Despite his warning, Pork also felt the mounting urge to dive in and
devour. He held back, though. With a crowd like this, you could feast
all night if you played your cards right - and no one would be any the
wiser. You just had to be patient, bide your time.

The girls returned with glasses of red wine and the four sat awkwardly on an old couch. While Lucy went to request a song from the
DJ, Shark took out a tiny ivory sliver from his pocket. Checking nobody
was looking, (especially that old wet-blanket Pork), he pricked his
thumb and allowed three large drops of black blood to fall into Lucy's
wine glass.

"I'm feeling a wee bit funny," Lucy said eventually. "I might have
a little lie down."

Pork raised a quizzical eyebrow at Shark who gave him a *how-
should-I-know* look. Pork realized Suze didn't look too good either.
He'd limited himself to a few sips but, even so, she seemed a bit
drained.

"Why don't you go on up with her?" he suggested. Suze gave a jaw-
cracking yawn and did an odd little stretch that ended in a fart.

"Oops," she giggled. "Don't mind if I do."

Off she waddled with a dazed giggle.

By two in the morning, Pork was starting to feel bloated. He'd done
the rounds and had more than his fair share of both blood and red wine.
Now he was feeling a bit merry, to be honest.

Then he saw her, sitting all alone on the far side of the lounge. She was an absolute peach. He headed toward the lovely lady who, quite astonishingly, had not a single soul to talk to.

He wondered whether he looked respectable enough and cursed not being able to see his reflection in any mirror. He patted his hair down and straightened his shirt for good measure.

"Hello lovely," he purred. "I'm Pork. What's your name?"

The girl simply sat there, staring straight ahead. Her red-rimmed mouth was gaping open, as though she had seen something obscene. He tried to follow her gaze and find out what it was.

"What's a nice lass doing in a place like this?" He gently nudged her with his shoulder. She was as insubstantial as air and leaned so dramatically in the other direction that he had to grab hold of an ample breast to stop her hitting her head against the wall.

"Whoa there, take it easy." He laughed nervously, quickly letting go of her boob.

She showed no signs of protest, so he leaned in to give her a kiss. Again, she made no move to stop him. She tasted strange. Unfamiliar. Exotic.

Passion overcame him and he tentatively gave her a little nip on the neck

BANG!

Pork jumped backward, lips stinging, eyes bulging from their sockets. He shook his head in disbelief.

His girl had exploded. In fact, she'd exploded with such force she must've vaporised. There wasn't a trace of flesh or blood left behind.

To his horror, nearby partygoers were openly laughing at him and elbowing their friends.

And they call us monsters! Overcome with indignation, Pork high-tailed it out of there to find Shark, before they got over their hysterics and had him up on murder charges.

Shark's signature odour (and the reason behind his name) brought to mind the redolent smells of an outdoor fish market at the end of a hot day. Pork's nose followed the scent to a dilapidated potting shed in one corner of the garden.

Shark lay on one side, fat belly protruding from beneath his filthy T-shirt. The crack of his backside was visible above the waist of his equally nasty shorts.

Boner was lapping crimson from Shark's face, while the lout slept peacefully in his blood-coma. Pork tapped the sole of Shark's workbook with the tip of one of his glossy winklepickers. Shark grunted and scratched his arse. Pork tapped again, harder this time.

"Hey buddy."

"Wha… whaaat?" Shark yawned, rubbed his eyes and stared blearily up at Pork.

"Get up."

"You ready to go?" Shark wiped his bloody maw on the back of one hairy arm and scrambled to his feet.

"Sure am," Pork said. "You would not believe how insensitive these modern youngsters can be."

An unearthly scream emanated from the upstairs bedroom.

"Change!" cried Pork, and the vampires quickly transmuted into their bat forms.

Pork shot up and through the open window, changed into his human form and landed gracefully on the floor of a very purple, girly bedroom.

Transmutation had never been easy for Shark. His sheer bulk made flying difficult at the best of times and a belly full of blood did nothing to help. He strained and wheezed with every pump of his leathery wings and bumped into the window frame, almost knocking himself unconscious. Finally, he landed, still in bat form, on the fuzzy purple rug. He tried in vain to push himself up on wobbly little legs that weren't made for walking.

"Change back, you fool," Pork snapped. There was a loud pop as Shark obliged.

Suze lay on the bed, a dark patch spreading beneath her head and neck. Her throat had been torn away.

Lucy hovered over her with fangs out, blood dripping down her chin and neck, a wild leering grin on her face. There'd be no use talking to her now.

Pork heard the sound of footfalls running up the stairs as Lucy went back to her meal.

"Damn you, Shark. We discussed this. Absolutely no converting the locals while on holidays."

"Yeah, I know."

Pork sighed.

"So, why'd you go and do it then?"

Shark shrugged sullenly.

Pork straightened himself up, bunged on his best smile and headed out the door, closing it firmly behind him.

"Panic over, folks. Just a big huntsman spider."

Using all his charm, Pork managed to turn the crowd of curious faces around and lead them back downstairs. The DJ was wrapping up, and Pork took it upon himself to escort any partygoers who could walk, crawl or ambulate, in any way, out the door. There were still a few bodies lying comatose about the place.

Looks like a scene from Night of the Living Dead in here, he thought and suppressed an ironic chuckle.

He considered helping himself to a nightcap but decided against it. He had a mess to clean upstairs and God knew what they were going to do with their new recruit.

The nightmare in the purple room had run its inevitable course. Lucy had made a meal of her best friend and, judging by the cat-that-ate-the-cream look on his friend's face, Shark had helped her out. The sorry pair sat huddled in the corner, Lucy sobbing into Shark's armpit. Pork suppressed the urge to punch Shark in the nose and slap her.

He had seen this pathetic remorse before. Newbies always had a hard time dealing with their first kill. They soon bounced back, though. Usually, the biggest bawlers turned into ones like Shark, who found their killer instincts virtually impossible to control.

Pork had a good mind to head back home and leave the bastard to deal with this mess on his own. But they'd been friends since they were in diapers and Shark being an idiot was just Shark being, well, Shark. He always took things too far and Pork would always be there for him.

Boner had flown in while Pork was mulling this over, and now the bed was swarming with vampire squirrels, ripping into the corpse like nobody's business. They each grabbed a chunk of Suze, transmuted into their squirrely bat forms and carried her off into the night.

That's the great thing about having friends, mused Pork as he patted Boner on his wiry forehead. Everyone mucked in and did their bit when the time came.

"Good boy. Thanks to your mates, we don't have to hide the body."

Boner wagged his tail, burped, farted, picked up his own hunk of meat and flew off after his minions.

"Look man, I'm sorry," Shark apologised. "I don't know what got into me. I'd never changed anyone before and I just wanted to see if I could do it. Never thought it would actually work."

"Sorry isn't going to fix this. Who's going to take responsibility for her? Train her? "

"I will."

"No, you bloody won't. You won't bloody well be here. You'll be bloody miles away."

"We could take her with us?"

"Just how is she going to fit into that bloody port-a-coffin? Not to mention the trouble we'll be in when the higher-ups find out. So much for my damned holiday."

Shark giggled nervously.

"What's so bloody funny?"

"You keep saying bloody."

Lucy turned toward Shark as though she was going to say something profound. Instead, she projectile vomited a stream of blood all over him.

"What a gal," sighed Shark. "I think I'm in love."

"Clean yourself up." Pork pulled the girl to her feet and handed her a large white handkerchief. "Pull yourself together, Shark. We've got to get out of here. Lucy and I will go down the stairs."

He took her hand and they walked through the house and out the front door without incident. Pork was relieved to see the pudgy silhouettes of Boner and Shark, in their bat forms, weaving across the slowly lightening sky.

Pork stopped by the park bench. Beneath a nearby spruce, he could just make out the section of churned earth where the squirrels had buried what was left of poor Suze.

"Gotta love an animal that hibernates."

After a respectful moment of silence, Pork showed Lucy how to transmute into a bat, which took a few gos. In one especially funny moment, she remained intact, except for a pair of twiggy bat legs. They couldn't hold her rotund form, so she toppled over like a bowling ball. Finally, they winged their way back to the attic, arriving before Boner and Shark, who had collided and landed in the rosebushes.

"Right," said Pork. "There's too many of us for the port-a-coffin, so one of us is going to have to sleep in the closet."

All eyes turned to Boner.

"Aaaaarroooofff," he barked plaintively. But, being a good vampire-dog, he ambled over and settled down with a sigh.

In the end, Pork felt Boner had actually drawn the long straw, as there was no way the three of them could sleep easily. After an interminably long day, trying to find a comfortable spot, he got up as soon as the sun was low enough. He sat brooding in the gathering darkness while the other two snored away.

Tomorrow they'd go out and get Lucy a bloody coffin of her own, then head back home. He'd had just about all the holiday he could take.

Harrow and Sons stood at the end of a cul-de-sac. The showroom with empty coffins would be through the back. Pork knew this because he'd worked in an undertakers before he met the vampire that turned him.

Leaving Boner to keep watch, Pork led his two friends down the side of the building. He lifted the doormat in front of the service entrance door and, bingo, there was the key. He escorted them to the main office and showroom. So far so good. One of the great things about being a vampire was the fact that you didn't show up on CCTV. It was like taking candy from a person giving away candy.

He motioned for the others to head into the showroom, pick out a coffin and carry it to the front of the building. Pork would meet them there with the hearse.

But, as they were leaving the office, Shark stopped to tie his shoelace. His rump smacked up against a cabinet and a large vase filled with glass beads and fake flowers came crashing down.

"For fuck sakes."

Pork could see it coming. The bane of every vampire's life. The compulsion to count anything that fell in their path.

Lucy was already on hands and knees, heedless of the broken glass cutting into her, sorting through the beads as though her life depended on it. Pork saw to his horror that the silent alarm had been triggered. Since the town was the size of a pimple on a maggot's bum, the police would be here any minute. He glanced at Shark.

His pal was holding it together, but his right eye was twitching and his knees threatening to buckle. Pork rugby tackled him, the pair slid across the linoleum floor, and Shark's head smashed into a wall. The jolt seemed to break his desire to count. Pork grabbed Lucy, blindfolded her with his hankie and frog marched her toward the showroom.

"Shark," he called. "Grab the keys and get the hearse. Meet us out front."

Pork ripped off Lucy's blindfold and demanded she pick a coffin.

"Weeellll…" She ran her hands along a shiny oak number. "This is rather nice but I can't say I'd die over the pink satin interior."

"If only," Pork muttered. But she literally couldn't.

Lucy walked past one perfectly good coffin after another, shaking her head and muttering, "Nah. Nah-uh. God no." until Pork wanted to pull his hair out. Or her hair out.

Finally, she pointed to a hideous looking thing.

"Oh, that's a lovely purple velvet. Purple's my favourite colour, d'you know?"

"I don't fucking care!" Pork shouted. "Just pick a bloody last resting place and let's get out of here."

Lucy's bottom lip quivered. Her mouth turned down and she began to wail.

"It's NOOOOT muh-my fuh-FAULT."

"I know, Lucy, I know. I'm sorry. Look, can we chat about this later?"

"I… I… I didn't ask to be changed into a vah-VAMPIRE."

"Believe me, this is the last thing I wanted either. I'm supposed to be on vacation."

"Wait a minute," she stopped sobbing and stared at him. "Did you say, vacation?"

"Yes, va-ca-tion. You know, holidays, R-and-R, that sort of thing?"

"Vacation from what? We're dead."

"Undead, actually, but I see your point. Now that I think about things, it does seem rather silly." Pork leaned against one of the displays. "I don't know what got into me, really. Just wanted a change of scenery, I guess. Now look at us. We'll be in ever so much trouble for hunting on another vampire's turf. We're allowed to enjoy ourselves, of course. A little drink here and there - but murder is out of the question. And then there's the matter of turning one of the locals. We'll never hear the end of this."

"I'll put in a good word for you," offered Lucy.

"You'd do that?"

"Sure, that's what friends are for, right?"

They smiled at each other and Pork wiped a tear from the corner of his eye.

"Gosh, thanks."

The wail of a siren pierced the air.

"Now, my dear." Pork pulled himself together. "If you could go ahead and just choose a coffin, I'd be ever so grateful."

"Hey, that one you were leaning on. It's perfect."

Pork stared at it. For the life of him, he could not tell what made it *the one,* but wasn't going to argue.

"Great, let's grab it and get the fuck out of here."

They bundled the coffin into the hearse and headed back to Mrs Wilson's house. The old lady was fast asleep in her seat in front of the telly and deaf as a doorpost, judging by the volume. They humped the coffin upstairs without her stirring.

Shark drove the hearse to the far side of town and left it in a car park.

Soon enough, all three plus Boner were in the attic. Pork rattled off a few last-minute instructions to Lucy about keeping a low profile and sticking to sheep or cows when the urge to kill became too strong. Then they said their farewells.

Pork, Shark and Boner piled into the port-a-coffin and headed home.

Lucy looked around her new home. It would do nicely - she thought - if it had a bit more purple. She'd get right onto that.

She heard a small scratching sound from the closet where Boner had spent the night.

She opened it and out popped Bruiser, looking immensely satisfied.

Yes, Prime Minister

K a r e n   L i e v e r s z

"Is this real?"

"Yes, Prime Minster."

"And legal?"

"Apparently."

Ken Davidson stared at the computer screen. He turned it to the left then the right, as if what was happening on the screen would make more sense at a different angle.

"I thought I'd seen everything. But this…"

"Seen what, sweetheart? Who are you talking to?"

Ken dropped his phone and slammed the laptop shut. His eyelid twitched as he looked up at the Prime Minister's wife. *His* wife, he reminded himself.

"Nothing, Linda. Just politics."

"You need to come to bed, honey. You've been working much too hard. I hardly ever see you."

Ken rubbed his eyes, hoping it would wipe away the images from the video he'd just watched.

No. They were still there, seared into his brain. In 3D technicolour.

"There's so much to learn," he sighed. "So much about running this country I don't know." He thought about the video again. "So much about ordinary people I still need to understand."

"And you will. But first you need to sleep." Linda took his hand and led him out of the study. He rolled his shoulders back. Everything ached.

Maybe sleep was the answer. It was still early days. He'd only been in the job for two weeks but it was already turning out to be much more difficult than he'd ever imagined.

Ken froze when they reached the bedroom. It was bathed in candlelight. Shadows danced across the king bed, playing come hither games with the duvet - while the tantalising aroma of sandalwood and rose cloaked the room in a sensual mist.

"What's going on?" He carefully kept his voice steady, hiding the fear that clawed at him.

"You haven't been the same since you won the election." Linda slipped off her dressing gown to reveal a black silk negligee. "It's time to spice things up a bit."

Ken gulped. Linda's voluptuous, creamy breasts spilled from the lacy top and long, long legs stretched out underneath. His face twitched as he backed away.

"Ken, please. What's wrong? I don't understand. Don't you want me anymore?"

Linda's eyes narrowed.

"You don't have some mistress tucked away now that you're Prime Minister, do you?"

"No, no. Of course not. I'm just under a lot of stress."

Linda's expression softened, her eyes dilating as she sashayed towards him. She pressed painted nails against his chest.

"I can help you with that stress," she whispered.

The candle flickered malevolently. Linda's hand slid down, towards the belt of his trousers and Ken broke out in a sweat.

The video! Oh God! She wanted him to do the things he'd seen in the video.

"No, Linda. I can't." He rushed from the room, his body pulsating with fear… and another emotion he couldn't quite put his finger on.

Safely back in his office, Ken shut the door and sat down, readjusting his trousers as best he could. They were tight. Again. What was wrong with his body?

He opened the laptop and picked up his phone.

"Flynn? You there?"

"I'm here. You all right?"

"I had a close call. She tried to get me in the bedroom again. I'm so exhausted, I nearly fell for it."

He was greeted with silence.

"Flynn?"

"I've been studying the video, Ken. Plus a few others I uploaded from *X-Hamster*. Humans seem to really like this stuff. You'll have to do it if you're going to blend in."

"Are you sure? It looks so wrong. Except for the elimination of waste, shouldn't other bodily fluids actually stay inside me?"

"We should have done more research before we implanted your essence into a human form. You'll have to wing it."

"What do you mean *wing it*?"

"Ehm… ignore your mind screaming to run and trust this body's instinct."

"Easy for you to say. There's so much blood rushing south I can barely think straight."

"Nothing for it, Sir. Don't think. Just do."

Ken scrubbed his face with the palms of both hands.

"I'm not sure I'm cut out for this assignment after all, Flynn."

"You certainly wouldn't catch me doing something so nasty," Flynn admitted. "But you've been working your whole life towards an extra-terrestrial posting and none is more important than this."

He wasn't exaggerating. The vile Tyreans had slaughtered eighty per cent of his planet's population, literally bathing in their blood. The savages.

The situation had been dire until Tyreans started falling like raindrops. A simple virus, harmless to Ken's people, had been deadly for them. And it came from the human race.

It was an avenue that offered a chance of survival and required immediate exploration.

The problem was, Ken's own people were propagated through cloning. This human desire to couple was a foreign and truly disturbing concept.

"It's not what I thought it would be, Flynn."

"Exactly! You're the first one of our kind to be fully engaged as a human."

"That's what I'm afraid of. It's playing havoc with my hormones."

Although his mind rejected it, the body he occupied throbbed with the longing to copulate. He feared, if he allowed it to happen, he would forsake his intellectual supremacy for the alien, baser needs that burned through him.

"You're thinking too hard, Sir. It's a wonderful honour. Your research on Earth gives our people hope that, one day, we'll be able to take over the entire planet. I'll call next week for an update."

"Wait! Don't go!"

"Sorry… you're on your own. I'll keep sending you videos. Study them. Did you see the one with something called a sixty-nine?"

"Yes. I threw up…"

"Good luck, Sir."

"Bastard!" Ken slammed the laptop shut. Flynn could be such an arse.

The doorknob rattled and Linda glided into the room. Ken eyed her warily,

"I thought you went to bed?"

"I couldn't sleep." Her sultry smile sent shivers down his spine. She licked her lips as if she wanted to eat him up. Flynn said that was normal. Ken wasn't convinced.

"Well, ah…" He shuffled the papers on his desk. "I've still got a lot to do before I turn in."

"I tell you what." Linda's smile widened. "How about a nice relaxing bath before… you know?"

She gave him a knowing wink.

"Oh, all right." Ken reluctantly allowed himself to be led into the bathroom. His frown deepened.

"There's no water in the tub."

"It's not for *you*, baby."

A bony blade shot from Linda's fingers and gored his stomach.

"We have scientists too." Her voice lowered to a guttural growl. "And they found we can't succumb to the virus if *we're* in human form."

Ken's eyes peeled back in his head, pain coursing through every muscle, as Linda bundled him into the tub.

"No," he groaned, blood gushing from his mouth.

Linda leaned forward and licked the sticky red fluid from his lips.

"Oh yes," she said, eyes bright with lust. "This is way better than sex."

Clink!

I s h b e l l e   B e e

Fish Quick Goal, Shoreditch, London, 1798.

I, Roger Featherybottom, The Most Honourable Marquis of Winchester, rotting in an accursed dungeon, recount my tale of mistaken identity most heinous.

After visiting the capital to absorb its exotic delights, I inadvertently wandered into the 'rough end' of Shoreditch and quickly fell afoul of a twopenny strumpet, shadowed by a colossus of a pimp carrying a length of pipe. It was no surprise, therefore, when I was bludgeoned over the head, robbed and left unconscious down a back alley, with my pantaloons round my ankles. Mistaken for a pervert, I was carted off in a wheelbarrow by the local constabulary and callously dumped in the nearby gaol. Confined within a dank cell, aquiver with slime and having only a stone slab as a bed and bucket to squat over, I wait. Whilst all about me inhumane screams electrify the air!

The turnkey, a suspicious-looking fellow named Grimes, clicks his jaw as he shuffles past my cell. He resembles some nightmare troglodyte vomited from the pits of Hell.

"Excuse me." I waft a frilled sleeve at him.

He stops and turns to look at me, spittle glinting on the edge of his lip.

"What's the problem?" he grunts.

"I have fully regained my senses and would like to reveal to you my identity."

He stares at me in gormless confusion as I blither on.

"What I am about to tell you will compel you to release me at once."

He seems unconvinced.

"I am the Marquis of Winchester," I announce.

A voice from the darkness wails. "AND I AM THE KING OF DEN-MARK!"

"What cretin attempts to ridicule me?" I shout. "Silence, you filthy peasant!"

Grimes chuckles to himself, sloping off into the darkness.

"NO. Please wait!" I yelp. But he's gone.

Oh, despair! I rattle the bars of my prison and weep.

Luckily, he returns a moment later, throwing parsnips into the cells. One whizzes past my head and hits the wall.

"Good, Sir. I must have your attention!" I cry.

He bows rather low.

"Is the parsnip to your liking, my liege?" He sniggers and shuffles closer to inspect me.

"I can prove I am the Marquis of Winchester. Give me quill, ink and parchment and I will send word to my cousin here in London."

He eyeballs me carefully.

"There is the matter of your crime."

"What crime?" I retort. "I was robbed and left for dead, with my pantaloons round my ankles."

"And here's me thinking you're a prostitute."

"How dare you, Sir!"

"No need to worry. You'll just get a good hard thrashing in the court-yard."

"WHAT?" I scream, outraged.

He leans in towards me, a dirty grin on his face.

"I am open to bribery."

"My monies and ring were stolen," I protest. "But I can pay you handsomely if you deliver a letter to my relative."

"I'll fetch the ink and quills," he agrees, scratching his arse.

"WHAT ABOUT ME?" the voice from the darkness complains.

"What about you?" Grimes shrugs his shoulders.

"I WANT TO WRITE A LETTER TO MY GRANDMA."

"Oh, for fuck's sake." He rolls his eyes.

"IT'S ONLY FAIR. IF HE'S WRITING TO HIS COUSIN, THEN I WANT TO WRITE A LETTER TO MY GRANDMA!"

"Fine," huffs Grimes and lurches into the gloom. I wait patiently, nibbling on the foul parsnip.

He finally returns with rolls of parchment, a bottle of ink and a quill, then passes them through the bars.

My scribbling is hasty

For God's Sake, tell them who I am!

Roger

I hand the note to Grimes, who tucks it into his trousers and grins.

"Tell me the address."

"Bramble Manor, Greenwich."

"WHAT ABOUT MY GRANDMOTHER?" the voice squeaks from the shadows.

"Fine. Whatever!" Grimes shambles towards the miscreant. "Write to your Granny. Just make it quick."

A scribble in the darkness and parchment is passed through the bars and into the hands of the rancid turnkey. My eyes catch a glimpse of the note.

FOOD IN HERE CRAP. PLEASE SEND JAM SPONGE.

"4 Dumpling Terrace, Shoreditch. Ta." The voice informs

Grimes lurches off, the keys on his belt jangling.

Alone in the gloom, I wait, pondering my fate. Suddenly a voice breaks into song-

There were three old gypsies came to our hall door

They came brave and boldly-o

And one sang high and the other sang low

And the other sang a raggle taggle gypsy-o

"I beg you, Sir," I assert. "Be silent!"

"I'M EXPRESSING MYSELF!"

"Please express yourself in a way that doesn't involve singing."

"I'M LOCKED IN A CELL. MY OPTIONS ARE LIMITED."

"Have you considered weaving a tapestry?"

"ARE YOU FUCKING SERIOUS?"

Three hours later, Grimes lurches into view, looking very pleased with himself.

"Thank God!" I cry. "Did you see my cousin?"

"I did," he nods.

"Tell me. What did he say?"

"He says he'll have his cook drop off the jam sponge tomorrow morning."

"Excuse me? What jam sponge?"

"WHAT ABOUT MY GRANNY?" the voice in the darkness yells. Grimes purses his ghastly lips.

"She denies all knowledge of you."

"YOU MORON!" I shriek.

Miss Nony is a C*nt!

Brad Cobb

A silence of such a magnitude as to seem incomprehensible presided over the fields of Dyess, Arkansas in 1920 - as it does today. The world there looked like row after raised row of turned earth and cotton, which stretched from wherever one stood to a horizon so distant as to appear unreachable. These alluvial plains were the home of Nonetta Vandegrift, known to all as Miss Nony, the final carrier of Vandergrift blood.

She sat barefoot beside a white column on the portico of the family manor. Gazing, with perfect stillness into the fields, considering things in back of herself, apparitions that only faintly made themselves known. Fancies spawned of the fecund soil of tedium blossomed within her, one being the idea that she was a tiny document covered in the scrawl of indecipherable runes, one that had become lost in a vast archive.

The palm of her slender hand covered her side and the tingling sensation beneath it had made its initial visitation on the forenoon of the previous day. To her, it felt like being sliced with a razor charged with low electrical current.

With a sigh, she arose and walked through the open double doors and into the cavernous front room. She started up the curving staircase where mosquitoes whined and drifted, grasping the balustrade but keeping one hand tight against her side.

Upstairs, she faced away from a scrying glass that stretched from floor to ceiling and undressed, returned her palm to her side, then turned to her reflection.

At 20 she was the picture of gentility, as refined looking as any of the Vandergrift matriarchs in the oil paintings along the staircase; tall and balletic, with an aquiline nose and eyes the color of rice fields in the deep of summer.

Her hand came away from her side as haltingly as the procession of time in the hinterlands, to reveal what seemed to her the lips of an imbecile. At any moment she expected them to drool or gibber, yet they persisted in their silence, unwilling in any way to expound upon their mystery.

What, she wondered, had summoned the birth of it there in her side? A malady spawned from a coupling of her kinsmen that bore too close a relation? Some curse cast by the rough magic of a root woman? Or rather Divine Sanction? She already, of course, possessed the one given to all her sex at birth, and though she was in no way ashamed of it, she had always been haunted by the absurd thought - *one hole, one emptiness.* The meaning of this mystified her as much as the new orifice which now made her two emptinesses. At first, she had suspected a skin lesion of sorts. But, as evidence to the contrary mounted, she accepted it for what it was and resigned herself to her new abyss.

That night, in the wee hours, her curious fingers drifted to both, and she found her lonely pleasures multiplied. With dawn came further bewilderment when she discovered yet another had blossomed on her opposite side.

She rang a handbell for her chatelaine, Rose Linehan, a frumpy young woman with ears like pot handles, who spoke nearly as sparingly as her mistress, yet from diffidence rather than depth.

Miss Nony said, "Summon Dr. Mashburn. "

"Is all well, ma'am?"

She didn't answer and laid there staring at, or beyond, the stamped tin ceiling - either at everything or nothing. It was impossible to tell.

"Ma'am? "Rose said. "Ma'am?"

The doctor serving Dyess and the surrounding provinces was Elton Mashburn, a typical country gentleman with a Van Dyke, hair the color of pearls and a monocle which somehow enhanced the good nature of his face.

Rose showed him to the room and he stepped in. He bent his head in greeting and said quite happily, "Miss Vandergrift! What seems to be the problem, my dear?"

Miss Nony arose from the gargantuan bed and strode as quietly as dawn around it to face him. She glided to a stop and let her robe fall with a tiny *hush* to the floor.

The Physician's fingers promptly unfurled, and his black bag banged against the hardwood. He gawped like a simpleton, while the monocle fell from his eye and spun in ever quickening circles. He reached to straighten what was no longer there and noticed its absence. Only then did he retrieve it.

"And, and… you have had *these*... always?"

"No," she answered. "One opened yesterday. The other, sometime in the night."

Mashburn swallowed hard and exhaled. He cleaned his monocle and redonned it.

"Frankly, Miss Nony, I don't understand how that could be. How could you have not borne them since birth? They don't suddenly appear like a wart. You must be mistaken. Yes. Mistaken."

"You delivered me, doctor."

Good God! He thought. He had. A perfectly normal girlchild, or so it had seemed.

At that moment, Rose entered and sent the tea service careening. She screamed and couldn't stop until the doctor administered an injection. After a short, troubled rest she packed her bags and abandoned her position.

Dr. Mashburn put on his head mirror.

"May I?" he asked, indicating he wished to examine her.

She nodded once and he approached like a man going to the gallows. Afterwards, he said.

"I'm just a simple country doctor. Your problem is *far* beyond my expertise. However, there are men highly regarded in their fields who I would like your permission to contact, so a more astute diagnosis might be rendered. Then perhaps some avenue of treatment might be found."

Nony looked back at him as she put on her gown, and somewhere in her peculiar gaze he was sure, despite her silence, he saw an affirmation.

"Very well." He attempted to appear buoyant. "It is my hope, given the nature of the situation, they might arrive forthwith."

Messages were immediately wired to his contacts, who were skeptical but intrigued and agreed to hasten to the peripheries for the germinal investigation.

Elton Mashburn canceled his remaining appointments for the day, then for the rest of his life. He never again practiced medicine. After that fateful morning it appears his existence took a turn for the worst. Increasingly he was given to strong drink, month-long bouts of inebriation, and chronic onanism. He began to eye his wife with the obsessive suspicion of a paranoiac, demanding she submit to nude examinations during which he pinched and pulled her flesh in various locations and scrutinized the tiniest skin abrasion with a magnifying glass for hours on end.

Psychiatrist Manfred Luge, author of the book *What the Doctor Saw* (Los Angeles, Bleucher and Holt, 1929) studied Mashburn in the years following the episode. Luge writes that Mashburn was haunted by recurring nightmares (ones that have since been profusely studied and interpreted with widely divaricated findings). In one, a whale beaches itself as Mashburn is standing and reflecting on the tide. He discovers the whale can speak and thus begins a lengthy discourse in which the whale argues for the possibility of scientific knowledge based on inductive reasoning, while Mashburn, outraged, advocates for deductive reasoning. The whale then slowly opens its mouth and makes a sound Mashburn equates with some Eastern religion.

Oohhmmm.

From the darkness inside, a species of screaming long-armed apes scamper out (some squirm from the blowhole) and fall upon Mashburn, who is then forced to wear a bustier and dance the Charleston, while the simians hoot, incessantly masturbate and throw feces at his ankles.

In yet another, he lives in a room by the sea and an unknown woman, whose presence fills him with horror (he doesn't know why) comes to visit. She never calls him by name but rather throws wide her arms and yells "My magnificent Aristophanes!"

She always bears a gift (one of the few variables in the dream); she brings wind-up toys that totter and glide and buzz like a hive of bees, figurines carved from jade or obsidian, fine German straight razors, polished seashells, boxes that unfold to reveal bottles containing liniments and healing tonics and marionettes so diminutive that it is impossible to manipulate their strings. In a filthy nest, in one corner of his room, lives a brace of vulture hatchlings and the woman always opens a cigarette case from which she removes slivers of fetid carrion that she dangles above their hissing snapping beaks, while talking baby talk. Then she stands beside him before the window holding his arm in a manner of restraint rather than affection, as they look out on the sea. Luge states that such was Mashburn's terror during the dream that often he awoke to find he had shat the bed.

The night following Dr. Mashburn's visit, two more pert and supple openings configured on Miss Nony's cream colored skin. One on her right thigh and the other in the center of her left buttock.

She stood this way and that before the scrying glass, using deft fingers to manipulate her labium, first one then another, into smiles or frowns or positions that indicated aghastment. She pontificated Shakespeare as she played the ventriloquist with them.

She tried not to move her lips, the ones on her face, as she said

To be or not to be. That is the question!

And

When we are born, we cry that we are born to this great stage of fools.

And

If you can look into the seeds of time, and say which grain will grow and which will not, speak then unto me.

And

Cover me, Pinkston. Lest this depth within me be revealed.

Concerning the last recitation, she could not recall if the Noble Bard had written as much, or if it was her own spontaneous creation. Anyway, who, pray tell, was Pinkston? The only person of that patronymic she had known was her nanny from early childhood, Georgia Ann.

By the time the august doctors assembled in Dyess, Miss Nony had 14 openings and could not help but wonder *how many emptinesses am I now?*

The patient disrobed and stood in the center of a large Persian rug of baroque design, while they revolved round her like moons around a planet, stroking their beards and making sounds of perplexity and astonishment. Cutting their eyes at colleagues, trying to discern, or at least theorize, some point of origin to what they had hastily decided to refer to as 'wounds', since they could reach no agreement that they were indeed vaginas. And, if they were, did each have a corresponding uterus and, if so, was each capable of producing offspring?

The prevailing word of the day was Dismay. Questions gave rise to more questions. More wounds or lady parts or vaginas or whatevers appeared each day. Debates between the doctors occurred every evening at the Vandergrift estate where they had quartered themselves.

Miss Nony gave herself to their probings and stuporous looks and questions (though she offered no answers).

Word of her ailment first escaped the farm's perimeter then the town's, and the curious and mercenary gathered outside.

Carnival owners with promises of main attraction billing came, only to find their hopes unrealized.

Lotharios arrived with their skimmer hats and gleaming big-toothed smiles. They wooed and lost and were sent away lacking. Handsome Jack of Memphis, defiler of over one thousand belles, hung himself from the lone Cottonwood on the estate, unable to bear the shame of failed conquest.

Peddlers of chastity belts and perfumed douches and yeasticides found no sales there.

One afternoon a group of men from a polyandry sect in Kansas knelt on the piazza with roses and boxes of assorted creams and engagement rings. In one voice they proposed marriage and, though Nony declined their offer, it was later that same night she disappeared and couldn't be found even after a thorough search of the grounds and surrounding area. (Thereafter, a permanent guard was stationed outside her bedroom).

At sunrise next day she reappeared, disheveled and wan, cotton detritus in her hair. She looked to be swollen at various points on her body, with what the doctors suspected were tumors, each in proximity to one of her wounds.

One wound, one tumor, they noted. She was unwilling to answer their enquiries or submit to an examination.

In the postprandial of that same day, her physicians became aware of a dilation of each wound but nothing was seen emerging, neither baby nor devil. Before long, she was groaning, then screaming. Then births, or what some later would argue were births, did indeed follow - and all at once.

They were described as Maelstroms that levitated around Nony. The siblings were circular in shape and slowly revolved, so they resembled whirlpools or stars imploding or whorled hypnotist coins or hurricanes from above. They looked to be composed of a thin mist or a sheer gauze or of webs spun by delicate minuscule spiders.

Then came something like a peal of thunder which so shook the ground that Miss Nony's fine teacup collection rattled in their saucers and Doctor Clutchner's false teeth shook from his mouth and clattered on the floor like dice. Every window in the place shattered and all the doctors dove for cover and peeked over the high backs of the divans and around marble statuary - to see the Maelstroms drift toward the windows and vanish out of them, as aptly as master thieves.

"This could very well be the beginning of the end of days," one colleague was heard to say to another.

Few things concerning Miss Nony were agreed upon by the Cadre and many different factions formed. Meanwhile, new wounds continued to appear, and not always that for which she was becoming known (one faction began referring to them as 'pseudovaginas') but also what appeared to be a mouth on her left shoulder and an anus in back of her right hand.

On closer inspection, one faction argued that the mouth was imitating a vagina while another was adamant it was a vagina imitating a mouth. Dr. Chapman tried to feed it a grape, Swiss cheese, a hushpuppy, and one of the assorted creams brought by the sect - but it would only nibble then spit it out like a finicky child.

Other debates ensued. The anus was imitating a vagina; a pseudo-vagina was masquerading as an anus. The grape was, in all truth, a cube of Swiss cheese imitating a vagina imitating a mouth.

At the forefront of all the unanswerable questions was a riddle - what exactly *is* Miss Nony?

A group that called themselves The Daughters of Transcendent Transmorphism appeared at the estate, clad in white robes and conical hats - which were folded along the front to resemble a vulva. At the point was another fold to give the impression of a clitoral hood. Despite the Cadre's objections they forced their way into the manor, their cones rocking back and forth and going askew with the effort.

They screamed RAPE! BLOODY RAPE!!! whenever a male laid hands on them. They gathered reverently around Miss Nony, who sat knitting a shawl and did not look up. She was dressed in a cream-colored kimono, rouge evening gloves and a pillbox hat with a lace veil. The Daughters asked questions in soft voices but they went unanswered. In a Eureka moment, members realized, en masse, that Nonetta Vandergrift was indeed speaking in the silence. Hidden Morse code messages were discovered in the clicking of her knitting needles, though they were cryptic (beautifully so) and subject to interpretation.

They would later be published under the title *The Nonettic Truths* (New York, Sapphic Rites, 1925).

Utterly flummoxed and lacking direction, the Cadre elected one member from each faction to an ecumenical council whose job it was to address the pressing questions concerning the patient and establish some common ground from which the group might move forward. As it turned out, lacking concrete answers and impoverished by empty theory, any agreement was hopeless and matters degenerated to the point where they constantly accused each other of Mashburnism[1], and several riots nearly broke out.

In the end, a single resolution was passed. It was agreed that Nonetta Vandergrift was incurably, and perhaps criminally, insane. That her wounds or buttholes or mouths or pseudovaginas or protoplasmic pudenda or openings or vents or whatever in the hell they might be, were a result of a psychosomatic disorder that was a by-product of her madness. Possibly.

On the day they had her removed from her ancestral home she resembled someone that had been ran through by a troop of sword-wielding Cavaliers. As before, for decency's sake, she was dressed in garments which left nothing uncovered. Her head (new ground for her sprouting wounds) was wrapped in bandages, with the exception of those haunting eyes.

The camp of onlookers moved from her estate and relocated outside the iron gates of Bensonhurst Asylum, where they observed from across the grounds on which cotton was planted right up to the Ivy covered rockwork of the building.

She was placed in a padded cell that reeked of pine oil and some faintly metallic scent that had no name. Shortly after her arrival the place became plagued by strange occurrences. Among the staff a high

---

1

[1] Term Coined by the Dyess Cadre which means an overly emotional reaction to a patient's affliction.

number of suicides began to take place. Some left notes claiming that Miss Nony's wounds, when no one else was around, whispered unspeakable things to them. Good news to the faction that claimed her openings were actually mouths masquerading as vaginas (or mouths masquerading as wounds). As an addendum to their original hypothesis, they proposed that the births of the Whirligigs were only emanations of a substance of indefinite expansion and Miss Nony's dilations, the opening of mouths to belch. Thus, once again, debate raged.

"If that's an asshole, Doctor McMurtry, you two-bit quack, I'll kiss yours!"

"And so you shall, you feckless son of a whore!"

"Philistine! Shitass!"

"Fellator! Buffoon!"

An inmate diagnosed with dementia praecox, a former union delegate from Chicago, organized fellow inmates in a strike - the first (and only) of its kind among mental patients. Their foremost (and most rational) demand being the right to have multiple vaginas like Miss Nony, or penises, or else a mixture of the two - and the inalienable right to fuck themselves to death. Miss Nony came to be seen as being affiliated with the bosses and greed, perhaps because she alone was the possessor of several whatevers. Strikers walked a picket around the Day Room carrying signs that read *Miss Nony is a Capitalist Stooge!* And *Down with Nonyism!* And *The Devil Is Trying To Steal My Soul!* And *I Threw My Watch Away So Now The World Will Explode!*

Rumors came of the birth of Abominations in other towns and cities. In Bastrop, Louisiana the glans of a penis was born, 4 lb, 2 oz, and in Warm Springs Georgia, a thing, neither penis or vagina, reportedly came into the world - an 8 pound, 1oz perineum - a taint.

Apocalyptocists and catastrophists preached sermons on every corner. The doctor's former pronouncement declaring the beginning of the end of days now appeared to many to be an undeniable truth.

A renowned interpreter of Miss Nony's knitting needle sayings, known by the acronym GAP, claimed some sort of ambiguous relation to the patient. A stern and humorless woman with an ankh tattoo, she led The Daughters of Transcendent Transmorphism to an isolated compound in the Ozark mountains to await Miss Nony's appearance, which would be in the sky and might possibly follow the blast of a female angel's trumpet (the Nonettic Truths weren't one hundred percent clear on this) - wherewith they would be caught up on a luminescent stairway to paradise.

The Doctors Council finally agreed, somewhat, on a name for Miss Nony's disorder - *Referential gynomulticommiseruntism**. The asterisk was placed afterwards at the insistence of Dr. Abraham Schwartz, a powerful proctologist and leader of the faction claiming the wounds were actually anuses and the births of the Pinwheels merely farts of a dense and rarified nature, usually seen only among the more gaseous mammals such as hippos and manatees and mules - yet flatulence all the same. Schwartz insisted, at the lunch preceding the so-called 'births', the patient had dined on speckled butter beans and collard greens with pepper sauce, a fact attested to by the kitchen staff.

Most of the patient's time was passed in her cell, segregated from the other inmates, except during Activity Hour, when she composed works of crayon and finger paint and glitter and glued macaroni elbows that were of such awe-inspiring quality as to draw representatives and monetary offers from art galleries around the world (more proof to the strikers that she was a reactionary lackey and the reincarnation of Napoleon Bonaparte).

On the eve of her first menstrual period since the onset of her predicament, in the space between twilight and darkness, Miss Nony's plaintive angelic voice, so rarely offered, was heard from her cell - like one calling from the depths of a cave. It was singing a *lied* by Schubert - *Leise Flehan Meine* (Plead Softly Mine).

The staff grew quiet and still. The strikers paused on their picket, let down their signs and listened. The voices in their heads ceased and hearkened. The electroshock machine stopped humming and surging as if it too had an ear. The throng outside the gates, even from across such a distance, hushed and turned their ears and listened to what sounded like the tiniest voice in the biggest world. After the *lied* she continued with *You Tell Me Your Dream, I'll Tell You Mine* but to a tempo with which it had never been paired. Then Purcell's *O Solitude*.

A long period of silence ensued and Miss Nony, as always, became as mute as her wounds. The listeners no longer listened and returned to the safe and suffocating banality of routine.

But the sounds that later came were so upsetting that neither doctor nor nurse was bold enough to slide back the slot on the cell door and peer inside. These grew progressively louder and more bizarre, at one point like radio static. Within this, the sound of rending flesh and the heavy breath of one either aroused or enraged or both.

At midnight a great concussion was felt and heard, which roused the crowd outside the gates and turned every eye towards Bensonhurst in the hope of catching a glimpse of what had come to be called 'The Great Aberration'.

The quietude which followed the concussion frittered away in an accumulating clamor, then a chorus of screams nearly inhuman with horror and agony. The crowd could hear doctors shouting orders in the pandemonium and people crying out for God. A huge physiognomy was glimpsed, dark red in color, rushing past windows that soon became splattered and streaked with what appeared to be blood. A squall arose over the sea of cotton and serpent tongues of lightning repeatedly struck the rods on the gables of the asylum. One by one, the lights were extinguished and, over the space of an hour, the screams and chaos fell away by increments like an old clock winding down.

The sheriff arrived at dawn and stood with the crowd staring through the mist at the dim Gothic outlines of Bensonhurst, with its pillars and pinnacles and archways. The place had never seemed more bound by muteness and no one took a step toward such a silence.

Dr Maximus Humboldt of New York, specialist in diseases of the female genitalia and noted skeptic of the mouth, anus, and pseudo-vagina theories of his inept hick colleagues, arrived from a boarding house (he refused to lodge with the Cadre). He began pushing his way through the crowd. In front he held up his hands for silence.

"Please, please, gentlemen! Quiet please, all you *brave* men," he said condescendingly. "I ask that you keep your place here with the women, where I am sure you all feel quite at home. I shall get to the bottom of matters presently."

"Fuck you Humboldt!" a voice shouted.

"Yes, "Humboldt muttered. "Quite so. Indeed."

He opened the creaking gate and haughtily marched up the path to the asylum.

In the years that followed, Humboldt wrote a book about the Nonetta Vandegrift episode, though it appears he had difficulty settling on the title. It was first released as *The Abysses at Dyess* (Memphis, Big Cotton 1929), then 5 years later as *Chasms* (Little Rock, S&S 1934). Then, only a year later, as *Hole* (Kansas City, Dreiser and Light 1935). A final edition was released under the enigmatic title, *A Tapper at the Window* (New Orleans, Juno 1938). After this Humboldt was lost to history.

He describes what he found that morning.

"Neither the operating table nor the butchery of the Great War were preparation for what awaited me. The majority of the men I came upon had their eyes gouged out and their scrotums ripped away, and, in place of their eyes, were the testicles like pink veiny stones. Many of the women were bent like the most nimble of contortionist, their entire heads shoved up their rectums so that they resembled some new species of invertebrate… Strikers were shish kabobbed with the handles of their picket signs… Tendons were used as rope to tie the corpses in macabre imitations of life - a group arranged around a table played cards - two played Leapfrog frozen in time - women appeared to gossip and whisper in one another's ears, mouths formed mirthless smiles beneath eyes of utter indifference... I came upon a wall of nailed ears that were looked upon by bodies seated in a semicircle of chairs around it, chins balanced on fists as though in deepest contemplation… The hallways were lined on both sides with severed heads decorated with a warpaint of menstrual blood…"

So continues Humboldt's description for 24 pages, none of which are broken into paragraphs, until he ends with, "It is beyond my powers of explanation, but there was a strange artistic quality about the massacre, like from the darkest nightmare of an Old Master."

Curiously absent from all the editions is the part where he departed the building after his investigation. Humboldt, as a true man of science, was determined to appear stoic even though his face was as white as Arsenic, and he hovered at the edge of incontinence. His tie was loosened and he continually dabbed his forehead and lips with a handkerchief.

At first, he was able to maintain a somewhat noble gait despite his clenched butt cheeks. But as he was descending the steps he was struck with the spell of dizziness; he staggered slightly left, then right, then at the last step he collapsed, and the forbearance of his bowels was loosed. Two men from the crowd came up the path, bent like soldiers under fire, grabbed the sobbing hysterical Humboldt under his arms and whisked him away, making faces at his rankness and calling him insulting names.

In his tome, *Pits of Mystery*, considered by many to mark the beginning of Nonetta scholarship, Cranston Verve argues (with scant proof) that Vandegrift actually escaped by train under the alias Nona Hunderfeld and traveled to Memphis where, just after her arrival, her wounds began to heal of their own accord. According to Verve, she spent the rest of her life in the City on the American Nile (as a spinster) raising orchids for a botanical warehouse and working as a crowd estimator at public events in Shelby County.

In her book, *Rage From the Alluvium!* (New York, Nightwood, 1936) renowned and outspoken feminist Athena Bergson claims the massacre was the revolutionary act of an oppressed woman. She also claims that, afterward, Vandegrift escaped but to a wildly varied list of locales. Bergson makes the bizarre claim that Vandergrift was responsible for the manufacture and planting of the bomb at the Haymarket Riot of 1886, a time long before Nona Vandegrift was even conceived. When the forever unyielding Bergson was confronted with this fact she stated:

"I don't have to know something is true for it to be truth. Rather I *feel* it."

She would go on to make the equally ridiculous claim that Vandergrift was actually a Native American Shapeshifter and not bound by time as we know it. In subsequent editions of her book, she claims her subject was also responsible for two Wall Street bombings and the founding of the Molly Maguires, the Irish terrorist and saboteur organization. Furthermore, Bergson insists that Vandergrift lived briefly in Germany as a Nonetta scholar herself, a professor of 'Womyns' Studies at The Institute of Social Research in Frankfurt and wrote, during her stay, the infamous and anonymously penned book *Die Perverse Frau* (Leipzig, Schmutzige Schlampe,1950), a celebration of female deviancy.

After the rescue of Humboldt, the crowd was clueless as to what their next move should be. Some suggested organizing an armed militia to raid the asylum; some said the place should be set aflame. There were many proposals, but no voice spoke with insistence.

At the height of the confusion a finger pointed up and, there in the ether, the Maelstroms were seen wheeling in sedate beauty.

Miles away at their Ozark compound, The Daughters of Transcendent Transmorphism took note of this apocalyptic sign (they kept a lookout in the Sycamore tree) and promptly flung themselves from a 200-foot bluff, white robes billowing and their cones drifting haphazardly as out of control rockets, and not one was caught up on the prophesied stairwell. Each Daughter was briefly aware of GAP's dreadful misinterpretation of the knitting needle aphorisms (more specifically *Aphorism #31*) before being crushed on the boulders below, something that would never have happened had they located their compound on the flat fecund plains which were the homeland of the Chosen One, as had been strenuously argued by new member, Rose Linehan, the former chatelaine of Nonetta Vandergrift and lone survivor of the Ozark fiasco. Her survivorship was apparently too much for Ms. Linehan's nerves, for she was committed shortly after to a mental ward in Little Rock and, for the rest of her life, only spoke four words, always smiling and shaking her head as though she couldn't believe her argument had gone unheeded.

"I told you so," she would say from sunrise to sunset. "*I told you so.*"

A procession of booming footsteps was heard coming from the direction of the asylum, and the crowd turned their eyes from the sky and narrowed them toward the distance.

A tall sleek figure bowed to fit beneath the doorway arch of Bensonhurst then strode proudly like a thing that had triumphed, across the veranda, past urns of Creeping Jenny and Passion Flower and the statue of the Venus de Milo. At the edge of the steps it paused, put hands on its hips and looked to be surveying its domain, which was not only Dyess, every observer could see this, but the world and all that was in it. The countenance of the women in the crowd looked to scowl and the men, with spontaneity and compulsion, leaned back their heads and sampled the air, their noses twitching and quivering like bawl hounds.

And, despite their fear of the intimidating figure, the world had never felt more right. Each man thought of the figure on the veranda by a poetic name of their own making - a Moist Fury, My Ravening made Flesh, the Lair Where a Splendorous Beast Dreams, the Cavern Where Ecstasy and Delirium Live in Harmony, the Crevice Whose Name is Grandeur, Cave of Wonders, Shaky Pudding... They had the inexplicable urge to yap and howl. What posed before them was a colossal magnificent vagina and, from the bullet-like clitoris that adorned it like a crown, to the immaculate perineum, the color of coral and smooth as a lake at dawn, everything about it spoke of perfection. And no one doubted it was Miss Nony, especially later when her body was not found among the victims in Bensonhurst.

The Cadre stood watch as well, and Doctor Turkington, leader of the faction that had all along insisted the wounds were vaginas, sauntered with a smirking smile over to Doctor Fuorquor, leader of the mouths imitating vaginas faction, spat in his face, kicked him in the groin with all his might, then sauntered back.

She walked down the steps and started along the road through the cotton at an ever quickening pace that was as elegant and weightless as a dancer of great renown until, finally, she was moving by leaps, like a gazelle, toward the front gate and the onlookers. Halfway there strange noises were heard, banging sounds like the closing of powerful electrical breakers, and every eye beheld that sections of Miss Nony's form began to close in upon themselves like a Chinese puzzle box. She was folding up like a bed sheet, and this strange redaction continued even as she leapt above the crowd like an athlete clearing a hurdle and folded so in upon herself that she vanished into a succinct multicolored asterisk like a burst of fireworks (though some would later claim it more closely resembled an exclamation point) to the brief accompanying sound of a tintinnabulation that resembled a wand moving across a line of hanging chimes.

Then the throng, already looking up, sought the Maelstroms, those manifestations that had made the distance between Heaven and Earth seem so less vast, and they too were nowhere to be found, and all that remained was an anguished union: the ringing silence of the fields, and the wind that came blowing through the cotton.

Very Well

Nathan Cromwell

The waitress noted Dan's bed hair, cheap suit and stapled-rather-than-knotted tie - and managed an encouraging smile.

"Big day ahead? What would you like?"

Dan tapped the menu, staring but not reading.

"Been married twice." He looked up. "Both my ex-wives met at the courthouse a couple of months ago and hooked up."

"That's sweet. Would you like?..."

"They opened a business together… today's my job interview."

"How 'bout I start you with some coffee while you decide?" she chirped before escaping to the server station.

Dan assessed. The fit brunette was clean, considerate, and had shown interest, meeting three of his two requirements. He sat straighter, channeled Humphrey Bogart, and waited for her return.

"I'm not what you would consider a successful man," he explained as she put down the mug. "But you won't find anyone easier to get along wi…"

"I'm just a waitress," she replied.

"Now, sweetheart," Dan said. "Ain't nothing low about slinging coffee. In fact, I…"

"I meant I'm not a social worker or a shrink. You wanna order?"

"What's cheap?" he grumbled. "Behind on alimony."

An hour later, Dan parked at a converted warehouse of wisteria-scribbled brick and baby blue trim. At the overly bulletined glass door underneath, a shingle announced: *Clay More!*

"Play More!" He paused, adopted a can-do attitude and slouched into the lobby. The female receptionist's enthusiastic smile waned to noncommittal.

"Yes?"

"Hello, ma'am. I have an appointment."

She leaned through the doorway behind her.

"Beatrix, the interview is here." She turned back to Dan. "Ms. Falchion is one of the owners."

"We've met."

A healthy brunette in glasses appeared.

"Come in, Dannie."

The windowless office had a fading Ficus plant, two padded armchairs, a filing cabinet, four framed posters shouting encouragement and a sturdy wood desk. Behind the nameplate, stack tray and pen-filled coffee mug sat a similarly fit brunette.

Bea gestured for Dan to sit and stood behind the other woman. "Dannie, this is Ginny Morningstar, my partner."

"We've met."

"Dan, we run a therapeutic pottery business." Ginny leaned onto her forearms. "Working with clay is magic. It helps people."

"Now that we've answered all your questions about our business," Bea said. "We'd like to explain the job."

A timer chimed. The two women swapped places. Bea flipped the nameplate and smiled at Dan.

"Our business is finally edging into the black but a little extra cash would let us invest in things like a second desk. That's where you come in."

Ginny edged forward.

"We need a nighttime security guard, someone to sit on his ass for hours while nothing happens. We thought of you."

"But that costs money," Bea explained. "No way around it. Now, you owe each of us back alimony, so we'll help you do the right thing and stay out of court by deducting from your paycheck each week. Everybody wins."

"Wait!" Dan gasped. "You two used to be such sweet, easygoing girls. What happened?"

"We married you."

He held out his hands. "Now…"

"Congratulations, Dan!" Ginny exclaimed. "You got the job."

Bea grabbed a form off the desk and stood.

"Dannie, follow me." She handed the paper to a young man who had replaced the earlier receptionist. "Dirk, could you start Dannie's employment paperwork? You can get his personal information off this judicial contempt citation."

Ginny strode out of the office.

"Okay, Bea, let's show Dan our baby."

"Here," Bea announced as they stepped into a room of shelves and tables. "We have the shop. Much of it is pieces on commission from actual potters. But, as our clients improve, more of it will be in-house. This is one of Lisa's. She shows such promise, don't you think?"

She stood to block Dan's view.

"Oh, and you are not allowed in here ever again because you're a klutz. Follow me."

The next room had kilns, potter's wheels, and worktables.

"Our workshop," Ginny announced. "We offer classes, but we also reserve large blocks of rentable time for clients to run free with their imaginations. But we're not soft about it, like some tired old community craft center. We drive our clients to 'level up' their skills by running our art studio like an addictive game app's rewards system."

"We post pics of well-executed pieces online, for the public to vote on," Bea explained as they stopped near an antique pumpkin pine display case. She tapped a fingernail on the glass door. "The really good work we place on these coveted shelves."

Dan regarded the morel-themed salt and pepper shakers, a terra-cotta airplane and sun-yellow trivet.

"Those are nice."

For once, they didn't question his judgement.

"As you can see," she continued. "We keep the shelves sparse, to make them exclusive."

"Everyone wants in here." Ginny turned slowly. "You gotta have ambition." As she stared into Dan's face, her eyes widened and her skin tone dropped two shades. "Bea and I have both seen, up close, what the lack of ambition will do to a person. We'll never let go of ambition."

"Never." Bea shook her head, blinked. "Then the best of these will make the trip to our store."

Ginny patted her partner's back.

"We close at 11.00pm and that's when you come in. We've had problems at night. Objects get moved, things get broken. Occasionally a work in progress will have a brutally honest comment scratched into it. We've had complaints. A big corporation can get caught dumping waste into school cafeterias and move on but we're a small struggling business - really can't afford something screwing us up now. So, your job is to stay in this room and find out what's going on. Hell, maybe you being here will act as a deterrent."

"You want me to stop it?"

"No. No, we do not." Ginny rolled her eyes. "Let's say it's rats. We don't want you chasing them through the workshop, knocking things off tables. Or, if it's bored teens or angry Native American burial ground ghosts, we don't want you throwing things at them. Just tell us what it is and we'll deal with it."

"But what if I can stop it?"

"You can't," Bea informed him.

"Suppose?..."

"You can't," Ginny iterated.

"But…" he started, as they leaned into his face.

"You…"

"…Can't."

At midnight the ghost appeared.

As instructed, Dan had spent the last hour on his ass doing nothing, lost in wondering if his wives would spring for a portable television, so he could watch classic movies. Startled, he jumped up and began backing towards the nearest door.

The blonde woman in lace boots, black skirt, white blouse, and fashionable hair bun wagged her finger.

"Those two uptight birds will have a sprightly ramble across your bum should you go into their precious store, don't you think? Come here like a good chappie. No? Fine, you stay there. My name is Sheila and I currently live in this display cabinet. I am under a curse and cannot leave. Yes, I am out now, but only for a five-minute interval around midnight - and within a small compass of my prison. I'd be awfully chuffed were you to hear me out."

Dan could sense when people were building toward asking for a favor. He grasped for derailing questions.

"How do I know you're really cursed?"

"Are you bloody thick? I'm a semi-transparent! Now, back in 1821, Peter Peters had a problem. He had a wife." She gestured to herself. "Plus two children - Margarethe and Hansel."

Dan stayed silent.

"They were poor but happy…ish. Now, Peter was easy on the eyes, and some sad old slag - she happened to be a witch - whammied the bloke into a besotted idiot. Peter divorced his wife and sent the kids to live in the forest with their new step-grannie. But a man can love more than one woman at time and Peter saw his old spouse on the sly, slipping her the odd pound from his new rich wife's trove."

"Why do you keep talking about yourself in the third person?"

"Why do you keep interrupting? The witch found out and imprisoned the wife in this display cabinet."

"What happened to the kids?"

"WHO CARES? I'm telling you MY story."

"They're your children."

The spectre walked over to a kiln and put her finger on the switch.

"Are you going to keep interrupting me?"

"I could turn it back on."

"But would that fluctuation ruin the pottery?"

Dan didn't know. And because his ex-wives had grown less tolerant, he shut up.

"The husband felt bad," she continued. "So, he searched the house and found the witch's spell book. He couldn't break the curse but he was able make it more comfortable. The wife remained, trapped in a gilded cage, cosseted and waited upon and fed sweet tidbits and delicacies - but ever so lonely. Will you help me escape?"

"If your husband couldn't free you, how can I?"

"My prison has a vast library. In it I discovered references to a spell that could release me. All it takes is gathering a few materials and reading some very, very short paragraphs aloud."

"That sounds like a lot of work and you don't seem so bad off."

She scowled, considered, smiled coyly.

"I'm not really a ghost because I'm not dead. And I'll be all warm and touchable again when I get out." She glanced both ways and lowered her voice to a husky whisper. "If you do the spell, I'll let you inside."

"Ain't you married?"

"Peter's been dead for a hundred and fifty years at best."

Dan scratched his chin. "You're a looker but I got a waitress seems hot for me who'd be less effort."

She walked to a nearby worktable and lifted a lopsided teapot by its handle.

"Dan, I overheard that your job is to prevent… this." She let go. "If I'm gone, that won't happen. Understand?"

Then he gloriously saw it. Without the ghost, he would have nothing to do. Nights and nights of doing nothing yet getting paid for it. Of course, he'd still be at work, so it wouldn't be as relaxing. Yet, with no fear of damage occurring, he could sneak out and do nothing in a more pleasant place and return before opening.

"What do I have to do?"

Sheila recited a list of items to collect and told him to be ready at midnight, when she would guide him through the ritual. A few seconds later, she was sucked back into the cabinet, somewhere between the salt shaker and the terra-cotta airplane.

Bea stood, palms on the desktop.

"What happened to Chi-chi's teapot last night?"

"I tripped on a shoelace," Dan replied, tipping forward and waving his arms wildly.

Ginny appeared baffled.

"We hired you to sit on your ass, something you've never had a problem achieving."

"I would move around less if you got a portable TV."

Bea pulled her hand back as if preparing to slap him.

"You… you have the gall to ask for a television when you owe us both so much money?" She yanked a fat crimson candle labeled 'Serenity' from a shelf, tore off the wrapper, and slid it under her nose, snorting loudly.

"Okay, I know you never expend effort without a reason," she sighed. "Fess up: What were you really doing?"

"Why do you two treat me like I'm lazy and stupid? Maybe if you…"

Bea lit the candle.

"I remember, often, watching you try to carry ten bags of groceries from the car…"

"Of which two usually reached the counter," Ginny added.

"And you telling me that fetching the dropped ones was easier because they were closer to the house than the car."

"That's simple logic, Bea. I saved tons of distance over the years."

"Exactly," Bea frowned. "When it comes to slacking, you're a hyperactive, insane genius."

She slapped the desktop.

"We'll tell Chi-chi the teapot sold and deduct it from your paycheck."

"What? It didn't look finished."

"Just think how empowered Chi-chi will feel selling an unfired, lidless teapot," Ginny grinned.

"I don't want to pay for something useless."

"Neither do we, Dannie. But sometimes you gotta."

At 10:30pm, Dan stopped at a gas station, already behind schedule. After that hectic first night on the job, he had unwound by watching *Casablanca* twice, which had led to waking up late afternoon. Most of the day had been spent pep-talking himself into starting the errands, only to discover, after much driving, that all the second-hand stores had closed at nine or earlier. As he pumped, he decided that acquiring the non-store-bought items first would buy time for inspiration.

Returning to the task at hand, he noticed he'd put eight dollars of gas in the tank and only had five bucks. Pondering this complication, he realized that - because this was a self-service station - he was thus a temporary employee. He divided the state's minimum wage rate by the minutes he had labored and subtracted that from the eight dollars.

Still more than five.

Thinking deeper, he realized that, as an employee, he should get an employee discount and took off 20%. He was still over and, come to think of it, actually needed that five bucks to stretch the four days until his first paycheck.

He wrote an IOU on the back of an old lottery ticket for the entire reduced amount and shoved it into the pump's credit card slot. As soon as he got paid, this station would be his second settling-up stop, right after giving a tip to the nice waitress who had her sights on him. He put his hand on the ignition key and took a deep breath. Stealth would be impossible.

The car backfired like a cherry bomb and he drove away fast.

Ten minutes later, he crossed Tick Creek Bridge into the parking lot of his old high school - a bland, one-story sprawl of windows and graffiti remover-stained bricks. He drove onto the sidewalk and parallel-parked next to the wall. Climbing onto the roof of his car, he pulled down the retractable fire escape ladder he and his friend had used for skipping school in senior year. Dan was pleased to discover the faculty's die-hard smokers still broke the roof's door lock every time it got fixed. He sauntered downstairs to the library.

Behind the librarian's desk was a bookshelf whose top was too high for students to reach unaided. And, because of liability concerns, the school supplied no step stools. Dan grabbed the librarian's chair and climbed up. He scanned the titles the district had added after the lawsuit mandating religions besides Christianity be represented. *The Tripitaka, The Esperanto Koran, Torah for Dummies, The Kitáb-i-Aqdas Coloring Book, The Spaghetti Monstrum Volantes in Evangelii* and a Seventeenth Century leather-bound *Necronomicon*.

From there he went to Ms. Mark's classroom. He'd hated Ms. Marks, who was rumored to have mastered the spells in the *Necronomicon*. Dan believed it: she had taught him, his dad, his grandpa, and his great-grandpa, though she remained as lively and scary and middle-aged as ever. Now he thought about it, she had been the one to sue about including other religious texts.

He snatched the brass 'shut up' bell from her desk, grabbed a few sticks of chalk and checked her confiscation drawer. He scored a cool plastic *Star Trek* tricorder with sound buttons.

Up on the roof again, Dan watched five squad cars disgorging eight cops. The chief of police deliberately overstaffed his force - budget be damned - to make the town the safest in the state. Any crime, no matter how inconsequential, resulted in a crowd of excited cops.

Dan suspected he could slip away from a catercorner part of the school. But then, getting back to work would require a whole lot of walking, he'd be late and his wives would dock his pay.

"Up there!" shouted Eva, his favorite policewoman. "Hey, it's that idiot, Dan."

"Did someone spot my car?" Dan asked the upturned faces.

The chief of police strolled across the sidewalk.

"No, the school installed cameras and motion detectors back when people kept breaking in and stealing their computers."

"I didn't see any computers."

"Maybe again, someday, when they pay off the security equipment. Say, how about you come down and we chat? I always enjoy hearing the logic behind what you do. Let's start with the gas station and work up."

Dan knew police were like wives. When they wanted to have a serious talk, you were doomed. He tried to think of a way out, and it hit him.

"I booby-trapped the school with explosives. If the best years of our lives are our teens, why make us get up too early, stress us out and force us to run endless laps around the football field? Unless society agrees to allow a five-year sabbatical from high school, I'm going to end it all and take out a bunch of rubberneckers besides!"

The chief of police put both fists on his hips.

"I'm going to count to ten…"

Dan waved the Star Trek tricorder.

"Everyone leave… now! Please."

The police stepped back in unison. The chief of police held up his palms.

"Okay, let's…"

Dan pressed a button and the plastic lid flipped up.

"This is for the kids!"

The police scattered, tearing toward the safety of the muddy creek's ditch. Dan supposed they wouldn't take the time to look back and zipped down the fire escape. His car started with a bang and he heard answering terrified screams. He drove off. By the time they reached their vehicles, he'd have a head start. Probably they'd go to his home or one of his usual hangouts - not to a job they would not expect him to have in the first place. In a day or two he'd drop by the station and smooth things over.

Thinking about the police gave him an idea for the item he hadn't been able to buy…

For years, the chief of police had bragged that his town was so safe he left his door unlocked. In fact, he kept a campaign sign with that slogan staked on his lawn. And he was currently out and about. Dan was banking on the man not wanting a home invasion robbery - no, 'borrowry' - widely known and that he would keep this visit quiet.

"Sorry, Eppie," he said to the chief's wife.

"Dan." She froze in her chair, using a half-tatted doily as a shield. "Polite thing is to knock."

"I'll return this in a day or two." He unplugged the side table lamp and jogged back down the entry hall. Back in his car, he grinned. The only items left were already at his workplace.

Sure, he was an hour and forty minutes late for work and the ghost woman would probably be sore about it. But if he stuck to the back roads and didn't run into any cops - Eppie was probably calling her husband now - he could get everything set up and done before the business opened.

Dan grabbed five scented 'Ambition' candles from his ex-wives' office, swept a space in front of the display cabinet clear of smashed pottery, drew a magic almost-circle, lit the candles and began reading the spell. Two-thirds of the way through, Sheila appeared. Sparks flashed inside her body.

"You… you're succeeding! And without my guidance! Soon I'll be free of this blasted hutch and live a… where's the lamb?"

Dan paused.

"You said lamp."

"I DID NOT! How do you sacrifice a lamp? You blithering fat-slapper! You damnable clod!"

She arched her fingers preparatory to raking out his eye. Dan sensed things were not going well.

"Since we're this far in, why not try?"

"Oh, fine. Ducky, even." She crossed her arms and leaned against the cabinet. "Do go on. Finish the spell and then offer up the heart of a living lamp to the Elder Gods."

Dan read to the end and then drove a clay-smeared trimmer knife into the smiling ceramic crawdad, shattering it.

The Elder Gods are so named for a reason. Those eldritch ones stirred, peered through squamous sheets of cataracts and knew, vaguely in their dementia, that something was expected of them. They gave an uncertain thumbs up before, once more, sinking into their city - dreaming of non-Euclidean bingo.

Dan felt light-headed and light-bodied. He floated over the floor, drawn toward the display cabinet. Sheila waved as she bobbed past.

"Thank you, luv, for everything! You'll adore it in there, really you will."

Sheila stepped away from the urinal and zipped up the pants on Dan's body.

"Well, wasn't that all… floppity-boo?"

She walked out of the men's restroom frowning, grabbed Dan's belt and adjusted the pants. The front door lock rattled and Gina blew in.

"Dan! What the hell's happening?"

"Good morning, luv. You're up and about early."

Gina paused and tilted her head.

"Ah, you want to know if your precious pottery has been damaged. I broke a planter or two, there is a magic circle drawn on the floor with chalk, five burnt candles and a shattered lamp and such. One must expect these sorts of things, am I right?"

Sheila fiddled with the pants again.

"But it's the janitor's bailiwick, not mine, eh? Well, must be off. A lifetime of adventures ahead for this gal. Tatty-bye."

She pushed past Gina into a glorious morning.

Finally, freedom! She could go wherever she wanted. Being a man would be odd, doubtless. On the plus side, she would not be dismissed and condescended to and belittled… and it was a man's world - her world, now. She would be able to take full advantage of it.

Where should she go? She was in America so, perhaps, New York City. First, though, she would shower. And get clean clothes. A trip to the barber might not go amiss. And definitely a dentist's visit.

She rounded a corner to the parking lot and spotted six vehicles. She assumed the well-kept green one covered in bumper stickers and window decals belonged to Gina. That left the purple rattletrap as the most likely suspect because, logically, the four police cars must belong to the officers leaning against Dan's car. They stopped talking and turned to regard her.

Sheila noticed the handicapped parking sign and decided that Dan had bequeathed her a fine of some sort. Happily, she'd be long gone before it became delinquent.

"Morning, fellows. Long night, that. Time for me to get home for a kip and off to adventures after. I say, would you be so kind as to allow me access to my jalopy?"

One of the officers removed handcuffs from a holster and started twirling them on her index finger. The police began approaching.

"There's good chappies," Sheila encouraged as friendlily as her impatience would allow. She grabbed her belt and adjusted. "I hope you don't mind my asking, but do any of you lads know how to make your willy comfortable in trousers? Mine's all odd angles and bunches."

A carpeted, door-lined white hallway, lit by candelabras, stretched both directions. Dan reached for the nearest doorknob and noticed the femininity of his hand.

"Huh." He looked down his chest, seeing less floor than usual.

Inside, the room had a long counter with toiletries and plush towels of many colors. Half the wide sunken tub was blocked by the corner of a giant sun-yellow trivet. Across the hall, he peeked into a conservatory full of plants and a table with two comfy chairs. He walked to one end of the hallway and opened a stairwell door. He chose down.

The first thing he noticed in this hallway was the tip of a terra-cotta airplane wing protruding from one wall. He'd seen this airplane before - as well as the trivet - in the workshop's display cabinet. Doors lined one side of the hallway, same as above, but the right wall had only one. Going through that, he retreated, momentarily dizzy. The library was round and spiraled upward for ten, book-lined stories.

How was that possible? He had only descended one flight.

Dan shrugged. Magic, he supposed. The lobby contained a variety of chairs and reading tables. In one corner loomed a giant, morel-shaped salt shaker.

A prickle rankled his neck, and he turned.

The short, fit, furiously clean man in the doorway wore polished black boots, white knee socks, a crisp cream shirt, red silk bowtie, black swallowtail lederhosen with wool suspenders and a bowler hat sporting a feather in its band.

"Willkommen, old bean. Must be surprised, ja? I am Ludwig, your butler-cum-manservant."

An Austrian man trying to affect a posh British accent threw Dan more than being in a magic mansion.

"Frau Daniel, though you are trapped here, every luxury has been afforded for your comfort. The beds are soft and the finest pajamas and robes hang in the many closets. This ever-updating library is stocked to the rafters; the dining room seats fifty; the bathrooms are simply cracking, supplied with both showers and sunken baths and the gymnasium is always closed for repairs. I do all the cleaning and cooking and every room has a bell pull to summon me."

Dan plopped into one of the seats.

"How do you get in and out?"

Ludwig ran to the facing seat and perched on the edge.

"Herr Peters was not a pious man, as one might divine from his dabbling in the dark arts and helping imprison a cuckolded wife."

He shrugged

"Frau Sheila fudged her tale a bit. When Herr Peters imprisoned his first wife, he was not thinking of her soul - as would a good Christian - just her body. Then his wife located, among this vast library, a grimoire that allowed her to swap her soul for another. She fooled some poor maiden into performing the ritual and got the hell out."

"So, anyone stuck in here can escape, as long as they find some sucker to swap souls?" Dan stroked his chin. "I presume it's happened a few times."

"Ja. The most recent occupant trapped here, Frau Sheila, is now encased in your body and you are inhabiting the centuries-old body of Peter Peters' original wife."

Dan relaxed into his chair and put his feet on a table. Ludwig frowned fretfully at the shoe heels on wood

"To continue. I was a humble tanner, so when Herr Peters offered this job as an immortal butler, I took it. One must have ambition. Unlike you, however, I cannot leave. Do you have any questions?"

"Not so far."

"'I have been studying the books in the library. You will find my knowledge unparalleled. In fact, so far, none of the women has stumped me - although after a while they stop trying - saying my prattle annoys them. They avoid me but I get so lonely. I'm doing it now, the too much talking, am I not? Please, ask me something. Please."

"Do I get periods? 'Cause I hear they suck."

Ludwig turned ruddy.

"I, ah, assume not. None of the previous ladies mentioned such. Wouldn't you rather hear how you may escape this pris…"

"Hold on. I don't have to work or worry about food and I can just lay around and be served? Why would I get out?"

The butler blinked, baffled.

"Don't you want to be in the real world, with people?"

Dan's eyes widened. He rose and gripped Ludwig by the suspenders.

"I've seen what ambition does to people. Always pushing, always angry, always in a hurry." He shuddered. "Never going back."

Ludwig jumped up and paced.

"But… human contact, mine old bean. My few conversations with your predecessors have kept me sane. If I had only known! The loneliness… a beer with friends, a laugh with the ladies. My reading, my always learning, keeps me sharp, fresh. But you, you want to just sit! What is to become of me? Nein! It will not do. You are human, like me."

He grabbed Dan's shoulders.

"Ask me something else! Show me you have some capacity for conversation."

Ludwig sounded desperate. The man needed companionship and someone to show off to, so Dan decided to oblige. He hit on something he had always wondered about. The succession of women in his life slapping him, shouting and swearing, rolling their eyes, clawing him with their fingernails. Could this man clear up why?

"Do women like sex better?"

Ludwig nodded.

"Ja, that is what the blind seer Tiresias claimed, and studies support this. Anatomically, women have more nerves in…"

"Follow up question. Would you be up for testing that?"

The man's eyebrows raised and no blinking occurred for some time.

"Guess you haven't gotten asked before, huh?"

Eyebrows still up, Ludwig shook his head.

Dan put his arm over the man's shoulder and led him into the hallway. Ludwig would see a door at the end, but Dan saw a never-ending path to contentment. Better sex. No pressure.

"I love to listen and you sound like you love to learn and talk. You're better than a waitress."

They skirted the airplane wing.

"Ludwig, this looks like the beginning of a beautiful friendship. With benefits."

Dances with Scissors (But Slowly)

E d w a r d   P a l u m b o

I don't look out my picture window anymore. The world outside my home is dark, so very dark. Of course, it is nighttime and that may have something to do with it. Lucienne is back in town. She will visit, and soon, sashaying her lithe figure into my condominium like she owns the place. No one can sashay the way she does. We will make love the first night she is here, or she will attempt to murder me, as if there is a difference. Lucienne loves me, of that I am sure. But I hardly feel special to her eye. I am her one hundredth lover, or so she once told me.

"I'm amazed that you have seen one hundred men in your life," I remarked. "You cannot be much more than thirty years of age."

"You would be amazed at who I have seen," she replied. "And what I have seen."

Lucienne is hard to define. She is not amoral, neither is she immoral, nor is she anti-moral.

What she is, is morally indifferent.

"I live my life, my way!" she shouts to anyone who will listen and that, most often, is just her parrot - who then yells the same thing back at her.

"When did you first realize I was a vampire?" Lucienne once asked me, as she removed her fangs from my postman.

"Just now. And, by the way, you could have let the man deliver the mail. I am expecting a check from an Arab sultan."

"We will always have Arab sultans," she promised, as she brushed blond hair from her jade green eyes.

"And we will always have Paris," I replied.

Paris. That is where Lucienne and I met, five years ago. I was there to enjoy Le Tour de France but should have read my ticket more carefully, as I had actually bought admission to Le Tour de Frank, which was basically just hanging out in a guy's house. A friendly guy, yes, but not a livewire. He didn't even own a bike, for Pete's sake. Frank was what the French would call a *personne ennuyeuse*, which translates as a 'boring person' or a 'pedestrian covered with cheese' - depending on whom you ask.

I met Lucienne at a café in Le Marais, on the second day of my visit. I was enjoying a coffee near the window and Lucienne was at the next table, scolding her croissant for its lack of resolve. Our eyes met. I stayed in her apartment for a week. Lucienne made love like a tigress, or so she told me, every night when she got home. One evening, I awoke at midnight and my love was missing from the bed. She had left a note on her pillow:

Just went to pee. Relax.

Lucienne has visited me, in Boston, many times since we met. I look forward to her arrival but I do get queasy, and my bilirubin count goes through the roof. It is not easy loving one who is undead but nothing worthwhile is easy, except eating and sleeping and reading. Come to think of it, there is a whole host of worthwhile things that are easy. There is my phone. Would you excuse me?

That was Lucienne. She will be here tomorrow at noon. My new postman will be here around one pm.

Things are going to get tense.

Giant Midgets from Neptune

K y l e   O w e n s

Inside the darkness of the Jersey woods, Ollie and Neville Kimball, brothers from way back, were by a river on a cold Halloween night. They were looking for bullfrogs with flashlights and sharpened sticks, as the full moon shone down on them through black trees.

Suddenly, they both heard a strange noise, like a hum. A bright light flashed above their heads and a spaceship shaped like a giant Big Mac calmly lowered itself from the sky, where it sat down in a clearing only fifty yards away.

"What is that?" asked Ollie.

"It's a freaking flying saucer, is what it is."

"Why would they come here for?" Panic filled Ollie's voice.

"I bet they came down here to explore our world and learn all about us."

"They had the whole world to explore and they came to New Jersey?"

"They obviously wanted to learn from the best," said Neville.

The door to the space capsule opened and out walked two beings with space helmets made of clear glass. They had hoses that ran from their helmets to their backpacks and stood about four feet tall. On their chests, written in bold white letters, were the words 'Alien One' and 'Alien Two.' These beings from another world stared at both Ollie and Neville.

"I see organisms," said Alien One.

"We'll eat them," replied Alien Two.

"No, you idiot. We're not here to eat anything. We're here to find our leader. That is all. When we find our leader, then we'll abduct a pizza delivery driver and eat *him*."

Neville was terrified.

"Ollie, they're coming over here."

"Don't do anything sudden. They can sense fear."

"Well, their senses are probably exploding right now because I'm scared to death!" Neville watched the two aliens walk up to him and Ollie.

"Hello, Earthlings. I am Alien One and this is Alien Two."

"Yeah, we saw your name tags," said Ollie.

"We are the giant midgets from Neptune."

Ollie looked at them, then at Neville.

"What's a Neptune?"

"It's a planet," said Neville.

"I didn't know there was a planet named Neptune."

"Didn't you take a science class in high school?"

"I did, but the only planets I remember are Earth, the sun and the moon."

"The sun and the moon aren't planets."

"What are they then?"

"They're the sun and the moon, you idiot!"

Alien One then said. "We have come to earth to find our leader."

"Are we your chosen leaders?" asked Ollie.

"We are not that desperate."

"Who *is* your leader?"

"The Jersey Devil or the Mothman," Alien Two replied. "We think they're the same thing."

Neville was in shock.

"The Jersey Devil is a giant midget from Neptune?"

"No," said Alien One. "He's a creature that roams the New Jersey forests. Have you heard of him?"

"Everyone around these parts has heard of the Jersey Devil," replied Ollie. "There are stories about him living around here that go way back as far as the 1970s. People say he has red eyes and large black bat wings."

"That sounds like our guy, all right," said Alien One. "Will you take us to him?"

Ollie thought it over for a few seconds in silent contemplation.

"Sure, why not?"

"Wait a second, now," Neville whispered to Ollie. "We're talking to aliens here. I'm not so sure we should be helping them out."

"It's the neighborly thing to do. Plus, it's more exciting than hunting bullfrogs. Now come on and let's help."

The four of them walked deep into the woods to a cave very few people knew about. They stood some hundred feet away and Ollie pointed it out to the aliens.

"That's it, right there. The Jersey Devil lives inside and at midnight he'll come out and fly around looking for food."

"Then we wish to capture him and take him back to Neptune to be our leader," said Alien One.

"How did you learn about the Jersey Devil on Neptune?" asked Neville.

"Leonard Nimoy's *In Search of* program. We would have chosen Mr Nimoy as our leader but he didn't have any wings. Plus, the Jersey Devil is a cooler name."

Without warning, a screech filled the forest. Red eyes began to appear inside the cave, which caused Ollie and Neville, along with Alien One and Alien Two, to scream. The Jersey Devil came out of the entrance and stood in the bright moonlight.

It was seven feet tall. Its face was like that of a horse crossed with a bitter mother-in-law. It had giant bat wings and its body was covered in hair - but the chest was like black leather and very muscular - similar to that of a gorilla.

"What are you all going to do with him?" asked a very nervous Neville.

"Alien Two is going to subdue him."

"Is he going to use a laser?"

"He doesn't have his laser license. He'll throw a red rubber ball at the Devil instead. He'll knock him out, then we'll put him in the trunk of our saucer craft and take him back home. You may proceed Alien Two."

Alien Two started to throw the ball to knock out the Jersey Devil when Neville yelled. "Stop!"

"What's wrong?" asked Alien One. "Do *you* want to throw the red rubber ball?"

"We can't just let you take the Jersey Devil," Neville protested. "He's very important to us here. He's part of our culture. A life without the Jersey Devil wouldn't even be worth living for us."

"I'm guessing that your life wouldn't be worth living even with the Jersey Devil here," said Alien One. "But we need his leadership. I mean just look at him. Wouldn't you want to be led by that?"

At that moment, the Jersey Devil let out a loud shriek and flew up into the air, where he disappeared over a far ridge.

"Now look what you've done!" screamed Alien One. "We've lost him and we'll have to hunt him down all over again. We can't leave here without our leader."

"Why don't you be the leader of Neptune instead?" suggested Neville.

Alien One immediately took to the idea.

"I like the way you think, earthling."

"You're the first being from any planet who ever said that to me."

"I *could* become the leader," Alien One pondered. "It's not that hard. All I have to do is fill out a petition and I'm on the ballot. I think I'll do it."

"That's the spirit," said Neville.

"If you win, what will be the first thing you'll do?" asked Ollie.

"Declare war on earth, capture the Jersey Devil and return him to Neptune as an exhibit. I'll see you all in about six months, maybe seven. I don't really know how long it will take the bribery checks to clear. Come on Alien Two, we've got an election to purchase."

Alien Two nodded as he put his red ball in his mouth and swallowed it. The two aliens then saluted Neville and Ollie.

"Leonard Nimoy to all."

Ollie and Neville returned the salute and watched Alien One get into the flying saucer. Alien Two opened up a small door on the back of the craft and started the engine with a pull cord, as if it was a boat motor. He got in the saucer, then they were gone.

Neville turned to Ollie

"I guess we better go home and load our deer rifles, if we're going to be at war with Neptune in six months."

"You got that straight."

The two of them started walking off.

"You know something, Ollie. I realize this might not sound right, but I kind of hope the little fellow wins that election."

"Me too, Neville."

"Do you think we did the right thing in keeping the Jersey Devil here?"

"I sure do. Even though it may have cost us planet Earth, I still think the Jersey Devil is worth fighting for. The people from earth might not understand, but the people in New Jersey will."

"That's all that matters anyway. Now let's go home and eat us some frog legs."

"Amen, brother."

Temporary Cavity

J o d i   S t o n e

My bone flap is buried in my abdomen, waiting for the surgeons to reattach it to my skull. It itches at the sutures and protrudes like a third rib. I'm thirty-three and my mom is a helicopter, asking me what it feels like all the time. Fluffing my pillows, feeding me soup. I want it out and I tell her that, but she ignores me, dusting around my bedroom and singing those old show tunes from the sixties. But I guess she heard or has the same thought as me cause, when they called, she screamed like she won the lottery. And I was sent back here to the hospital, slopped up on antibiotics and opioids.

The clots were caused, they say, by the impact of my head hitting the steering wheel. I don't remember any of it. Nothing after dropping my last date home, wine still pouring out of her. She was mad that I didn't walk her to the front door. Took two steps away before spinning back around and poking her head in the passenger window. The gold chain of her purse scraped against my paint job and all I could think was it was better than getting keyed again. My car wore the scars of lovers' trysts and the local autobody shop had given me a stamp card, I was there so often.

I wasn't really listening to what she was yelling but I made damn sure she'd stepped back before I rolled up the window and pulled out. Say what you want about me but I'm a gentleman that way. I was thinking about the guys at the autobody shop and Johnny in particular. He'd pull that smirk on me, snap his fingers and say "Aw yeah, Lady Killer" when I rolled in for another touch-up job.

"Unlucky in love," I'd reply.

I was imagining the scenario when, out of nowhere, a wall, solid and cruel, popped up from the centre of the earth. It stopped me so fast my tires didn't even screech. Don't put your faith in airbags. They are unreliable children, fickle gaseous things that only show up on *their* terms.

So, surgeons removed the bone flap right after the accident to relieve some pressure. Said it would only be temporary until the brain swelling shrunk. They drilled at the scalp, unfolding the skin like smooth pages of an unread book. The drill they used to make holes in my skull looked like any you'd have in your garage, something you'd use to make decks. I researched this all on my device, after the first surgery, when it didn't hurt as much to look at light and illuminated things.

The holes in my skull were connected by cuts from a saw that looked a little less residential, a little more refined. The size of the bone flap was the surgeon's call. He could form the shape any way he wanted. Triangular, square. For me he was cavalier with his cutting, creating a bold kidney shape of bone that sat on a surgical tray for a full ten minutes while he sliced a new home into my abdomen.

I can touch it now but it freaked me out a first. The strange hardness just there below the liver. I still don't touch my head, though. I'm terrified it will collapse into a freakish crater. I picture it, soft-boiled beneath the skin, the brain sloshing around, shrinking, and expanding without its shell. This is more common than you'd think, this occurrence. It has names like *Syndrome of Trephine* and *Sinking Skin Flap Syndrome*. It's caused by changes in the gradient of intracranial and atmospheric pressure. I've been reading up on it when I can't sleep, which is often.

If that happens, they'll have to cut the bone flap out of my abdomen sooner than later and hope the brain swelling has reduced enough. Then I get to worry about post cerebral contusion expansion, which usually occurs within the first two days, where my head bulges like rotten fruit.

I also fret about bleeding complications or hydrocephalus, that can happen one-month post-operative. And don't get me started on surgical site infections like dehiscence. Or ulcers. Or, worst and most terrifying, necrotic skin on the flap contour, which would spell certain brain death.

I can't sleep at night worrying about these things.

Someone told me in passing today that my body is rejecting the bone flap, again. My memory is muddled and mixed. One, maybe two bodies in scrubs. That's the thing about hospitals, everyone is wearing the same thing, so you don't really know who does what. I think they should, at least, have a colour coding system. Green for surgeons, pink for nurses, blue for the cleaners and orderlies.

So, they are standing near me, close to the head of the bed, when someone else in scrubs comes in with a step stool and places it beneath the clock. It is an hour ahead, unchanged from when all clocks went back last week. I'm busy watching her wrestle with it, chipping at its face to reach the hands. But they won't move and she throws up her own hands, to no one in particular, because I am the only one paying attention. The people next to me keep talking, stressing how important their words are.

"Do you understand, Victor?"

I look up at them, then back to the woman dragging the stool behind her, clock face unchanged. I try to listen but can't focus. I try harder. I turn my face to them and blink, like I've been listening all along. One of them puts her hand on my wrist, tells me it's infected again, the bone flap. They've already tried to put it back in once, back on my brain but it got infected. She repeats this, like I don't know. Like I don't remember that first attempt. Cutting a wider hole in the abdomen, its temporary cavity looking more and more like a permanent home. And the waiting. God the waiting, until my body was ready for them to try again.

That's when my mom screamed like she won the lottery. This last time, this third surgery, when they said we should give it another shot.

I am getting to know the staff on this unit pretty well. Repeat patients like me have outside lives narrowed into prescriptions and observations and appointments and restrictions. The medications we take to prevent seizures and the medications we need to offset stomach burning from anticonvulsants. The opioids for pain and the laxatives to neutralize them. Time consuming, all-consuming stuff. And we're still not experts. We don't know what our bodies will do from one day to the next. The brain is a delicate beast. Delicate and in control of everything, like petal soft businessmen.

I can hear the new nurse in the next room, propping herself up on self-deception, turning faults into pluses. Convincing herself that her speed and efficiency doesn't make her cold. She's talking to a recent admittance, a woman's voice, something new and sweet. I want to be near her. I want her to see what I can do with this strong body. But my body has holes in it now. There are IV sites in each of my arms, immediate portals of entry for urgent procedures. They've got something different pumping through the left one that stings and clouds my eyes. Maybe it's making me hear things, but that new admittance's voice sounds sort of like home. The way she speaks draws forms in thin air that spiral and twist. I swear I can see her standing next to me, this new woman in room nine.

The lights go out early on this unit. Truth be told, they never really get turned on, with most of us light-scared after neurosurgery. Just before the night shift arrives, the halls dim down low and all the lights in the rooms go out like clockwork. We never properly see the night shift nurses or know what they look like. They lumber into rooms, darkness at their backs, shuffling with the odd groan. They tap us and poke us, shine torches in our eyes and mumble our names, maybe, if they're feeling spirited.

There is a warning bell that sounds like a clown horn which goes off when any of the wanderers get too close to the exit. Darryl is the most persistent wanderer and, lucky me, his room's just a few doors from mine. I think he may have been a neurosurgical mistake, though nobody would admit it. He's not getting any better.

He forgets his room and why he's in here. He forgets his name and how to eat. But he doesn't forget how to move and that's all he wants to do. He's like an angry toy nun that can only walk forward and spit sparks. His feet keep going, even when he butts right up against a wall. When the clown horn goes off, someone emerges slowly from the nurses' station to turn him around and direct him down the hall, back toward his room. It has three A4-sized papers that say DARRYL, written neatly in varied coloured markers.

So, it's dark at bedtime and, once in a while, I'll hear this clown horn go off. It wakes me out of hard-fought slumber and I know that one of us is, at least, trying to break free.

I think her name is Alice. That's what it sounds like, at least, when the doctors come around.

Alice, you've got a subarachnoid haemorrhage. Alice, you've got some pressure on the brain. Alice, we'll need to operate again if the swelling doesn't go down.

I think I hear her crying when the doctors leave and I want to get up and walk to her room, hold her hand and tell her it's not that bad. Maybe get a kiss.

"You can get through this," I'd say. "It's not a day at the amusement park but it's bearable."

The thing is, I've gotten a little cranky and I don't think Alice would like to meet me in this state. I have a temper. I've punched a few walls in my day. I have it under control most of the time, because I've learned deep breathing patterns and how to count to six. But these drugs they have me on. Dexamethasone to fight the swelling, Levetiracetam for seizure prophylaxis. They make me irritable.

The nurse on the night shift labelled me a BSR. He started off by warning me. Then he began to withhold my painkillers. Then he marched right in, opened my drapes wide and turned on my overhead light, telling me I was a behavioural safety risk. Me! That he was going to pop that BSR sticker right on my chart if I didn't calm down.

I hadn't really noticed I was yelling. They said I was disturbing whoever was on the other side of the drawn curtains. The nameless patient, a sleeping zombie.

They moved me into a private room just like Alice's, on the other side of hers. I tried to get a glimpse while they rolled me past but there was someone hovering over her bed. A relative maybe. Or a specialist. Someone not in scrubs. I sat up a little, even against the mag-waisted restraints, and yelled out to her but she didn't hear me. The nurse made sure I was sleepy, because there was a new pill in my cup when he did the 2100 med pass. I started nodding off and fell into some deep dreamscape that ran amok, filled with haunted eyeless children.

Next morning my restraint belt is off and my knuckles are bloody, which is strange because my hospital gown doesn't have a speck on it. I pulled out my IV in the night, or my IV had been pulled out and now it is sitting tidily on the pillow beside me. I swing my legs to one side of the bed and steady myself, my head spinning a little. I try to bear weight on one leg, pumped by the possibility of walking. I attempt standing and instantly fall. I expect a nurse to run in, those specialized ears tuned to the exact pitch of bone hitting cement. I wait for help that doesn't arrive. My gown is open at the back and a cold draft hits me right up the crack. When I pull myself, commando style, to the toilet, it takes most of my strength.

I don't remember eating the day before, or even the day before that. When I look in the mirror, using the sink for strength, I see my beautiful, chiselled cheeks have turned hollow. Then the shape of my face starts shifting, like ice floats under a hot sun.

I must have been standing here for an hour. Just staring at myself in the mirror, watching my skin sink into the hole where my bone flap should be. And, you know, it isn't exactly terrifying. Not the freakish crater I expected. The longer I stare, the more I like the way I am looking. I tell myself that facial asymmetry is perfectly normal. My face felt boring before this. I am feeling unique. Singular.

I want someone to see me, so I start to let go of the sink and slowly place one foot in front of the other, holding onto the wall. Then the door. Then the air in front of me. That's when I drop again but, this time, someone comes running. I see one, then two, then three sets of worn, dirty trainers in front of me and I can't raise my head from the weight of its transformation. The heavy work of its evolution. I can only hear muffled shuffling, as the shoes dance for me, enacting a dirty ballet of dropped plastic IV ends and forgotten peri cloths.

The Hoyer lift comes and they roll me on my back, making various tsking sounds. Within minutes they have hoisted me into bed and raised the rails up - all four of them.

I am hoping the nurse who stayed behind will comment on my crater. Tell me how impressive it is, to encourage its growth. But she says nothing while she straps me in with a magnet waisted restraint belt. I don't have the strength to fight it. She's inserting a fresh IV line when someone resembling a doctor enters. He is wearing a green jogging suit and can't be much more than five feet tall. The nurse adjusts my bed to the lowest position, so I am almost eye to eye with him. He is unblinking and direct. He delivers some news and I look between him and the nurse, who nods solemnly. She seems to agree with his diagnosis.

"Sepsis-Associated Delirium," he repeats, over and over, until I'm forced to listen. He is talking slowly, like I'm a brain-dead child. He claims these snakes I saw crawling all over me last night are really just IV lines. He says the infection has reached my brain. They confuse me when they say SOFA.

"I am in bed," I point out. "I am already restrained. Why would you move me to a sofa?"

The nurse shifts her body into a regal slant and holds my hand firmly in hers.

"It stands for sequential organ failure assessment," she explains and that sticks.

Organ failure. It can't be right. My brain has been a little off from the accident. I forget things sometimes, I'm often cranky. But, once my bone flap is taken out of my gut, I'll be right again.

I tell them as much and then they shake their heads in unison. They say my body can't handle any more surgery at this time. Everything has to stay put for now. They'll increase my dose of antibiotics, a broad spectrum that might kill most pathogens. Add something for the pain.

I keep saying things, blurting out great ideas to resolve the issue and they look sheepish. Orderlies and interns come to the door and look sympathetic.

"No," they insist. "No, Victor, I'm afraid you're going to die."

This should bother me. I should be a little upset. Maybe it's the new liquid coming down through the IV line that is making me calm but I start nodding. I get what they are trying to say. I don't agree with them but I understand.

"I need a sandwich," I tell the nurse. "Some sustenance. My body will fight this infection if I only could get a sandwich."

She grabs my wrist with her forefingers, looks at her watch and counts. She pops a thermometer in my mouth.

"Preferably rye," I mumble around the thermometer. Then I have this idea that caraway seeds would kill the infection. I insist that the sandwich include caraway, or poppy seeds, in a pinch. I am really getting into this idea, trying to convey what condiments could kill the infection, when my mouth stops moving and everything goes dark. It sounds like I am under the sea, where the soft ultra-sonar of submarine signals bounce off underwater boulders.

My mom is there when I wake, staring out the hospital window, clinking rosaries against her many metal bracelets. She's never attended church a day in her life.

"Oh, you're awake." She looks frightened as she turns around.

Something is different. My head hurts incredibly, like someone has sucked out every last drop of liquid and it is just brain on bone. I want to touch it but my hands won't cooperate.

"Mom," I manage. "You're finally here."

"I've been here the entire time." She doesn't move from the window. "You don't remember? I was here all yesterday and all last night."

My head. Why wasn't someone giving me something for the pain? I say as much and she walks a little closer. She pats my foot and doesn't make eye contact. She tells me that she has to go away for a few days but will keep in touch. She says I am in good hands and looks out the door, likely at Darryl wandering about. Then she leaves.

I'm stunned. She's never left without squeezing the life out of me and smearing lipstick on my cheek. But my head is pounding and the light hurts. Thinking isn't helping it. I press my call bell and a voice asks if she can help me. I mutter the word *pain* and she asks me to repeat myself until, I guess, I'm yelling it.

The nurse comes in, takes my vitals, and asks me how bad the pain is out of 10. I say 20, or worse.

I must have nodded off after she administered the morphine. It is night when I awake again and my restraints have been lifted.

There is a calm eeriness to a hospital at night, as if I'm hiding under an old wooden porch that's cool and quiet but just might collapse. The two-phase fluorescent bed lights hum, filling the space between infusion pump drips and telemetry beeping. The clock on my wall is still one hour ahead, since the time changed back two weeks ago.

A quiet bald man, as tall as he is wide, shuffles by with his water cart, sometimes forgetting me tucked behind the wall of my bathroom in this L-shaped room. The wanderers must be sedated tonight, no clown horns going off in terrifying intervals. But all the other bells and beeps continue.

The regular nurses have gotten alarm fatigue and respond slowly to calls. There's one nurse in particular who's been on this floor for fifteen years. Small. Loud. Likely Filipino. Takes her a full hour to respond. When she does, she comes in flapping her arms and saying something that sounds like the pitch and fall of my Filipino neighbours. From that, I assume I know her, so I say as much. That I know her culture.

She goes quiet and that's when I start feeling scared. She leans over, real close, pulls out a flashlight as long as her arm and flashes it in one eye, then the other. Suddenly I'm blind but she tells me I'm fine. I hear she thinks we're all drug seekers, so she'll never give me opioids on the hour. You hear a lot lying still for days on end with no devices of distraction.

Around this time, when it's dusk and the light lets go its grasp of my small square window, I am at my loneliest. My mom would usually be here. I once had a phone but they took that away, saying I was making flagrant 911 calls, reporting my kidnapping and subsequent murder. They must be making that up because it doesn't sound like me, and I certainly don't recall doing it. My eyes tune in and out of vision, blurring until the details are soft blobs of colour. I can't imagine I could make out the correct numbers to dial.

There aren't even any televisions on this unit. They tell me it is to protect our brains after surgery but I'm beginning to think it's because they want to make us crazy, cutting us off from the outside world.

I'm sure I hear Alice breathing next door. If I was able to bore a hole through my wall, I could watch her. I wonder what she looks like. I wonder how she is feeling.

It's usually just old people on this floor, suffering the brain bleeds caused by leaky old bodies. Or the tumours and abscesses of high-grade gliomas that get cut out by irritable young surgeons. The gliomas will just keep growing back, mutating and becoming cancerous, as their old DNA is broken and can't write itself into healthy new cells. I saw a woman being wheeled by without a nose and a hole for an eye, because they cut the cancer away and keep on cutting and the young nursing students dressed in their Caribbean blue scrubs hold new butterflies to poke her with because she's just turned palliative.

But Alice isn't like that. She's fresh and strong and has my attention.

I don't hear her crying anymore. In fact, I don't hear any sounds coming from her room. I generally have a good idea of the flow of things around here. The nurses busy themselves at the beginning and end of shift change. Then there's the midnight lull. According to the clock it's 2300, so I know I have an hour to kill. I start gathering some supplies around my bed and try to rest my eyes, save my strength. I wait until the familiar dip in the evening, when fewer sounds drift down the hallway.

Getting to my feet is hard, so I steady myself on the guardrail. I swing my feet to the floor and find my slippers, the ones my mom bought me, not my style. They've got sequins on them. Not terribly manly. I can abide a bit of velour but no glitter or shine. She knows that and I told her as much. But they're all I have and they're anti-slip.

My head is woozy, yet I feel no pain. Not sure what the nurse administered but it's strong and still coursing through me. I take my IV pole and its bags of magic liquid. Someone kept the bathroom light on, so I poke my head in and see that the crater has deepened. It has lowered to my right brow bone. It looks cool, unique. I feel like an evolved man with nothing but a thin flap of skin between the power of my brain and the world. Can practically see the synapses firing in the mirror, little sparklers humming above the soft curve of the fissure, as it dips in a smooth wave toward my ear.

I turn the light out in my bathroom and poke my head into the empty hallway. No wanderers. No staff. Just the feminine sound of soft sleeping coming from Alice's room. I'm out of sight from the nurses' station. I put one foot carefully in front of the other.

The hospital smells make me gag. The stale odour of shit from adult diapers that are called 'briefs' to protect dignity. Oozing fluids from ostomy bags. Necrotic toes of diabetic patients, black, shrivelled and just moments from falling from foot to floor. The smell alone is impetus to be off this unit again. To be walking in the street, to be driving coolly in my patched-up car. And, in this newly evolved heightened state, free of the encumbrance of excess brain bone, I can see and hear and think things that I've never experienced before. It's like the universe is funnelling pure electricity into my brain, forming bold new truths. It's so simple, the answer. I laugh but no one hears me. The tired, care-worn ears of these caregivers are tuned only to terror.

Alice's room is exactly as I'd thought it would be. There is a certain smell in here and I know that my senses have been heightened. My evolved brain is bigger, not swollen. It touches the air around it. It is one with everything. I come to Alice as her saviour, her lover, her personal best friend. I can feel she notices the temperature in the room has shifted when I enter. I hear her moan as I approach.

With the IV pole in my left hand and the bedside flashlight in my right, I find the edge of her bed. I am not as primitive with the light as the worn-out nurse. I don't flash it directly into Alice's eyes. I play with the darkness, easing the light into it by zipping the torch from side to side. First on the floor, making little swirls of light that start opening the blackness from the ground up, until it has fully unveiled her.

I knew it. She is lovely. That shade of pink in her hair from the surgical antiseptic doesn't become anyone but her. She is fair, likely platinum blond before all of this. The same side of her head is shaved as mine, from ear to centre. We look like half-hearted punks. Her staples run around the right parietal lobe and are raw. I flash my light to the Vancomycin bag attached to her IV pole: she is fighting a serious infection. Her body has rejected her own bone flap, or if it hasn't yet, it will. I know the drill. I can see the truth.

I reach for her hand and it's warm, soft. I can sense the energy of the universe streaming through her fingers and it makes me gasp and clutch my IV pole for strength. I gently replace her hand on the bed. No bone-bound doctor could feel what she needs.

I know what to do.

Neither of us has had solid food for weeks. It's strange how not picking up a utensil alters you. All the nutrients poured directly into our veins informs an evolution that most humans won't experience.

I am light. I am air. One positive about this hospital is that they encourage self-care. They never take away your toiletries and my mom got the leather shaving bag right, three birthdays ago. It is fully stocked with one of those trendy straight razors with a pearl diamond pattern in the handle. I like the easy access of my gown. When I get out of here, I am going to wear something similar, something as accessible. Maybe a cape or a sari. I want to be more open to everything. Every touch. Every breeze. Every bit of electricity that pours out of people.

The spine of the razor is sharp, and I've had some practice pivoting it and holding it by the jimps and the tang. I rest the flashlight on Alice's chest because it's the perfect height to project the light on my abdomen. I touch the outline of my bone flap poking out and it feels like it's ready to go. It's been trying to leave this temporary cavity for weeks.

It doesn't take much coercion and the incision is perfect, warm and drippy, like I'm letting out all my poison. I smile at the goodness I am doing, giving part of myself to Alice so she can heal. Her body may reject her own bone flap but mine is different and different is good.

I can feel myself transcending into lightness and consider that maybe I'll become a neurosurgeon when I get out of here. My mother would scream at that too, just like she'd won the lottery. Her son a surgeon! A lifetime's supply of hair salon bragging.

My mind is so vivid now, I can hear her screaming clear as day. The sound filling the surrounding air, flooding out through Alice's mouth, over my tingling head and into the hallway.

I feel a wonderous calm.

That Old Time Religion

Gary Battershell

Lily stepped back from the microscope with a look of pure frustration.

"I just can't get this thing to focus right."

"Let me help," I said eagerly. In a moment, the erythrocytes on the slide were sharply defined and I was, yet again, Lily's hero.

"I just don't know how I'd get through microbiology without you as a lab partner, Stanley. This must be the hundredth time you've helped me out."

"Really? I haven't been counting. But I know I always look forward to Thursday morning lab."

"Me, too," Lily said. "I've been wondering if you were going to ask me out."

My mouth went dry and my knees weak. I mean, literally. Lily Palmer was, without doubt, the most beautiful girl I had ever seen, including models and movie stars. From her platinum blond hair to her pink toenails (she always wore open-toed shoes), she was five feet, five inches of feminine perfection. I know her height because it's exactly the same as mine.

"Well, it looks like you've thought about it," she said.

"Uh, yeah, but…"

"You don't have a girlfriend, do you?"

"No. No, no. Absolutely not."

As I stammered, I backed up into a student at the next table.

"Excuse me, sorry."

"It's okay, bud," he said, winking at me and ogling Lily before going back to his microscope.

"Great," Lily beamed. "How about we start kind of slow?"

"Slow's fine. Fast would be fine, too… don't care about speed. Safety, that's what counts."

"Okay, how about we go for lunch after class? Do you know Smitty's?"

"Yeah, the little burger place across town."

"You don't have an afternoon class, do you?"

"Just comparative religions. I know all that stuff anyway."

"If you're sure. I wouldn't want you missing something on my account."

"I've never been surer of anything since I was conceived."

After lab was over, Lily drove us to Smitty's in her Volvo. The place was popular with the college crowd, so it was pretty well packed, but we found a little table against the back wall.

Smitty's is known for its burgers but they serve plate lunches too. Lily ordered rare steak and mushrooms and she seemed to like it a lot. I've never seen a person so enchanted by raw meat.

"Looks like you're enjoying your lunch," I said.

"It's amazing. I can't believe there are Vegans in the world. I mean, what's up with that?"

"Yeah, what?"

"You know." Lily dabbed a red smear off the corner of her mouth. "You remind me of somebody famous."

"You remind me of somebody famous, too."

"Really, who?"

I reddened. "Aphrodite."

She laughed.

"That's funny but I was being serious. You look like a young Woody Allen."

I smiled weakly. "Great, great."

She thought I looked like an undernourished, geeky movie director. *Hooray. I'm in like Flynn.*

As soon as I returned to my apartment, I called up Aaron. Aaron was, like me, pre-med - but he had stayed home in Hartford and enrolled at the local university. My folks were well off and well-connected, so I'd wound up across the country at one of the best schools. I'd rather have stayed at home, but they had mapped out my future since I was in diapers.

"Hey, Stanley," Aaron said. "I was getting worried. Hadn't heard from you since last night."

"Ha, ha. Funny. Are you saying you don't want to talk to me anymore?"

"Of course not. You're a diversion. You know this town. Nothing ever happens here. Nothing much happens to you either but, at least, it's nothing in a different place."

"Something's happened. Something big."

I told Aaron about Lily. It took close to half an hour convincing him I wasn't hallucinating. After he started believing me, he brought up something that had been in the back of my mind too. Something I didn't want to think about.

"She's not Orthodox, is she?"

After a long pause, I said, "I didn't ask but, of course, it's not likely."

"You know how important that is to both our folks."

"They just told me not to marry outside the faith. They didn't say I couldn't fool around."

"Stanley, you're fooling *yourself.* Let's say this girl and you really get serious. Could you just walk away? That's what your folks would expect."

I began to feel defensive.

"I'm my own man. What could they do?"

"Cut you off?"

"Oh, yeah."

"To be fair to her, maybe you should bring this up. I mean, your faith is important to you too, right? It's not just something you do for your folks?"

"Yeah, it is. It's in me deep. Lily invited me to dinner at her parents' house on Saturday. I'll find some way to talk to her about it then."

On Saturday, Lily picked me up at seven for the drive to her folks' place. Before she arrived, I spent some time in my prayer room, a bedroom I'd fixed up as a chapel. I prayed for guidance but didn't get an answer. That was maybe just as well. I don't know what I would have done if the answer was to stay away from Lily.

On the way, I tried to broach the religion issue a couple of times but couldn't go through with it. I was having a great time with the girl of my dreams and, while I might eventually have to ruin it, I didn't want to do that any sooner than was absolutely necessary.

Lily's folks lived in an exclusive part of town called the Heights. At the top of a ridge, near her folks' house, she pulled into an overlook with a breathtaking view of the Pacific.

"This is where I grew up," she said, leaning back in her seat and taking her hands off the wheel. "I spent half my childhood playing on that beach."

She put a hand on my thigh and looked at me soulfully.

"I hope you like them. My parents, I mean. They're very protective of me and insist I bring home any boy I might get serious with before…"

She paused and blushed.

"Before what?"

"Before we get seriously serious, if you know what I mean."

"Have you brought anyone home before?"

"Two. They didn't work out."

Lily leaned in and kissed me, our first kiss. I'd been kissed before - not often, but it had happened. This wasn't like previous kisses. It was as if everything in the universe had narrowed down to two soft lips and a moaning sigh. And, for the first time in my life, I felt as though I was exactly where I was supposed to be. They say when you find the right one, you'll be willing to die for her. I realized now that it was true - but no real sacrifice was involved - because life without Lily would just be a sort of prolonged dying anyway.

Lily and I snuggled for a while, then she drove us a short distance and turned down a paved drive flanked with expansive lawns and ending at a mansion. I can't think of any other word for it.

I thought that my folks' house was big, but Connecticut big and California big are evidently two different things. This place made my parents' six-bedroom neo-Tudor look like a toolshed.

"They've let the servants go for the night, so it will just be the four of us." Lily got out of the car.

"Yeah," I said as we walked to the door. "I'd have done that, too. Servants can be so in-the-way and… servanty."

"Ready?" Lily took hold of the doorknob.

"As I'll ever be."

She turned the handle, and we went in.

The door opened directly into a living room roughly the size of Rhode Island. The peaked ceiling was punctuated with skylights and supported by exposed timbers that, given their size, could only have come from California Redwoods. The opulent furniture looked like it might have been purchased at the liquidation sale of an upscale Byzantine brothel.

"Hello! We're here! Mom, Dad? Come meet Stanley!"

A man and a woman emerged through draperies that hung on the room's far side. The man was tall, blond, and athletic. The woman a statuesque brunette and, despite her age, strikingly beautiful.

"Stanley," Lily said. "I'd like you to meet my parents, Dr. and Mrs. Bertram Palmer."

I stepped forward and offered my hand to Lily's father. He smiled as we shook and looked at me in a way that let me know my evaluation had already begun.

"Good to meet you, Stanley."

"Delighted, sir," I replied.

I shook hands with Mrs. Palmer next.

"Lilith says you've been a great help with her schoolwork."

Lilith?

"We help each other," I said.

"That's not true," Lily corrected. "Stanley's a brain. He's going to be a wonderful doctor someday."

I looked at Dr. Palmer.

"Lily didn't tell me you were a doctor, sir."

"Not that kind of doctor. I'm a researcher. I have a Ph.D. from Caltech, in biochemistry."

"That's uh, that's something."

"Keeps me busy. How about we have dinner now? We've put together a little repast out on the patio."

The 'patio' was a cobblestone courtyard behind the house. It abutted tennis courts, an archery range and a swimming pool, overlooking a curve of private beach fronting a natural lagoon.

"This view is really impressive." I followed my hosts to a table laden with a dizzying array of platters, bowls, and trays.

"Try the quail." Lily pointed to a pile of what looked like tiny roasted chickens.

I did try the quail, and the veal, and the trout, and three different desserts - two baked and one frozen.

We ate our food in lounge chairs facing out over the ocean and washed it down with wine, switching from white to red as the dish demanded. As we ate, we talked and, I have to say, I found Lily's parents to be friendly, forthcoming, people. I thought that laudable, since they must have known my ultimate goal was to sexually defile their daughter in every conceivable way - and twice on Sunday.

When we were all finished, Mrs. Palmer and Lily cleared away the dishes and carried them inside, leaving me alone with Lily's father.

"One thing, sir…" I began, finishing off a glass of excellent Riesling.

"Call me Burt," he insisted.

"All right, Dr… Burt. I didn't know 'Lily' was a nickname. She never told me her real name was Lilith."

"Yes. It's an old family name and related to our religion."

"Oh. Are you Jewish? That name comes from Hebrew legend and folklore, I think. In some stories, Lilith is the first wife of Adam, before Eve.

"No, we aren't Jewish, and we're not Christian, either. In fact, that's something I wanted to talk to you about this evening. If you get serious with my daughter, you'll have to understand our religion."

"I'm glad you brought that up, sir. I come from a very religious family and have strong personal beliefs of my own. I was worried that might be a problem but now I don't think so. You're obviously good people and the fact that your beliefs aren't exactly the same as mine shouldn't make any difference."

I amazed myself as I said that and wondered if it would have been possible without the wine. Still, I meant every word of it.

"That's wonderful, Stanley. Because this *would* be a problem for many people."

"What's so problematic about it?"

"I don't really know. Our religion holds that people are born with great potential. And that potential should not be suppressed by outdated tradition and adherence to mythology."

"I believe that, too."

"Then you believe in the liberation of the individual and the right of people to seek happiness in whatever form they desire - without harming others, of course."

"I do, sir."

"Have you ever seen this?"

Dr. Palmer extended his right hand and showed me a silver signet ring he wore on his middle finger. The design was a five-pointed star with a goatlike face inside the pentagram. I recognized it as the image of Baphomet, the symbol of the Church of Satan.

"You're *Satanists*?"

"We are. As a young man, I was involved in creating our church and its doctrines. Lilith was raised on it and I think we can agree she turned out rather well."

Still too stunned to form a reply, I just smiled and nodded.

Palmer smiled back.

"Since you seem to know something about our faith or lack of it, I suppose, you probably realise we don't literally worship Satan, or any other mythological entity. We believe in science and reason. Satan is the symbol of our rebellion against conformity and intellectual coward-ice."

Wonderful. Satanism is just institutionalized atheism.

The rest of the evening was sort of blurry. The Palmers talked about their lives and Lily's childhood, while I sat beside her and drank wine until I was numb. There was no more talk of religion. I think that was intentional, for the purpose of this evening had been simply to introduce me to all of that, with the indoctrination to come later. I supposed I should be grateful for Dr. Palmer's candor. This would not have been a good thing to discover *after* the wedding.

Lily dropped me off at home about midnight. There had been little conversation on the way back and our goodnight kiss in the car was perfunctory.

"Is something wrong, Stanley?" she asked as I opened the car door.

"Just a little too much wine, I guess. See you in lab."

A few minutes later, I called Aaron.

"Hey, dude," he said. "How'd it go? Meeting the parents is always a big deal."

"You don't know the half of it."

"Fill me in."

"They're Satanists."

"Whoooah!"

We talked for a while and Aaron finished with the obvious.

"You know you have to break it off."

"Of course. If she'd been a Baptist, or a Jew, or a Buddhist, I might have been able to work with that. But they're a direct affront to my religion, all I *am*. They don't even believe in a real Satan, any more than they believe in God. Satan's just a symbol for them and Baphomet simply a boogeyman to screw with the Christians and Jews."

"Yeah, dude, I know all that. My folks and yours go to the same church. We learned the same stuff about blasphemy."

"Yeah,"

"Like I said, you got to break up with her."

"I know."

"Guess labs are gonna be kind of awkward now."

"You think?"

After we finished talking, I decided on a devotional before bed. What I had experienced tonight had left me feeling sad and bereft and I thought prayer might improve my mood.

I went to my closet, took down my red robe, put it on, and entered my chapel. Once inside, I put on the hood, lit the black candles at each end of the folding table I used as an altar, and shut the door.

I knelt on my goat-skin rug and contemplated the bronze image of Lucifer, horned and enfolded in thorny wings, on its stand behind the altar. How ignorant they were, I thought. To deny His Majesty his very reality. How sterile a faith with no God.

I said the prayer I had been taught as a child.

"Mighty is the Lord of the Abyss, the bringer of chaos, perfect in his aspect, unparalleled in his wisdom. May he make good use of this unworthy flesh in the accomplishment of his divine mission. Hail, Lucifer the Risen."

I felt the familiar whoosh of warm air as I was lifted up off the rug, safe and contented in the arms of the God to whom I had been consecrated so long ago.

A Helpful Guide To The Men's Bathrooms of R.J. Fortune University

Anthony Neil Smith

The bathroom closest to the classrooms where I attend most of my classes is a horror show. This is Bleacher Hall, the oldest building on campus, and it looks it. In the winter, bleak granite walls, dead ivy, architecture only a gargoyle would love.

At least it has an elevator.

However, the ancient professors complain modernization such as elevators and copy machines and computers have destroyed not only the spirit of R.J. Fortune's vision, but also the air of scholarship that has guided many lucky generations of America's One Percent for the past one-hundred-and-nine years.

The elevator installed thirty years before - 'recently' according to the ancients - is usually slower than climbing five flights to the top floor, home of the English, Philosophy, Polish, Humanities & Religious Studies Department. Not too long ago, those were five different departments, now budget-sliced to sharing one floor. Take your chance on the elevator. It's slower, crowded, freezing, and makes noises that should be red flags.

Now, the bathroom.

Two urinals, almost always unflushed, plus two stalls. One has no door, only a ripped curtain. Your choice is either the disabled stall, with its uncomfortably high toilet seat and risky morality if you're abled, or a regular stall exposing you to every man who zips back the curtain without checking first.

I only ever used that stall once, in an emergency, which was the first time I met Harold Pickwick - loud, bald, pale as a dead squid. A sociology major. His protruding bones looked like rocks. His eyes bulged.

"Dude! Hurry!"

I shrank. "I'm in here!"

"Man, I need to go!"

"*I* need to go!"

"Go faster!" He paced the whole time. Scuffed work boots, stylishly worn with the tongue out, mostly untied. I was very sure he hadn't scuffed them that badly himself. Probably cost more to buy them pre-worked. Paced real close past the guys using the urinals.

"Scuseme, scuseme."

One chopped back, "Watch it."

Harold got behind him, grabbed a couple of belt loops, and braced him flat against the urinal, soaking his entire front.

"I wouldn't *need* to watch it if you'd *stand closer* like a considerate person."

He made a quick escape.

I wasn't halfway done. I'd eaten a rich lunch - our cafeteria chef has two Michelin stars - my stomach is touchy and I needed more time than Harold wanted to give me. So I wiped off quickly, knowing it wasn't good enough. I squeezed hard to hold in the rest, which triggered my nervous cough, worried I wouldn't be able to hold it long enough to find another bathroom.

I flushed and zipped and buckled, and he was already in before I was out, almost singing.

"Aw, thank *you,* thank *you.*"

It wasn't a real thank you.

The other guy at the urinal stared at me like it was my fault.

I didn't stop to wash my hands.

Zero out of ten.

2.

There are eight full bathrooms in L&G Science Hall — three men, three women, one unisex, and one disabled private.

Private.

The building had recently undergone a monumental upgrade thanks to global tech giants pouring money into STEM. The exterior looked like something you'd only see in Dubai - spacy, artistic, chrome and glass. The classrooms astounded me. It felt like I was on the International Space Station, if rich people built it.

Large touchscreens everywhere. State-of-the-art analyzers and computers. The most comfortable-looking desks I'd ever seen.

Enough about that. I want to talk about the private bathroom.

One big square with only one extra-long toilet, one sink, one hand dryer. Brand-new when I discovered it. Beautiful tiles in cerulean blue, mellow yellow, earthy brown, and white. The sink was untainted and gleaming. The toilet smelled like lemons and bleach. A full-length mirror, not smudged, cracked or pitted. An extra-fast air dryer - the only real negative since it's a bacteria farm. But the fact there was *only one* of them was glorious.

It had a heated floor.

I discovered it by accident on a snowy day, as close to a blizzard as possible without the President canceling classes. My coat was thick with a half-inch layer of slush. Still, I had to push through a horde of smokers to enter the building. They would smoke in any conditions. Blizzard? Check. Typhoon? You got it. Scorching sun? In bikinis if they had to.

It had a thick wooden door, a wheelchair symbol in the middle and a button at hip level (or head level for those in a wheelchair) to make it swing open.

I punched the button and, luckily, the door swung wide. Inviting.

I was in awe.

Unfortunately, some nosy individual soon learned I was using it as my primary restroom. It wasn't marked *only* for the disabled. Since disabled students enrolled on campus constituted a small percentage of overall enrollments, reserving the restroom only for them would be a massive waste of resources. In order to receive the best return on their investment, the non-disabled should use the facilities as well. I would even argue some of us – diagnosed with anxiety, perhaps – could argue that using this private bathroom was important for maintaining our mental health.

Nonetheless, I emerged once to find a disabled woman student sitting next to the school's Public Safety Chief. The student said, "Finally!" and ran over the tip of my shoe in her rush to get into the bathroom.

Meanwhile, the Chief, who looked like a brick wall in a pullover sweater and pristine baseball cap, with our team mascot - the Moneybags - gave me a look like I'd sexually harassed the girl instead of, you know, keeping her from the call of nature.

"You do know this restroom is reserved for the differently-abled, right?"

"There's nothing saying I can't use it, too."

He chinned the wheelchair symbol.

"Really?"

"Not all disabilities are visible. Maybe the privacy is important for my…"

"Stay out of that restroom, alright? Catch you again, it's grounds for expulsion."

Then he told me to beat it.

Leaving me with the difficult task of finding a new bathroom able to hold a candle to this Holy Grail of toilets.

Normally the perfect ten, I deduct five points for its lack of inclusion.

Did I mention it smelled like cinnamon?

3.

The other bathrooms in L&G Hall are adequate, if old, smelly, and poorly ventilated. But there is one immaculate set of restrooms right across from the main two-hundred-seat science auditorium for basic biology lectures. This one pair of restrooms stood out on campus for its capacity. Eight urinals and eight stalls, arranged in an L-shape, and eight sinks and mirrors. The stall walls are sturdy with smaller gaps at the door hinges. They have relatively strong locks for this old-school set up. The air is bright and crisp - apple turnover air freshener?

It's a strong contender.

Definitely avoid it right before and after the big lectures, but other times of the day, it can be a temple, a sanctuary, a shrine to Mother Nature herself.

It was empty when I sneaked in with my copy of *Heart of Darkness*, hoping to catch up before the quiz in Prof. Clement's class. It's a story wrapped in another story, wrapped in a riddle, wrapped in *Apocalypse Now*. However, there was no Dennis Hopper here, no Brando, no Martin Sheen.

I'd had chili for lunch.

My tummy was a bubbling, burping cauldron of lava.

Now, I had a decision to make about which stall to occupy. A very serious decision. Count out the closest and farthest, automatically. In a men's bathroom, the first stall is typically the most trafficked, meaning the filthiest. Even if cleaned several times a day - which I'm pretty sure they weren't - the buildup of bacteria and fecal matter and sticky urine would be unbearable.

The farthest is the disabled stall, meaning it is twice as wide and the floor twice as wet, muddy with soaked scraps of toilet paper.

Nor should I choose the stall in the dead center of the row, although with eight, there wasn't really a dead center. There were two stalls I'd classify as such, and they were likely to be the second most used of the row. Why? Something about human psychology? I wasn't there to argue the validity of it. I was there to empty my cramping bowels.

The correct stall to use was two up from the disabled stall.

I entered to find a pristine toilet and full roll of paper. As I guessed, it hadn't been used *once* since the maintenance crew had cleaned it that morning.

Nirvana.

I made myself at home. Plenty of room from wall to wall. The floor was *dry*. I kid you not. The overhead light flickered, but that was all right by me.

My natural effusions filled the bowl with loud farts and splats. I sighed. A good deep satisfying sigh. I felt safe.

Even when the bathroom door swung open and echoed down to my stall, I felt no uptick in anxiety. The man just needed to pee, I told myself. He had those gleaming urinals to himself. No need to worry.

Heavy bootsteps headed my way.

I cringed. I clenched. I felt a tight high note in my brain. A tuning fork ringing *No no no no no…*

Scuffed work boots, stylishly untied.

They stopped outside my stall door.

I could think of no universe in which this was a coincidence.

He peered through the thin space between stall and door.

"You again?"

"Occupied."

"Of all the bathrooms on campus…"

"You're telling me! Take your pick, though. Nobody else here."

"I want this one."

"I'm…occupied?"

"I want this one."

"I don't care, I'm in it right now."

"This is the best one. The cleanest. I know how to do the math." He slammed his fist against the door and I flinched. "You can move to the next one. Or the handi stall. I hear you like using the handi stall."

"I'm not…I'm in mid-crap, man! I'm not going…"

Another slam.

The latch held.

"Stop it!"

Another slam. "It's my stall. I want to use my stall right now."

"It's not your…"

Slam.

"Stop it!" Near tears, I'm not ashamed to say. "Leave me alone!"

He took a step back, lifted his left boot and kicked the door so hard the latch broke off the stall and the door swung wide, slapping me in the knees and skull. I barely registered the pain before Harold grabbed me by the shirt, pulled me off the toilet out into the bathroom, my offending bodily discharge dripping all over my own pants, my shoes, and the tile floor, before he tossed me aside. I tripped. My hip and right hand hit first. My little finger bent back far too far. *Crack.* I screamed.

Harold stared down at me, then walked into the stall, stood before the toilet, unzipped and let out a stream, loud and proud.

He watched me over his shoulder while he did it, too.

I wished I was dead.

When Harold was done, he shook off, zipped up and stepped over me.

"Don't use my stall again."

Before that happened, I would've given this bathroom a seven out of ten.

Instead, negative one.

4.

In the administration building, six stories of unnecessary positions draining our funding dry, you'll find the absolute best bathrooms on campus. I heard they had heated seats, only on the sports program's floor, and I've never been able to fake a reason to sneak up there.

In fact, at our university, the President's office is on the fifth floor. The sports program? One above. Tells you something, eh?

However, I have had occasion to meet with the Associate Provost of Student Affairs for a dispute I had with a commie professor in

Composition. He disagreed with the politics in one of my papers and failed it, even though it was immaculately sourced, logical, and free of grammar errors.

I'm not saying me winning the 'battle' by carrying it up the appeals ladder all the way to the eighth floor caused them to push his stubborn fat ass towards the door sooner than he wanted. However, it was true that after my grade was overturned, he retired the next semester, then fell dead out of a basic economy airplane seat on his first true vacation in twelve years, right before take-off.

The Provost and his many assistants, associates, office workers and student interns all shared two bathrooms - men's and women's, although I didn't see that distinction lasting very much longer - rivaling the private handicapped bathroom I'd coveted in the science hall.

Marble. Gleaming silver fixtures. Four sinks in each. Three giant stalls. Warm, quiet, peaceful.

The scent of freshly washed linens.

For several days, the men's room on this floor became my refuge. I learned if I came and went as if I truly had business with one of the Provost-lites, looking like I belonged, no one would bother me. I even smiled and nodded at a particularly attractive assistant, with dark, severe hair cut straight at the shoulders and bangs across her eyebrows. I'd give her a "Mondays, right?" or "Sweater weather!"

She'd smile and nod back and I thought I might have a chance there.

Until I stepped out, one Thursday afternoon after a long constitutional and leisurely round of Candy Crush, to find her standing with her arms crossed.

I smiled.

"Chill in the air. Almost Fall." Then kept on my way. I was late for Ethics.

"Excuse me, did you have an appointment with us today?"

"I'm sorry?"

"I've seen you here a lot. Are you meeting with someone?"

"Well, I had spoken with Carol a week ago." The Vice-Provost's name, although I had never met her. "And, um, my appointment with Reg keeps getting pushed back." The real Provost. I'd shaken his hand once.

"You know," She said. "I can simply turn around and ask them if any of this is true."

I shrugged. "You got me. I'm shy."

"It's very strange, seeing the same student here so often."

"Okay. I only wanted to use this bathroom. It's so much better than the ones…"

"I think you should leave."

"Whatever you say. I'm sorry about this. I'm leaving." One step backwards. "Hey, would you like to get a cup of coffee later? Or come over and watch some Netflix?"

She shook her head. "I'm calling security."

"You could've just said no," I spat before heading for the stairway.

I'd had about enough of this place.

Great bathroom, though.

Nine out of ten.

5.

I've saved the crème de la crème for you, though. The best kept secret on the whole campus.

Our library is empty all of the time. Four stories of cobwebs and mold.

Sure, there are some students using computers in the state-of-the-art labs, reading magazines in comfortable chairs and couches, sleeping in study nooks or making out in the empty unused microfiche aisles.

But the two floors of the library containing paper books are nearly always deserted.

Which means the bathrooms on those floors are also nearly always deserted.

Cleaned daily. Untouched for days at a time.

The men's rooms were the same on each floor. Two stalls, one an extra wide handicapped. One urinal tucked at the end of its own stall, giving a man more privacy than he might usually feel in a row of porcelain fountains.

There was no particular smell associated with either restroom. A neutral scent of *clean*, a subtle odor of soap when lathered in the sink. Both hid the foulness of the business we did in there quite well. Good ventilation.

This particular session, I remembered to grab a book from the section nearest the bathroom door - movies. This one a giant book of criticism about Kubrick's films through to *Full Metal Jacket*. Sixteen hundred pages, hardcover, over a foot tall. The largest section covered *2001*. Hundreds of pages on Hal, Dave, and the monolith. I was more interested in *Barry Lyndon* which, although boring, made me sound like an expert at parties.

Jeans at my ankles, book open on my lap, a solid turd working its way out of my anus, slowly, steadily.

All by myself.

Three better words in any language I know not of.

The door opened.

Oh no.

A shuffle of feet. I couldn't see his shoes. He approached the urinal, unzipped and unleashed. I calmed my heartbeat. Deep breaths.

The stream kept up a good ten, fifteen seconds. Then sputtered to a stop. His belt buckle jangled a few times. He zipped up, headed to the sink for a three-second wash, then banged the air dryer. I heard the door open and close well before the dryer stopped growling.

Simply a man who needed a break. A man who minded his own business.

Even after I'd finished my duty, I stayed, continuing to read about Kubrick's vision, his failures, his accidental successes. The hefty weight of the book comforting.

I remember thinking, *I should direct movies.*

I thought I had found my ten out of ten campus restroom experience. Until…

The door opened again. No shuffle this time. Very deliberate, heavy bootsteps. Slow, deep breathing.

When the boots stopped in front of my stall door, I saw the tips – scuffed, laces loose.

I drew my feet up from the floor, held them in midair, hoping he hadn't seen them.

The boots. Unmoving.

The breath. Unwavering.

I closed the Kubrick book on my lap.

The boots. Still unmoving.

The breath. Still unwavering.

I lowered my feet to the floor.

Harold said. "This is my stall."

My heart sank into my stomach. My neck began to cramp. My stomach roiled.

Harold said. "Did you hear me? I said this is my stall."

I stood and pulled up my pants. I reached for the latch, slid it open as quietly as I could, but of course we both heard the *click*.

The door swung open, Harold gently pushing it.

I hefted the Kubrick book, screamed, and brought it down on his head. Once. Twice. Three times.

He dropped back, held his arms over his head and tried to swat the tome away.

I wouldn't let him. My unzipped jeans fell to my ankles but I followed like a prisoner in leg irons, Shouting and slamming, connecting.

He almost made it out the door.

Almost. Mere steps away.

However, he didn't make it because he slipped on some water blown off the hands of the guy who'd peed not long before Harold followed me inside.

He slipped. Fell backwards on his derriere.

I kept hammering away. When he had exhausted the energy in his arms, they dropped to his chest. I kept smashing his face with the book until his nose was flat and he was gagging on his own blood.

I kept on.

I kept on.

I kept on.

Harold stopped gagging. Stopped moving. Stopped everything. Eyes wide, unblinking. He'd lost a boot, on its side back at the stall.

I dropped the Kubrick. Covers broken, slick with blood.

I slid down the wall, trembling, the tile cold on my exposed skin.

What had I done?

Eleven out of ten.

6.

When you, dear reader, find this post, I hope it will help you carefully consider where you take your constitutionals. We all need to feel safe, do we not? A safe space to perform the most basic of human functions. We need to feel comfortable as we cleanse ourselves. Each and every one of us should hold this as one of our most natural, god-or-self-granted rights up there with speech, religion, and the right to bear arms.

Once I hit 'post', I'm afraid this 'missive' will be used for other purposes.

For one, evidence.

I'm sure people will refer to it as my manifesto, as ridiculous as it may seem. I mean, my parents paid an obscene amount of money for me to attend R. J. Fortune University, which should have included access to private bathrooms.

Is that too much to ask?

If you happen to read this before you hear about it on the news, call the local TV. Tell them to find me on the fifth floor of the Administration Building, probably in the men's room. Probably with something deadlier than a book this time.

Tell them to bring a mop.

What's In a Name?

M a r c   S h a p i r o

Gordos on a Friday night. It was the place to be after an evening of cruising the boulevard.

The atmosphere? Pure Tijuana trashy. The drinks? Cheap and powerful. The women? Sometimes legal. Sometimes not. But always easy. Gordos was where the hardcore Cholos and bangers went to cool out after a night of strutting real or imagined machismo and defending their turf. Only the baddest of the bad were allowed inside.

Everything was cool...

Until the door creaked open. The bad asses physically and mentally backed away. The bartender made a move underneath the bar. On most nights, that meant The Peacemaker was about to come out and play. But this night, his hand returned to view, wrapped around the finest bottle Gordos had to offer.

Only the best for Crazy Loco.

Crazy Loco moved uneasily into the bar. He was not the scariest looking guy on the block. A pot belly jiggled vigorously from under a ridiculous Hawaiian shirt and played fat rhythms against the top of his faded blue bellbottoms. His hair was 60s long on the sides, framing a slow but steady receding bald spot. No tats. No bling. He was seemingly the image of a loser, who walked through life wearing a sign that said *Kick my ass. I deserve it.*

But then, there was that face.

If it was possible to be human and look like a reptile... A deep knife scar bisected his face. Eyes that reflected no soul. One look at Crazy

Loco and you could see how he got his name. The cat was just not wired right.

He had proved it many times, if you believed the stories that had grown up around him. Nobody had ever seen Loco lift a finger to remove somebody from the picture and, although many claimed Crazy had personally ordered them out on hits, no one ever had the balls to say as much with him in the room.

Long story short. Piss Crazy off and you died, disappeared or a combination of both. Bodies were never found, at least not complete ones. Crazy was never a suspect. The locals were convinced he did his damage through some kind of Satanic/Voodoo shit.

Crazy didn't say a word. He didn't have to.

It was legendary in the barrio that he could convey more with a look and a gesture than any ten F bomb laden rants. He shuffled slowly over to a corner table that was occupied by a leather-clad dude and his old lady de jour. He gave them the death stare. The bad guy instantly got the hint and dragged his squeeze out of her chair and away from the table. She'd be pissed at his cowardice and he probably wouldn't get any that night.

At least he would be alive and, perhaps more importantly, in one piece.

Crazy sat down at the table. The bartender brought over his liquid offering with a clean glass and set it down. Almost mechanically, Crazy began pouring and downing shots. The vibe turned painfully tense. A couple of rough looking toughs got up and left. The rest went stone silent, watching Crazy Loco for that something they knew would soon bubble to the surface. And mentally crossing themselves in the hope that, whichever way his madness turned, it would not be directed at them.

They did not have long to wait.

Crazy Loco had no sooner drained the last of the bottle then the empty glass flew across the bar, barely missing the head of a slutty young thing, and thudding against a far wall. He slammed the bottle on the table; shattering it to a sharp jagged point, which he waved threateningly in front of his face.

"Rodriguez!" he screamed. "I want the head of Rodriguez!"

Those in the bar knew what the drunken Loco was on about. They had heard this rant countless times. But it was a declaration of violence that seemingly had no answer.

Because Rodriguez was a ghost. But, for Crazy Loco, he was very much alive and somebody who needed to be put in the ground.

It had started a bit over a year ago. Crazy Loco's seeming stranglehold on street-level organized crime and, in particular, the crack and prostitution trade, had been in steady decline. A tougher crowd with better shit, better prices and pimps who ruled their stables with a violent hand were slowly taking a serious bite out of his lifestyle.

That was the reality. In Crazy Loco's feverish brain, however, the reality was a mysterious mastermind named Rodriguez - who had chosen to grind his enterprise into dust. He would rage on about Rodriguez at the drop of a hat; mostly idle threats that listeners knew would end up going nowhere.

Those listening to this latest tirade rolled their eyes. They all knew Rodriguez. Or *a* Rodriguez. Hell, in this part of town, you could hock a loogie and hit one. Rodriguez was what the Gringos likened to 'Smith and Jones'.

But Crazy seemed to have a method behind this night's madness.

"That's right! I want the head of Rodriguez laying at my feet! Fresh blood pouring from his neck, forming a red lake at my boots."

Then he landed his bombshell.

"Whoever lays the head of Rodriguez at my feet will get free drugs and women for the rest of their lives!"

Crazy suddenly had their attention. Many in the bar lubricated their macho with a major 'jones' fed by petty crimes and hopelessly dead-end jobs. The rest were always looking for some 'strange' to supplement their wives and girlfriends. Whether they realized it or not, they were leaning forward in their chairs.

"Bring me the head of Rodriguez and some kind of proof that he's the one muscling in on my business. All the drugs and pussy on the planet will be yours for the rest of your days."

They were interested in Crazy's drunken offer. Beginning to fidget in their chairs. Even the women were getting flushed. The madness of the pep rally was grinding down, as the effects of grade-A hooch began to take its toll on Crazy. He stood uneasily, looked insanely to the heavens and half shouted, half slurred

"So, who wants crack and tail for life?"

He ended his offer by falling face first through the table, wood chips and splinters scattering everywhere. Then he was out cold on the floor, the only visible sign of life a string of saliva curling down his cheek.

The bar patrons got up and quietly made their way out of Gordos. The place was soon empty, except for the bartender, who stood over Crazy Loco and the wreckage and sighed at the absurdity of it all.

It was just Crazy being Loco. Surely nobody was going to take his rambling seriously?

But he already knew the answer.

It was late and the cops were expecting the usual shit.

The drive-bys, the domestics, the drug deals gone sour. In this part of town, it was everything that began and ended with shots fired. But, for some strange reason, it was *not* the usual shit. The police choppers shining their lights witnessed nothing. Cop cruisers moved through silent streets. All they saw was blocks of empty.

Word had spread along the Chicano Hotline like wildfire. Every crack head and whorehound for miles around was on the hunt. In their fevered minds, everybody and anybody was a prime suspect.

They were all looking for Rodriguez.

Crazy Loco staggered into Gordos the next night. It was Friday and the joint should have been jumping. But the only person in the place was the bartender, who grudgingly acknowledged him, then went back to staring blankly at a big screen showing the Dodger's game.

Crazy sauntered over to his table and sat down.

"Hey motherfucker! The usual!"

The bartender brought over the good stuff and laid it in front of Crazy, who took a healthy swig straight from the bottle. It went down smooth.

"Where is everybody? Did immigration swing by and round all the losers up?"

"You know where they are. You told them what you wanted and what you'd give them. They're out there trying to collect."

"Oh yeah. That head of Rodriguez shit. And I meant it too!"

"I know you did. Which is why I told every Rodriguez I knew and gave a fuck about to stay indoors and carry a piece."

Crazy got that look in his eye that everyone prayed they would never see. He rose from the table and took a couple of unsteady steps toward the bartender, who crossed himself but stood defiant.

"Senior Loco?" A mild-mannered voice called from the other end of the bar.

Crazy and the bartender turned to find a slight, elderly man - visibly shaking and obviously in need of a fix - framing the entrance to Gordos. In his hand twitched a leathery pouch. Crazy eyed the mess in human form, then offered a nod that was the key to his shot at glory.

The man moved slowly forward. He stopped mere inches from Crazy and, without saying a word, tipped the pouch upside down and shook it gently.

The bloody human head hit the floor with a pulpy splat.

The bartender took an instinctive step back. A tremor rumbled through Crazy's face. He bent over and took a closer look. The head was smeared with glistening blood. The eyes a lazy lull of pain and resignation. The cut across the neck which sprouted pulp, slowly dripping blood and entrails, was ragged and sloppy. The kill looked fresh.

"My God!" gasped the bartender. "He's so young. Barely a teenager!"

"His name was Rodriguez," the junkie protested meekly. "Word on the street was that he used drugs."

"Where did you find him?" Crazy sneered. "Passed out in an alley?"

The shaking old junkie nodded weakly in agreement.

Crazy bent down and studiously looked over the grizzly orb, going eye to eye with every element of this bloody mess.

"Any ID?" he sneered. The old junkie shook his head.

"Well, shit, man! Then how do I know this is a Rodriguez? It could be a Sanchez. A Martinez. A Rojo... Hell, we fuck anything that moves! This could even be a Kirby!"

The old man was about to make his case when Crazy held up his hand to stop. He was looking wearily past the head-hunter, toward the door. A crusty middle-aged Chola, out of shape and looking disturbing in tight black leather, walked in. A Trader Joe's bag, dripping blood and virtually disintegrating, was held in her hands.

She sauntered up to Crazy, jostling the junkie out of the way and ignoring the head on the floor.

"I've got your Rodriguez right here," she boasted. "Now where's my shit?"

The bottom of the bag ripped open and another head hit the floor. The eyes were open with a 'last moment on earth' stare. He looked to be somewhere between 30 and death. The bloody cut was even and clean. Most likely a meat cleaver massacre. Crazy did a cursory inspection, carefully tilting the head to one side with the point of his boot to get a better look.

"So, this is Rodriguez?" he asked, matter-of-factly.

"Sure is," responded the woman. "Know it for sure."

"How's that?"

"I've been sleeping with this motherfucker for five years. I've seen his ID millions of times. He's definitely a Rodriguez."

Crazy flashed an ironic smile in the direction of the bartender, who returned the same. They were both too cool to admit they had just had their minds blown.

"You killed your old man?" Crazy laughed.

"Why not?" the woman snapped. "He was so much into the chronic he couldn't get it up anymore. A woman has needs, you know? If he could have popped a chubby a couple of times a week, I might have kept him around. I always gave good head. In the end that's all he was worth to me."

"He's givin *you* plenty of head now," Crazy deadpanned.

Throughout the night, other heads just kept on coming. Family members. Out-of-towners who happened to get caught in the hunt. Even a couple of Gordo's regular customers - all came to a splattering end in a bloody pile at Crazy Loco's feet. Those who brought them in stood silently as the pile grew, with the look of expectant puppies who were hoping for their master's favour and a bite to eat. Finally, as the count grew to 15 and things were starting to get a bit foul, Crazy stepped before the group.

"Good job. We've got plenty heads here. A bunch of Rodriguez's."

A lot of smiles, some with teeth, from the masses. Each thought a lifetime of drugs and ass would soon be theirs.

"Unfortunately, none of these is the right Rodriguez." Crazy swept his arm over the pile of flesh. "I know who I'm looking for and he isn't here."

There was low grumbling and a couple of F-bombs. Those who weren't high or suffering from the DT's looked downright angry. But they knew enough about what Crazy could do and didn't want their skull joining the party.

"Don't give me any shit." Crazy roared, feigning anger for effect. "Get out there and bring me the head of Rodriguez and we'll all live happily ever after."

The crowd slowly thinned out, leaving Crazy and the bartender to deal with the rotting pile of flesh. There was a moment of silence as the pair turned eyes on each other. The bartender countered Crazy's stare with his last ounce of mock bravado. He turned to the pile of heads, laying mere inches from him.

"None of these are gonna be the right one, are they?"

Crazy laughed, a slow sardonic crowing.

"Of course not."

"Then why?"

"Because of the barrio telegraph, baby! Word gets around that I'm looking for Rodriguez. Then heads start turning up. The real Rodriguez shits his pants and gets outta Dodge."

The bartender was stunned but not surprised at the revelation.

"And if it doesn't turn out that way?"

Crazy's eyes bulged. His mouth spread into a wide grin. For the first time in his life, the bartender visibly shuddered. Crazy raised his booted left foot and began stomping on the stack of heads. The sound of squishing skin, bone and spurting blood provided a slow, lazy echo around the bar. The trophies were quickly reduced to a massive blob. Crazy raised his blood and brain matter splattered boot out of the misshapen mess and glared at the bartender.

"Then, eventually, I'll get the right Rodriguez."

Behind the Blue Door

Dale L. Sproule

Some of the voices were gruff and some were screechy.

"Where'd he go?"

"Fi, fie, fo, fum."

"Aw, give that shite a rest, arsehole," thundered one of the trolls or orcs or whatever the hell they were. "You think this is still the middle fucking ages? You think you're talking to children?"

"He's gone into the water," squawked a smaller voice. "Under the ice."

"Follow him!" came the imperative.

"I can't swim," croaked the bogun and the vampire.

"It's too cold!" groaned the demons and the djinns, sounding like a swampful of very large frogs.

"What do I look like? A duck?" asked the griffin.

"He's getting away!" Shouted the bogun.

"Olive's got him back," said one of the vampires. There were moans and growls all round.

By this time, the lamia named Olive had indeed pulled Aaron back out of the water and dragged him to a path on the other side of the bushes.

"If you humans keep getting bigger," she whispered. "I won't be strong enough to do this sort of thing in a few more centuries."

Aaron's teeth were chattering so hard he could barely hear her. Even now looking at Olive made him gasp. If you took all the girls that had fueled Aaron's wet dreams since adolescence and rolled them into one, that's what the lamia looked like. And, of all the girls he'd ever crushed on, Olive was definitely the smartest - which made her even hotter, if that's an adjective which can be used when it's so cold. Aaron recalled the conversation that had precipitated his escape attempt.

"You don't look like these other creatures," he had asked innocently. "What are you?"

"A lamia," she'd answered.

"We studied a poem about lamias in first year English," he'd said, hoping to impress her. Then he remembered what the poem was about. Lamias seduced and ate people.

As they came to what seemed to be a clearing, he broke into a run - before falling through the ice seconds later.

"You need to understand." She lifted him into what was known in Aaron's world as a fireman's carry and wove through the trees. "That this realm only exists within the collective unconsciousness of humanity. Without a mortal context for our existence, we are naught, dust, diddly-squat..."

"If that's true, why is my imagination trying so hard to kill me?"

"First of all, we're not imaginary. We're as real as you but only because you need us to be. It's complicated." She set Aaron on his feet and he rubbed his belly where her pointy shoulder had dug in. "Secondly, if you stick with me, the other creatures aren't allowed to kill you. That's how our system works here. A bit primal - the whole possession-isn't-just nine-tenths-of-the-law-it-is-the-fucking-law aesthetic - but they're not allowed to touch you, as long as you stick with me."

"Are you going to eat me?"

She shrugged.

"I admit some lamiae - over the centuries - were attributed with seducing and consuming young men. But I'm not one of those. I promise. I will not harm you."

When she locked him in her manga-eyed gaze, only Aaron's unyielding tumescence prevented him from wetting himself in the full-on intensity of her stare - and this was standing in the frigid air, still soaked from his icy swim.

"My place in the archetype is strictly as a devourer of small children," Olive said, like a chemistry teacher talking about an interesting quality of chlorine.

"Wait. You eat babies?" The giant lump in his pants was replaced by one in his throat.

"Not babies. Not as a first choice, really… no." She turned away. "Toddlers are more filling."

"Seriously?"

"One thing we are not is trendy," she continued in a small voice. "There are no vegan lamiae. Although I do like carrot cake. And kids who eat their vegetables are tastier. Look, I didn't come up with my own back story. And I really do like you. That's why I saved you just now. So cut me some slack, okay?"

"If you're not trendy, how do you know slang like that?" Aaron was suddenly suspicious of the whole setup.

"We've come out of the deep freeze twenty times in the past fifty years."

"You didn't save me just because you like me. What are you going to do with me?"

"Get you out of here. Back to your own world."

"Why would you do that? In one breath, you tell me you eat small children and, in the next, say you want to get me back to my world. I may not be the brightest crayon in the box but leading you to the exit strikes me as a really bad idea."

"Okay, fine. Good luck on your own, then." She turned, ducked under some branches and was gone, quickly and simply. Aaron had already experienced what would happen if he left her side. Wasn't in a hurry to do it again.

"Olive? Olive? Olive!" he whispered, louder and more desperate each time - until it became more of a soft shout.

Which was answered by a very masculine grunt. He heard crashing and thumping of birch and fir trees bending out of the way, along with the occasional loud snap.

Alongside them, Aaron could see the shadows of smaller creatures darting hither and thither toward him. Although, how he could perceive shadows in a landscape with no identifiable light source, was still a mystery.

The stand of fir trees in front of him parted like a curtain and a head as big as an Easter Island statue peered through. Its heavy brows rose and its mouth fell open, revealing row upon row of shark-like teeth. Aaron could smell its breath from three trees away.

"Changed your mind yet?" The lamia said in a lilting voice as she stepped out from behind a big oak.

Aaron nodded like a bobblehead.

"That's far enough, Stuffy. He's mine," she warned the creature reaching for him.

"But you left him behind."

"Well, in case you've gone blind my friend, I'm baa-aack. And I beat you to him."

The troll's fingertips reminded Aaron of ham hocks, calloused with thick white rind. They had claws instead of fingernails. The troll called Stuffy grabbed Olive. She looked like a porcelain toy in its giant fist. It reminded him of Ann Darrow in King Kong. How could he be this freaked out and turned on at the same time?

"Eat it or give it up to someone who will," the troll rumbled.

"Fe, fi, fo, fum," came another voice. "I smell the blood of an...."

Setting Olive back down gently, the troll turned and drove a huge roundhouse into the face of the giant behind him. Blood sprayed everywhere and there was a crash like a falling oak.

"Foooooockkk! What'd you do that for?"

"I said to can that fairytale shit! You don't hear me yelling *who's that walking across my bridge*."

"Well... that's because there's no bridge."

"And there's no Englishmen!" The monster whirled back and pointed at Aaron. "Are you an Englishman?"

"No. Canadian."

"So, there ya go. We can't eat yet." The argument continued as the pair departed, fading to thunder in the distance. Olive released a huge sigh.

"So. Are you ready to talk to me now? At least consider my proposition?"

Aaron nodded. "Let's just get away from them."

"Oh, Stuffy and Sven are the least of our worries. Your scent is on the wind. There's gotta be at least a thousand others who know you're here."

"Okay, I'm listening. What do you want me to do?"

"I'm gonna take you back to the door in the underground parking lot where you came in. And out you go."

"Huh. After all this, why would you let me go?"

"You'll come back."

"Why would I do that?"

"Any deal we make here is as binding for you as it is for me."

"What do you want from me?"

"You just need to fetch me some supplies."

"I'm not bringing you any babies!" he said.

"Of course not."

"No toddlers? Or kids of any description?"

"I promise," she shrugged. "Only inanimate objects. But you need to make up your mind now. The passage won't stay open much longer. I'll give you five seconds to decide before handing you over to the hungry bestiary… four… three…"

"Fine. I'll do it. But how do we even find our way back to the parkade?" He peered forlornly into the darkness.

"Easy," she said. "I oversaw its creation. The whole bottom level of the parking lot doesn't exist in your world. It's just a mirror image we made of the floor above. Drivers don't realize what's happening until the blue ramp door closes behind them and the asphalt gets bumpy."

She raised an eyebrow

"Why were you even down there?"

"Security guard. First day on the job, so I thought I'd look around."

"That's why nobody saw you coming in. My people were preoccupied with the car."

"People? You call them people?" he muttered, closing his eyes against the memory.

He'd never forget what happened to the middle-aged couple who had been sitting in their red Audi convertible when the blue door locked behind them. Before Aaron had a chance to run up to their idling vehicle, a creature half the size of the car jumped onto the hood, its weight lifting the back tires right off the ground. The creature had glistening green skin, a whip-like tail and claws as long as Aaron's fingers.

With a grin like a discoloured ivory comb, it plunged both arms straight through the cloth roof. Aaron heard screaming and watched the creature haul a male passenger through the breach. As it opened its enormous maw and took his head off with one bite, smaller creatures swarmed into the shell of the car for the shrieking driver. A cyclops and a small dragon tried to pull the passenger from the first creature's grasp. Crowing and grunting, they dragged it to the ground in front of the convertible. In the glare of the headlights, Aaron saw them tear the man open like a package under a Christmas tree. A cry of ferocious joy went up and he turned his head away. Something plopped onto his shoe.

Looking down, he saw it was a human finger.

A froglike creature scampered after it but came up short when it saw Aaron.

"Another huuuu-man!" It shrieked triumphantly. "Another!"

Dozens of eyes peered in his direction and he ran from the howling pack.

The dark terrain changed and he found himself sprinting across a forest clearing that looked like an automotive version of Stonehenge.

As he passed, Olive stepped out from a half-buried PT Cruiser and took him in her embrace. Much like she was doing now.

Only this time, instead of pushing her away, he embraced her back, reduced to hormones by the soft pressure of her breasts against his. She stroked his jaw and drew him down into a kiss.

"Let's mess around before we set off," she said.

"Here? Now? You're joking, right?"

"Just following my nature, like I told you." She cupped his crotch.

"You said it was your sister who was the seducer. Not you."

"Maybe I don't eat young men." She unzipped Aaron's fly. "But my sister and I do share some enthusiasms."

"Ohhh," he moaned, helpless. But just as she was about to take him in her mouth, he thought about all the flesh-eating creatures in the forest and jumped back.

"What's the matter now?"

"Show me your teeth," he demanded.

She stood up, opening her mouth to run her tongue sensually over her small, even and very human teeth. Then she shrugged out of her filmy dress and grabbed his pole again.

"Nnnnnnmmmyyyyyyaaeaeah," screamed Aaron, ejaculating up her arm, all the way to the shoulder.

"No way!" Olive cursed as he went limp in her hand.

"Nnnnooommmyyyyyyygawwwd," Aaron's scream morphed as a huge, wolflike creature jumped out of the woods directly behind Olive, fangs bared.

"C'mon Lonny," She turned around. "You promised me an hour. And it's only been like 40 fucking minutes!"

"You blew it!" the wolf chuckled. "You've given it your best shot. It wasn't consummated. Now you gotta give someone else a turn."

"If he can't get it up for me, you're probably shit outta luck."

"I'm not looking for a chew toy boy. I came for dinner." He turned to Aaron. "You got nice shoulders."

"I have twenty minutes left," declared Olive.

"I'm lodging a formal fucking complaint this time."

"Drool me a river, dogbreath. Now be a good doggie and shoo!"

"I'm keeping an eye on you." The wolf, pointed at Aaron. Dropping to all fours, he ran back into the deep, dark woods.

Aaron didn't let go of Olive's hand the rest of the way back to the parking garage.

"What if I die of frostbite before we find the gate?" he asked.

"You won't."

"I can barely walk," he snapped. "Hypothermia is a thing. Not a mythical thing."

"You can't actually die in this world."

"Oh, is that right? So, if I walk away, that pack of monsters won't eat me before I get ten steps. Can't die, my ass."

"While I imagine that being eaten alive would be most unpleasant," she said sanctimoniously, "It wouldn't be your real, earthly body getting scoffed."

"How does that work?"

"You're not physically here. Just metaphysically, y'know?"

"No." He shook his head. "I don't. I clearly remember coming down the stairs at the car park and through a blue door." He waved his arms around vigorously to assert his presence. "If I'm not really here, who are you talking to? Who am *I* talking to?"

"If you don't understand by now, you probably won't get it." She stopped and looked him in the eye. "But think about this. It's 32 below. You fell in icy water. And you've been walking around soaked to the core for however long it's been. If you were going to die, you'd already be dead."

He tried to scratch his head through hair that was practically solid ice.

"When you opened the door, it was your consciousness came through," she continued, "Your shadow self."

"Came through to where?" he demanded.

"Here. The zeitgeist. The spiritus mundi. The archetypal circle. The collective unconscious. The place where we live."

He pursed his lips and creased his brow until the ice cracked and fell off his face.

"Well then, what *would* happen if I was eaten?"

"I dunno." She shrugged. "You might just wake up in your own body."

"Well then, I should just allow it to hap…

"Or, more likely, you'd simultaneously die of some other cause in your world," she continued with a sly smile. "How should I know what happens over there?

As they passed through the technological henge, with its rusting hulks of antique cars buried nose-first in the frozen ground, he listened for a place to cut into Olive's steady stream of chatter.

"…not really sisters. More like different iterations of me. Lamiae are not fixed mythologies, at least not compared to the classics. Aphrodite's attributes were predetermined by historical record and academic debate. But we lesser stars in the archetypal firmament have remained part of the darker animus. Whenever we do show up in your literature or art, everyone imagines us differently. So, we get to be all those different things at the same time. Sorta fun. My six sisters are nothing compared to the forty or fifty iconic variations on werewolves. Lonny is closer to your Red Riding Hood wolf…"

He finally saw the first of the concrete pillars from the parking garage. This one had a blue stripe with a circle that said *2E* backwards.

Right; a mirror image. He could see the blue door from here.

Olive slammed him up against the concrete pillar.

"Can you feel it getting warmer? We need to hurry."

"What do you mean?"

"The gate to your world only opens at 27 below." She unzipped his pants, grinning to see that neither the cold nor the paralyzing fear could dampen his ardour. "There's only one key that can unlock that door,

Aaron. The only way I guarantee you get back in one piece is if you agree to work for me."

"Work for you?"

"Promise me you'll take up my banner in our mythic quest!" She wrapped her arms around his neck and her legs around his hips.

He nodded.

"You need to say it out loud."

"Yes! I promise."

She lowered herself onto his personal Excalibur. He lasted only seconds after her hips began to gyrate but she seemed delighted about his quick trigger this time.

"Okay! Deal signed and sealed." She jumped off nimbly, shouting like a cheerleader. "Let's go find that gate!"

His heart began to pound when he saw the light switch he had flipped to illuminate this entire world. On the floor was the broken cell phone that had failed to prop open the heavy door. But now the door was hanging open.

"Oh my God," said Aaron.

"What is it sweetie?" Olive was hanging on his arm - so deliriously happy she was like a drunken teenager.

"They've broken through, into the rest of garage."

"Who has?"

"Your friends."

"Oh, no. Don't worry. I keep telling you, we can't cross over." She looked deep in his eyes before giving him a long kiss. "You know that you're mine, right? Whether it's next year or ten years from now, you have no choice but to come to me when I call, wherever and whenever the gate opens again. When it opened in 1945, it had been over a hundred years, but with nuclear testing and pollution and changing weather patterns… it's been opening every second year since then. So I have no doubt I'll see you again soon."

Her words were just babble, as his brain tried unsuccessfully to put the pieces together.

"Oh, and here's your task. I need Clomiphene. Too bad we don't have a pen. I'd write it down for you."

"What the hell is Clumpopee?" he shouted.

"Clomiphene," she corrected him. "I'm pretty fruitful as it is, but with the fertility drugs, I've been known to pop out ten or twelve at a time. They're only half-human but pretty tasty for all that. See you in a year or two. And don't forget the Clomiphene. C-L-O-M...."

As he scrambled through the door, he lost consciousness, waking up on the stairs. Staggering up to the main floor of the garage, he appreciated how cold he really was, but managed to keep putting one frozen foot in front of another. He made it out of the door at ground level before hypothermia took him down.

One of the nurses told him someone else had died at the car park the same night. An older couple succumbed to carbon monoxide poisoning.

It bugged Aaron when that same nurse laughed at him.

"Lots of patients ask me for morphine," she said. "You're the first who ever asked for Clomiphene."

Catfish

Geneve Flynn

Bruce crouched, one hand on the fridge for balance, gut squashed against his thighs, knees aching. He twitched the piece of ham.

"Here, puss-puss."

The kitten approached at an angle, ducking and darting away.

"Come on."

Twitch.

The little cat was thin and long-legged with patches of dirty white-and-grey fur. Its eyes gleamed yellow out of sooty sockets, like they'd been rimmed with eyeliner.

Nasty looking thing.

It sniffed and crept closer. Took the ham, warm tongue rasping gently at his fingertips.

"Good kitty."

With a purr, it rubbed a scruffy head against his hand, coiling a crooked tail over his thick fingers.

"Bah!" Bruce shouted.

The kitten shot sideways, fur bristling, claws skittering on the kitchen floor, desperate for a way out. The lino was slick and the cat careened headfirst into a cabinet. Bruce threw his head back, snorting with dull glee. The cat staggered and righted itself. It scrambled between his legs towards the screen door. On reflex, Bruce put his foot down to stop it. But his boot came down too hard, too quick.

He stared at the crumpled body, mouth open in shock.

He hadn't meant to. Not really.

It can't be the same cat.

Bruce swayed on his feet, blinking stupidly. He fumbled for his glasses on the kitchen counter. Yesterday, he'd buried the thing down behind the compost heap. It had been a boneless rag in his hands.

The little cat watched him from the open back door. It closed its amber eyes and cracked a yawn.

With a slow frown, Bruce picked up the can of stew he'd been about to heat on the stove. The kitten's nostrils quivered. It skirted him, a thin bib of saliva dampening its chin.

There must be a litter of the bastards.

"Here, kitty..."

He blew across the open can, sending a beefy waft towards the cat. It meowed, yellow eyes tracking him as it crept forward.

He clamped down on its bony neck. It twisted free, clawing and biting up his leg. With a scream, Bruce dropped the can. He tore the kitten off and hurled it across the kitchen. Crunch. It struck the fridge, dropped to the floor and lay still, chest panting like tiny bellows.

Bruce limped over, teeth bared.

Blood on his shovel mixed with clay, as Bruce smoothed dirt over the body. The head was buried deep in a second hole behind the chook pen. He turned and limped back to the house, leg throbbing.

He stopped.

No.

The little cat watched him from the kitchen windowsill.

A crushing agony struck Bruce in the chest, lancing down his arm and up his neck. He folded over, vision narrowing into a tunnel. All he could see was the cat.

He wheezed, fumbling for his pills. The tablet dissolved with a sharp tingle under his tongue and, within minutes, the pain eased. Bruce straightened and lurched up the path, rubbing his chest. The cat jumped down and darted past. Bruce lunged and missed, crashing to the ground.

The cat stopped halfway along the path, the pink pucker of its bum taunting him. It swivelled its head around and hissed, ears laid flat. Bruce roared and hauled himself up.

It bolted over the back fence into the easement between the two estates. He flung the gate wide with a bang and saw the cat at the end of the lane. He blundered after it, boiling with hot, rancid thoughts.

I'll get it. This time, I'll get it for sure.

The cat waited until Bruce was almost within reach, then leapt over the opposite fence.

Bruce eased the back neighbour's gate ajar. The yard was trim and pretty. Beds of roses, a wind chime hanging from the patio, the weatherboard house painted a pale mint. The kitten preened on the threshold of the open back door. Bruce saw a smear of blood - his blood - on its whiskers, before it disappeared into the dark interior. He swore, clutching at his shoulder again, as he hobbled after it.

The aroma of apple pie filled the dimly lit kitchen. An archway led down a short hall. Cross-stitched pictures of felines hung on the walls. A calendar showing fluffy kittens was tacked above the spotless counter.

Bruce hesitated. This wasn't private business anymore and the thought of explaining himself to the coppers made him shrivel a little.

Something streaked past, sunk needle teeth into his ankle then shot away.

"Right!" he bellowed. "That's it."

He chased after the crooked bottlebrush tail into a darkened living room. Its curtains were drawn and the smell of talc overtook the fragrance of cinnamon and pastry. Bruce peered into the shadows.

"Here, puss-puss..." he whispered.

A hiss answered and a pair of golden eyes blinked open in the corner.

He grinned.

"Gotcha."

Bruce took a step then faltered. A second set had blinked open, followed by another and another and another. Too many glowing yellow eyes. A final pair opened, larger than all the rest, in the silhouette of a stuffed armchair.

Bruce took a step backwards, skin tight and clammy.

"I was... I was just looking for my cat."

"That's quite all right, dear," an old woman's voice answered from the chair. She clicked on a lamp with a lacy shade, flooding the room with mottled light. "Which cat was it?"

Gnarled hands were busy with something in her lap.

A fresh sheen of sweat broke out over Bruce's body.

It was a hand fishing reel.

She was slowly and patiently winding in many clear filaments.

Cats crouched on every surface. Each one a dirty, white-and-grey, long-legged kitten, with kohl eyeliner around amber eyes and a crooked tail.

Each cat attached to a fishing line.

The old woman smiled.

As he folded to the ground, heart seizing like a rusted engine, Bruce saw the sharp glint of her teeth.

Prince Charming Finds His Sleeping Beauty

Ann Wuehler

I looked across at the man I loved, who was staring down into the grave we had just dug up. His mouth had come open, revealing a slender pink ribbony tongue... a snake's tongue.

Lee had become my Prince Charming. My soul mate, my other half. And his hobby was not about to distract me from that.

"She's fresh... seventeen. Car accident."

His voice held chimes, those tiny wind chimes in all the female empowerment movies. Tiny bells of heaven.

Lee lifted his eyes, which were full of holiness and greed.

"I love you, Heather."

My name. The name of the girl in the grave was Summer or Autumn or some other ultra-dumbshit feminine handle.

Thrills. Better than the sex we seldom had. But I was a girl, he often argued. Girls prefer cuddling and long talks and understanding. I was his first girlfriend and often thought... *what does he really know about women?*

So it was up to me to forgive his stereotyping. That's what men do, stereotype women. It's what they're comfortable thinking. And it's okay. Love is about forgiveness and tolerance, right? That's what's taught on all the talk shows. In every movie I've ever seen.

Lee broke through the casket and the smell... ripe and intense. The dead girl lay there, hands folded on her still firm titties. She wore a blue dress with lace about the throat and big black buttons all down the front. My boyfriend stared at her, stroked her face. She did not respond and she did not tell him he was ugly and short and going bald or that his breath stank. The perfect female.

How womankind had destroyed him over the years, the insults right to his face! This one did not argue or criticize or have any sort of opinion... the ultimate Stepford bitch. One who just lay there and let the man act as he wished. As I was learning to do.

Lee squeezed her breasts and I heard the fabric of her dress rustle and creak in his small flabby hands. His short fingers moved around and I realized he was looking for the nipples.

I waited, obedient and passive and full of a fierce pity for other women who just did not understand what it was to love. To give. To bend. Those lonely fat women, those lonely skinny women. And everything else in between.

The night air made my breath plume. Frost was forming on the grass of the graveyard. After he was done, we would lay beneath my purple comforter, eat popcorn from a common plastic bowl and watch old Cary Grant movies... because the women in them were dead. So, he could fantasize placing Myrna Loy from *Mr. Blandings Builds his Dream House* on a silk-covered bed and then enter the bones of her pelvis; she unable to refuse. Because she was a skeleton. Any old movie would do, really. It was the unable to refuse part that really got him going, made his hands move and whirl.

Next, he lifted her dress until it covered Autumn-or-Summer's cold, distant undreaming face. With a pocket knife, he sliced her bra off, then her underwear. There was her cold little pocket between her rigid thighs. The vee of her mortician incision. Purple-white skin. Lee reached into his coat pocket, took out the Vaseline and smeared it all over his erection, using my hands to help, as his were shaking too badly with excitement and joy. How hot he felt against my palms and fingers.

Stop. Judge not, lest ye be judged. What sins do you crave to commit, have already completed if you are honest enough to admit such things? We must accept the good and the bad in those we love. That is the great lesson of life itself, surely.

He climbed on top of her, his white hairy pimpled buttocks moving deliriously. The sounds... of flesh ripping open, of his grunting, of the mingled rustling of their clothes. I watched from above, holding the shovel so we would not forget it, raising the flashlight so he could see. Lee pulled her dress down so he could kiss her. He did other things to her body... all of her orifices made ready with lots of Vaseline. I loved him and supported his choices for happiness. I felt fulfilled because he was fulfilled.

Back at home, Lee sighed beside me, his uncleaned fingers dabbling in our mutual popcorn as Myrna Loy acted calm and wise to Cary Grant's frantic and hysterical.

"I wonder?" He turned suddenly to me, his eyes soft and inquiring. "I wonder if they could be fresher. Just after the moment of death. Just after... What's the matter? Does the popcorn taste burned? I microwaved it for exactly the time it said."

"It's fine. I just don't want any," I replied diplomatically. I am a consummate diplomat. All women should be. It's why so many are without a man. No diplomacy. No looking the other way and not calling attention to faults.

"It's wonderful popcorn. Just right. It's simply... you're talking about... about murder."

Lee sighed again, that glow leaking from his face. I had done that.

"But," I continued in my sweetest voice. "Maybe that wasn't what you meant. "

His greasy finger traced circles on my nightgowned leg. Round and round and round. I would never wash that stuff out. There would be spots where his fingers had pressed. Grease spots. My favorite nightie.

"I don't know what I meant. We'd get caught. I don't wish anyone to know. You never make me feel ashamed. You're so perfect."

He placed his head on my small breasts as if he were a child come seeking solace, after a particularly nasty monster scarefest dream-o-rama. His warmth soaked through me at once, like an oversized heating pad. Some nights, it was rather like lying next to a volcano. I would sweat and stick my legs out from under the covers to cool down - but he slept without apparently noticing our combined body heat approached the temperature of the sun. I suffered this in near silence for, after all, women love to cuddle. I would just have to learn to love it. Love is also about patience.

"No... tell me what you were thinking. How... how was it? Tonight." I kept my tone gentle and welcoming.

"Wonderful. She'd have told me no... before. But she was so loving and accepting. A feast. I wanted to eat her hips. Her just-rounding hips. But I would never do that. Never. That's... that's sick."

"It's all right," I cooed, stroking his long strands of gingery hair. He needed me, he needed me desperately. All was right with the world. And his yen toward cannibalism, after his acts of love, nothing to deal with yet.

"You're so nearly perfect," Lee amended, eyes now closed. "You still move too much. I can hear you breathing."

"I can't hold my breath that long," I snapped, remembering our last attempt at mating. I had to play dead, as Lee put it. I'd held my breath and my body as rigid as possible until the calf muscle in my right leg went into righteous spasms. It had spoiled his enjoyment. We had tried again. My arms went to sleep. Playing dead took lots of practice and discipline.

"So... how could they be fresher?"

"That moment, right after. Death." Lee breathed out, his voice barely heard. "Maybe strangle them, tie them up and strangle them. And then, as they cooled... so much nicer and fresher and cleaner. That girl tonight had a smell and she'd only been dead a few days. Maybe some of that chest rub stuff in the nose. We got any of that stuff?"

"Yes. But... after you're done with the strangled girl... what about her body? What do we do with it?"

"Practical Heather! That's why we were meant to be together. Together forever. You're my lobster, my wolf, my eagle." Lee kissed my lips and I tasted dirt on them. Grave dirt. Sour and bland at the same time. "Bury them? The river?"

"I'd say the river," I agreed at once. "Take all their clothes off and dump them in the Snake. Or drive them somewhere to some other river. The Columbia. Maybe the Colorado. Washes away all evidence. And they have to be strangers. I read on this website that the reason so many killers get away with stuff is they can't be linked to their victims. And that crime scenes get messed up royally all the time. It's not like on CSI, or those other shows with smart cops. Ed Gein was a nice guy to his neighbors. Ted Bundy was a nice guy. Jeffrey Dahmer was a quiet guy who lived alone."

I racked my memory

"Jack the Ripper. They're still looking for that Black Dahlia killer. The Hillside Strangler is sitting well fed, even now, in a jail cell after what? Thirty, forty years? Luck is on our side. And, if we're careful. If you want this... we can do it."

Lee smiled.

"You're the only live girl I'd bother with."

"I know," I said proudly. I was giving him a great gift. I was giving him what he truly wanted, not some sweater or gift certificate to Home Depot. The chance to fulfill his basest desires. To finally be sated and full and too worn out to continue.

She said her name was Lisa Mathers. And she also whispered to me, when we went into the bathroom together at Joe's, a bar in Payette, that she liked women. As in... really liked them. Lisa stood five ten and weighed about two hundred - but it was well distributed, not all lumped beneath her chin or swinging from her arms. She was big and solid. A farm girl out for a good time. Twenty but could pass easily for forty, with her tightly permed hair and heavily made up brown eyes.

"You're a dyke?" I asked as she washed her hands.

"Shh!" She giggled and clutched at my shoulder with wet fingers. She had just thrown up her ten rum and cokes.

Lee had stayed at home, this having been my idea to scout out a suitable first victim. We couldn't be seen taking her down together, I'd said laughingly.

"I think so. I've done a few guys! Does that count? You wanna go out in the parking lot? You're nice, Heather. You're so nice."

Sometimes, God hands you a broken-legged gazelle on a silver platter. I licked my lips and giggled. I had taken diazepam from the vet clinic where I worked. Stupid. I should have to come up with something better, something that could not be linked to me.

I followed Lisa out and no one noticed us. There were prettier prey at the bar that night, girls far drunker and far more clingingly desperate. But Lee would love Lisa. There was so much to her. She was not delicate or easily broken. And perhaps God or Jesus had meant for her to be a sacrifice. Who am I to question divine decisions?

Lisa drove a battered green Toyota, something vaguely square and oddly Japanese. Japanese/American. A car one saw every day on the streets. She fumbled about for her keys and I fingered the pills in my pocket.

"Hey," I said craftily, "I got something here. You wanna try it? Ever wanted to sniff glue? Ever taken animal tranqs?"

Lisa turned gracelessly around, the way very drunk people do, as if balance and grace were taking a night-long smoke break somewhere deep in the brain. I had to look up, as I'm short. Lisa smiled vaguely, her voice masculine in its lowness.

"Glue, baby? I don't do glue. Jump in my car and get those jeans off."

I smiled, her lust throbbing against me, oiling the very air between us, as if she were trying to dip me in Wesson. Then deep fry me.

"It'll make it better... you know, like X. It's kinda like X. Or Valium."

Lisa laughed, placing her hand on my face.

"Anything you want. You are so cute. God, you are so cute."

Then she leaned in and kissed me, her lips tasting like vomit and rum. The taste of women. I could smell her perfume and body odor. Something oddly high-school, too sweet, too strong. And her sweat and the aroma of her skin, that living aroma of life, frenzy, blood, sugar, salt, hair. A living stink. Lee surely would turn up his nose at such a rich, real smell. I let Lisa kiss me, then pulled back. Her lips were soft... different from Lee's, more giving, less quick.

"I need a Tic-Tac," she laughed

"Are you gonna try this or not?" I grinned back. "I can give you a Tic-Tac."

Lisa jerked as a group of young men staggered out of the bar and headed toward their cars, howling like coyotes, yodeling like mountain climbers. The world at their feet at one-thirty on a Friday night in Payette, Idaho. How joyous they sounded, easy and floating on beer rivers.

Something in my groin loosened and burned. They wouldn't want to cuddle and watch women long dead... but that was disloyal.

"I'll try it," Lisa slurred. "I'll try anything once."

"Yes," I murmured, helping her to the diazepam, guiding her down into her own car, over the backseat. She went easy, already half passed out. I looked around, checking for witnesses. None. No one had noticed the two bar hags leaving together, two plain misses, not worth a second look.

I drove the Toyota, thinking all the while about fingerprints and trails of evidence. And how Lee would be so happy. He would finally get what he wanted and all because of me. I drove carefully, obeying every law, speed sign and change of light. Not weaving over the painted lines. Lisa lay in her own backseat, covered with my coat. My car was still back at the bar... we would have to retrieve it tonight after Lee was done.

I kept the window down, though it felt about twenty degrees. The reek of Lisa was making me light-headed, not to mention the alcohol I'd thrown back. I got to the apartment building and went to fetch Lee.

He looked in the backseat, then at me, his skin oddly slack and repulsive for a moment. Then his lips split in a giant grin.

"Heather... oh my god, Heather. Let's get her upstairs... she's still breathing." He drew his hands back as if her rising and falling chest blistered his fingertips.

"We can't take her upstairs. We have to take her somewhere else, where no one can hear us through the extra thin crappy walls, Lee. Go get the Vaseline and your coat, maybe some cash? You know, in case we drive a long ways. We can go out to Owyhee somewhere! Dump her there. And... we gotta get my car. Let's do that now. Let's leave her covered and take your truck, get my car, and come back here... so you can have what you want. She'll be out until morning. She put away a bottle of rum and I gave her some stuff from the clinic. Okay? I got it all figured out."

Lee sighed but obeyed me, wanting obviously to strangle her and get started.

So, after retrieving my car, and being stared at by a biker with a beard down to his silver belt buckle and slab-like bare arms sticking out of his vest at near right angles, we returned to sleeping Lisa.

She had moments before her prince arrived, not to wake her but crush her windpipe. She would be doubly violated. As a dyke and a person. Her take on it, not mine. Except, she would have no opinion on it now, would she? And what sort of life would she have had before her? She was nothing before and she would be nothing now. A blank canvas for Lee to paint. She would be left a ghost to wander out in the grim sere hills of Eastern Oregon.

There was good company out there. Murdered Indians, pioneers who had starved or frozen to death, young Chinese girls torn apart by their new lives of slavery and prostitution. Lisa would join their transparent ranks and make the wind moan, adding her voice, her low, mannish voice. Just another girl who didn't make it home from the bars. Just another girl.

I drove Lisa and myself out to the Owyhees, roughly forty miles or more, Lee following in his truck, with his shovel and flashlight and lubricants. No one was out driving. I felt invincible. And so, warned myself to be careful. This was too easy. Perhaps God would grant us this one... this one perfect time.

That was why those others had been caught... they got greedy. Wanted more and more. Jack the Ripper stopped killing. Or so they thought or speculated. The Black Dahlia Killer... only once. Just the one time would be all we got. Everything would fall into place. Lisa had been a gift to Lee and me. She had not fought or struggled, she had willingly sucked down the diazepam. She had given me a kiss of blessing.

Only once, only this one time, I thought as the dark road curved and twisted before me. That terrible, narrow road that led up to Lake Owyhee and beyond, to the back country. I wanted, suddenly, to find 97 South, to roll toward Nevada, McDermott and Orovada and Winnemucca. To huddle far out in the nowhere wasteland of the Silver State. Far, far from Joe's in Payette, burning Lisa's body, giving back her ashes to the blind, bland heavens. No river, no hasty shallow grave... no chance of finding her at all. Burn her. Burn her voice, her ghost. Burn everything. A clean ending, after her remains had been put through their paces.

We could burn her, build a campfire where no one could see what we were doing from the road, incinerate her remains. Though it might take a mighty hot fire to do that. Lee's headlights splashed through the dirty windows of Lisa's Toyota. I noticed she had a tape deck, nothing as modern as a CD player. Celine Dion... Barry Manilow... Air Supply... Journey... Faith Hill. Love songs. Soft, sugared love songs.

Tears stung my eyes. Lee would have to be respectful. This was not some dead girl we'd dug up. Lisa had given herself to us... to me. The universe would watch and make sure she was treated accordingly.

But what kind of universe was it that allowed her to be so used in the first place?

I chose a road and followed it, a dirt track that juddered me and nearly broke the car in two. It threw Lisa about. She never stirred or complained, but slumbered on, Sleeping Beauty, Snow White. Those passive girls, waiting so politely for the knowledge of penis. In the original versions, the sleeping women had been raped. Or perhaps the princes had thought them dead.

Lee turned off, his headlights blinding me for a moment as he tailgated me. We drove along slowly, deer leaping before us in outrage and white-eyed fear. The road widened and some instinct in me whispered *here*. I flashed my brake lights and put the car in park. Lee stopped his truck and came right to my door, bending down, his mouth open.

"This is perfect, Heather. I love you."

But he was looking at the passed-out woman in the back seat. I did not mind... this was his moment, Lee's ultimate pinnacle. He was a salmon returning to his native waters, to spawn and then to die. But what a glorious spawning Lee would have!

"Get her in the open," I said. "Her name is Lisa."

Lee struggled and pulled, puffing, huffing, as we both managed to get Lisa onto the cold, rocky earth. He kneeled over her, fingers flexing.

"Hold the flashlight, Heath."

"Of course." I fetched it and returned. Cheerleader, perfect girlfriend, perfect woman and helpmate. Lee placed his short-fingered flabby little hands around Lisa's Amazon throat and locked them, his thumbs pressing inward, almost disappearing into her flesh. She gave vague twitches. She grunted, coughed. Farted. A long ripping one. I bit my lips, anything to keep from braying out giggles like an insane donkey on crack. Dead girl farts, film at five and ten! Her feet drummed in protest of her life's end... I had not given her lots of pills, just enough to keep her under. Her eyes came open in the cone of the flashlight's glare. Brown, senseless, blind. They swiveled toward me but surely the light blinded her, dazzled her. I did not want her to see me. And Lee kept pressing her throat inward. His shoulders bunched and rippled with the effort.

"God damn," he whispered, a little crankily. "Die already."

"Shh," I cautioned. "She's a gift. Just break her neck if you have to. One of those head-turn moves, like on Xena."

"I think you have to have special training to do that sort of shit," Lee snapped.

Then we both heard the absence of her breath. He had done it, pressed down hard enough to end her days. He staggered back, fell on his bottom, cutting his hands on stones, which he would not notice for some time. But I noticed.

"Naked... help me."

Stripped, she was just meat. Just dense inanimate meat. Her bulgy, strong body lay before us. Before Lee. Stretch marks on her limp breasts, her pubic hair trimmed sloppily. He kissed her cooling lips and skin and worshipped her in the odd spotlight of his own flashlight. He left little smears from his rock-lacerated hands on her pale flesh.

Her legs were freshly shaved and there were tiny nicks on her knees. Bruises necklaced her throat. Lee's fingers had done that.

I watched, listened, calm at my very center. This was what love called for... complete and utter understanding of another person's deepest, basest wants. Peering, unafraid, into whatever awful heart beats and lives beneath their fake, shown-to-the-world heart. An act of charity so profound that only a woman was capable of it. Men would never understand the fragile shell they walked on... the fragile shell of women's souls, given up in service to all mankind. They would die without us, it was that simple and that far-reaching. Did they not understand? Every act of rape and violence and sheer stupid cruelty only served to hurt them... didn't they, men, get it?

Of course not. Women forgive... and the world limps onward toward Armageddon or whatever's coming to end it all. And we women will forgive when Armageddon is done, too.

And, did not Lee understand that, now, he could never leave me?

Let him cheat all he wanted with his dead girls. My necro boyfriend was all mine, forever. And, when I was dead, he would either be dead too or be waiting for my soul to flee - so he could get started. Finally love me without any resistance on my part, with no signs of life to distract him, confuse him or make him feel small, worthless and not a man at all.

For hours, he used Lisa's flesh. I recorded each detail in my mind. I wanted to understand his habits. I wanted to understand him. I held his hand during some of it, our fingers linked as he bucked and hunched, driving himself into Lisa, into the limp folds of her still body.

When he withdrew, panting and sore, it was almost morning. The horizon was starting to glow and soon the sun would ruddy the Eastern sky. Red sky at morning, sailors take warning. Rain or snow... snow up here.

"What do we do with her?" Lee asked, like a child might ask a question of his mother. I stroked his face and he flinched, smelling of Lisa's too-strong, too-sweet perfume.

"Burn her. We gather wood, build a giant-ass fire and burn her." I stared deep into his bemused, satiated eyes. For once, he had had enough. For once, the scarlet tides of his shameful needs were quiet and peaceful, not churning bloodily against his stark black inner shores.

"We can't burn the damn car, but we can take off the license plates. Incinerate them with her, maybe. Leave the vehicle up the road somewhere. Lock it. Leave a note. *Went for help, be back. Out of gas. Broke down.*"

"You're like Albert Einstein." Lee rested his head against me. He was pleased, I had pleased him. He would never leave. "No plates? Can't trace it."

We watched the orange flames eat her. It was hard to watch, so we huddled with our backs to her crematorial fire. She melted rather than burned. For some reason, I thought she would turn to instant ash, like paper does. But she was more like a tire.

"Heather?" Lee's arm was around me, very tight. "What if I can't trust you?"

"You can. But we can only do this once, only get away with it once. We'll be caught if we try it again. Ontario, Fruitland, Payette... Vale... just too small to keep doing this. Hell, even Boise's too small. And... Lisa was a gift, a pass from the universe. A lottery ticket with a winning number. You only get one."

"Just one?" How petulant he sounded. Sulky and arrogant.

"Yes, Lee. Just one," I repeated firmly.

"We'll see," he replied, trying to sound devious and dark and scary-movie-like.

The fire cracked and spit, as bacon does when it gets to that out of control frying stage. Lisa flamed behind us, burning pork roast, something sweet and pig-like. Something bitter. The smell of sagebrush assaulted my nostrils and perhaps a dead deer, something bloated and dead for a while, hidden in the sagebrush off to my right.

Yet all was excellent with the world. Love meant everything and I loved Lee beyond the strings of my own mind, beyond the poor tatters of my grubby little soul. Everything was shiny and clear with the coming of morning.

Love was patient and kind and sought only what it could get for another.

Just like that Bible verse they always recite at weddings.

Deemed Consent

Robin Pond

Louise, following Elliot into the room, paused at the entrance, surprised by the décor. The room had a slight odour of stale food lingering underneath the strong stench of bleach. There were cupboards and a counter with a microwave, coffee-maker and a number of mugs. There were also a few dirty dishes in the sink.

"Everyone," Elliot announced in a perfunctory tone. "This is Louise Spencer, the new humanist."

The others made courteous introductions. A large middle-aged woman identified herself as Beth Butler, the doctor. The smaller man in the grey suit was Jackson Fuller, the lawyer.

"We had to use the lunch room," Elliot explained. "All the conference rooms were taken."

"I guess you're really busy."

"You don't know the half of it," Elliot snorted. "Ever since they introduced WASTED..."

"The Wherewithal Act to Support Termination Ethics Decisions," Jackson interjected for Louise's benefit.

"The Ministry's been adding more and more of these Panels, so we'll just have to make do."

Beth and Jackson sat down at one of the tables and Elliot motioned for Louise to join them. There were thick black binders arranged in front of each of their seats and a large silver obelisk in the centre of the table.

"This," Elliot told Louise. "Is an Omega 4 Secretar. It records everything. All proceedings are made available to the public thirty days after each meeting. Everything becomes a permanent record, subject to review."

Louise nodded, slightly awed by the magnitude of the Panel's responsibilities, despite the modest surroundings.

"Let's get on with it," Jackson prompted. "We've got a quota to meet."

"Secretar commence!"

The obelisk glowed faintly. Elliot launched into a detailed enumeration of what he called 'the rudimentary facts', reading from his binder and other prepared notes. He outlined the case of Eleanor Upton, a woman just past her eightieth birthday, who was being kept in a medically-induced coma, subject to the Panel's assessment. His monotone review continued for several minutes and then abruptly ended.

"Right then," Jackson announced. "Given our careful review of all the facts and circumstances in the case of Eleanor Upton, I move for an affirmative assessment."

"For the purposes of the Secretar," Elliot reminded them. "We require voice confirmation from all Panelists."

"I also agree in the affirmative," Beth stated. "To termination on humanitarian grounds."

They all focused on Louise who sputtered nervously.

"I'm sorry. I don't really feel up to speed. I mean, I don't even know what's wrong with this woman."

"It's all in the binder." Jackson waved his hands impatiently. "You should already have read it."

"Unfortunately," Elliot explained. "Louise's appointment was quite recent, so we weren't able to get her the materials in advance."

Jackson regarded Louise disapprovingly.

"That's the problem with the constant turnover of humanists."

"The medical history is always in Appendix A," Beth explained.

Louise opened the binder and began to quickly skim the contents.

"I don't fully understand these terms."

"As the doctor on the Panel," Beth assured her. "I've reviewed the file."

"Are these conditions likely to be terminal?"

Beth shrugged.

"Given the right circumstances, any number of conditions can be terminal."

"And she's old," Jackson added. "Which is the right circumstance."

Louise continued to flip through section 1 of the binder.

"I don't see any living will."

"She doesn't have one," Jackson confirmed. "A terrible oversight. Everyone should take care of their own business, including a standard provision for an expedited death."

"But," Louise reasoned. "We have no way of knowing what this woman would have wanted."

"That's why we have these Panels," Elliot explained."

"I really don't feel comfortable." Louise shook her head. "Perhaps the three of you could vote and I'll just abstain."

"First of all, I don't vote." Elliot drew a deep breath. "I'm not a member of this Panel. I serve as the Ministry Coordinator. And secondly, under the terms of the Act, a unanimous vote is required. There can be no abstentions."

Louise continued to search through the binder, while the others stared at her. A large man dressed in a plaid shirt and corduroy pants entered the lunchroom. He extracted a small bag from the fridge and inserted it into the microwave, pushing the buttons.

"Secretar cease!" Elliot was clearly annoyed. "Lloyd, what are you doing?"

Lloyd, the large man at the microwave, responded without turning around,

"I need a muffin, and they're getting a little stale so…"

"Can't you see a Panel is in session?"

"I need a muffin at this time every day. It's a blood sugar thing."

The microwave beeped. Lloyd retrieved his snack and retreated.

"Lloyd's a Resolver," Elliot explained, watching the man go. "They implement the Panels' decisions. And a good Resolver's hard to find, so they're accorded a certain leeway."

"They get away with murder," Beth commented.

"There was a time," Jackson sighed. "When muffins and juice were provided at these meetings."

"Budget cuts," Elliot confirmed. "Secretar commence!"

The discussion continued. Louise was becoming defensive, feeling the others were all aligned against her. She told them she wasn't comfortable voting in favour of assisted termination without some indication of the woman's own wishes.

Jackson glanced at the time on his phone. Elliot sighed.

"There is a provision under the regulations to allow testimony from close friends and relatives in determining a subject's intentions. In this particular case there is a son, Bernard Upton, who might be called upon to provide further insight."

Louise agreed that, if the son could speak to his mother's wishes, it would do a lot to increase her comfort level with such an important decision. Elliot explained that the family was notified when a loved-one's case was pending disposition, so the son happened to be onsite, waiting in one of the Staging Rooms.

After a brief pause, the Panel reconvened, with Eleanor's son in attendance.

"Secretar commence!"

Bernard had a round boyish face but his curly hair was already greying at the temples. He appeared to Louise both middle-aged and child-like at the same time. He glanced at Jackson and then focused his attention on the Secretar in the middle of the table.

"I understand you want me to tell you my mother's wishes in regard to assisted termination."

"We appreciate this is difficult for you, Mr. Upton," Jackson commiserated.

"Please take your time, and in your own words," Elliot prompted. "If you could just tell us of any conversations you and your mother may have had on this subject."

"Yes…" Bernard began his recitation, seeming like a schoolboy doing his best to remember lines. "We discussed this issue on many occasions. My mother was very clear about, when the time came, not wishing any advanced heroic measures or artificial extended-life provisions. She has always wanted to be terminated in a timely fashion."

Elliot thanked Bernard for his input 'at this difficult time'. He then escorted Bernard from the room. Jackson flipped his binder shut.

"I think the intention's clear in this case."

Louise slowly shook her head.

"No. No, it's not."

"What more could you possibly want?"

"If Mrs. Upton was so clear on this, I'd have liked her to actually write down her directions."

"A lot of people never get around to it," Jackson told her. "They procrastinate. They can't be bothered."

Louise was unconvinced.

"Are there any other family members who could corroborate?"

"No. Bernard's an only child. There are no other close relatives."

"So Bernard is the sole heir?"

"You're putting me in a very difficult position," Jackson growled. "I'm not at liberty to comment on a client's…"

"Bernard's your *client*?" Louise exclaimed. "Isn't that a massive conflict…?"

"Secretar cease!" Elliot screamed, having just returned. "I would ask you not make accusations against your fellow Panel members, especially during a recorded session."

"Besides, it's not a conflict," Jackson retorted. "The regulations are very clear. If the subject herself were a client, it would be a conflict and the case would need to be assigned to a different Panel. But family members are not referenced at all in the regulations."

"I was expecting to be able to bring this to a vote." Elliot regarded Louise. Louise stared back.

"No."

"So," Jackson sighed. "I guess we're at an impasse."

After a few seconds of silence, Beth said quietly. "Perhaps there's one more approach we could try."

Jackson frowned at her but she continued

"We have a Psychic Practitioner on retainer, for really difficult cases where the intensions are unclear."

"This case is not that difficult," Jackson complained. Beth ignored him, calmly discussing this new option with Louise.

"Would you like us to contact Dr. Julianna Nightingale, the Psychic Practitioner?"

Louise considered the suggestion.

"So this would be like a séance?"

"No, not really," Beth chuckled. "The Psychic title is unfortunate. But I assure you there's a scientific basis, even if it's still experimental. There's been a lot of research regarding stimulating certain parts of the subject's brain to retrieve memories, to ascertain the subject's belief systems and wishes."

Louise nodded.

"Yes that would help."

"We're never going to meet our quota," Jackson muttered.

Elliot went off to put in a call to the Psychic Practitioner and arrange transport to the Hospice, remaining in his office to check emails. Jackson strode to a guest kiosk and made phone calls. Beth and Louise remained in the lunchroom. Louise studied her binder while Beth checked her messages. Then they began chatting.

Beth asked Louise about her family and Louise proudly told her all about her husband, Ron, who had recently been promoted to Senior MetaSystems Designer. They were in the process of moving into a larger apartment.

Beth told Louise she had a son in university and a daughter who was a high-school senior.

"The education costs are staggering."

"Yes," Louise agreed. "I've heard that."

"You don't have any children?"

Louise shook her head, her mouth contracting into a thin line.

"We've been on the list for some time now but they've been very stingy issuing permits."

"Yes," Beth commiserated. "I know it's become quite restrictive under the Balanced Population Directive. But you're still fairly young."

Elliot came to collect them. He picked the Secretar up and led them to the elevator. When they arrived on street level, a large black van with tinted windows and the Ministry crest was waiting for them. Elliot slid back the door revealing Jackson, Lloyd, and Bernard already seated inside. Louise, Beth, and Elliot awkwardly climbed in beside them.

They made the short trip in silence, everyone reading or texting. Arriving at the Hospice, they disembarked and assembled in the main lobby, gasping slightly as they became acclimated to the warmer and more humid air.

"This whole outing is unnecessary." Jackson removed his jacket.

Beth took control. She had several patients who were residents at this facility and she was able to lead them directly through the beige lobby, up the main stairway to the second floor and down another hallway to Eleanor Upton's room. They all clustered around the foot of her bed.

The room was small but clean and bright, sunlight streamed in through a large window on the left side. At the front, on either side of the bed, was an array of machines on rollers, connected to Eleanor Upton through countless cords and wires. They rhythmically chugged and hummed and beeped, externalizing her breathing and heartbeats and other bodily functions, publicly displaying what should normally be the personal private functioning of life.

Eleanor herself appeared tiny, inconsequential, resting peacefully in the large bed, with the covers pulled up to her neck. Standing beside her was a tall woman with dark features and a prominent nose, dressed in a long black cassock. She was introduced as Julianna Nightingale, the Psychic Practitioner. She had already taped numerous electrodes to Eleanor's head and was now in the process of affixing the other ends to her own temple, smoothing each receptor in place. All the wires ran through a small square black box that was lying on the bed beside Eleanor.

After a few minutes, Julianna straightened up and commanded in a husky voice. "Dim the lights."

Elliot switched off the light. Lloyd plodded over to the window and closed the blinds.

"Bernard," Julianna instructed. "Take hold of your mother's hand, so she can sense your presence."

"Should *we* join hands?" Louise whispered to Beth.

"It's not a séance," Beth whispered back.

"Quiet, please!" Julianna stared at them sternly. "We want to induce, if possible, dreamlike conditions."

Yet the procedure did seem to Louise to mimic a séance or possibly some other ancient religious rite. Julianna was a neural priestess, murmuring in a low incomprehensible rumbling before holding her hands out over the bed, moving them back and forth, so close to Eleanor that her long bony fingers were almost brushing the edges of the old lady's hair.

The murmuring became louder but remained incomprehensible, as if Julianna were speaking in tongues. Then she suddenly cried out in a strange new voice.

"Make it stop. Make it stop. Oh, how much longer?"

Bernard clutched Eleanor's right hand in both of his.

"I'm here, mommy. We're all here. We just want to know what you want, what you would like to happen."

"Make it stop," Julianna again cried out. "I've endured too much. I've waited too long. It's time to end it."

Jackson spoke up.

"We just need you to confirm, Mrs. Upton, what you told your son on other occasions. That you don't want to be continued once you've reached this state."

"Yes," Julianna hissed. "Make it end. Now!"

She screamed and collapsed beside the bed. A few seconds later, in her own huskier voice, she told them. "That's all I can do."

"It must be terrifying," Jackson concluded. "To be trapped inside like that."

Louise studied the old lady's impassive, stone-like face.

"She seems so peaceful."

Beth nodded.

"When the brain stops being able to control the body, internal states can no longer be communicated."

Elliot was still clutching the Secretar, which he now ordered to commence. It began to glow.

"In the case of Eleanor Upton," Jackson stated. "I vote for humanitarian termination under the auspices of the Wherewithal Act."

"I also vote for termination on humanitarian grounds," Beth agreed.

"Yes, so do I," Louise sadly concurred.

"The vote of the Panel," Elliot concluded. "Is unanimous. Secretar cease!"

Elliot announced the van would be there in approximately fifteen minutes to return them to the. Ministry. Louise, Jackson, and Elliot went down to the lobby to wait for it. Eliott and Jackson stood flipping through messages on their phones. Louise decided to double back to a washroom on the second floor she'd noticed in passing.

She was returning to the lobby when she saw Bernard and Julianna Nightingale standing around the corner, on the other side of a deserted nurses' station, shaking hands as if they were concluding a business deal. Louise instinctively slowed when she spotted them.

Nightingale's phone beeped and she checked it to confirm, "Money's been received."

"I want to thank you for all your help," Bernard told her.

"A pleasure doing business," Nightingale responded giving his arm a pat. "And you'll probably receive a brief client satisfaction survey. I'd really appreciate it if you could provide me with a positive review saying you'd recommend us to your friends."

"For sure."

When they saw Louise approaching they fell silent and moved further apart. She stared at them accusingly but then, without uttering a word, set off down the hall, returning to Elliot and Jackson in the lobby.

"I just witnessed Bernard Upton paying the Psychic Practitioner."

"Of course," Jackson said curtly. "Everyone's got to get paid."

"Isn't she paid by the Ministry?"

"No. We can't afford to. Budget cuts."

"But, if she's being paid by the son who stands to inherit, then she's not independent."

"She's an independent contractor," Elliot explained. "Provided through the Serene Passage Foundation."

"I thought she was a doctor."

Elliot and Jackson laughed at this.

"The Dr. Nightingale persona's just a stage name," Elliot told her.

"Serene Passage's main goal is to provide comfort to loved ones who may not want to let go," Jackson added,

Louise was appalled.

"I want to change my vote!"

"You can't do that." Elliot patted the Secretar he was holding. "Your vote's already been recorded."

"Secretar, commence!" Louise proclaimed.

"That won't work." Elliot smiled. "I've put it into extended sleep mode."

"And besides," Jackson said. "It's already done. The Resolver was in the room when the vote was taken. It's in his hands now."

Louise raced back up the stairs and down the hall, bursting into Eleanor's room. Lloyd was standing at the head of the bed holding a pillow.

"Stop!" Louise screamed. Lloyd dropped the pillow.

Beth, standing at the foot of the bed, put her hand on Louise's shoulder.

"It's too late. The process is complete."

Louise looked around at the machines. They had been disconnected and rolled further away from the bed. The humming and chugging and beeping had been replaced by silence.

"Reverse it!"

Lloyd slid away from the bed.

"That's not how death works. It's not reversible."

"I pronounced Eleanor Upton dead several minutes ago," Beth quietly informed Louise. "We're just waiting for the Parts Retrieval Team."

"You can do that?"

"Yes, even at her age, a number of pieces are still viable."

"And I suppose somebody gets paid for that?" Louise asked indignantly.

Beth was clearly offended.

"Just the standard commission."

Louise gazed back at the bed, studying Eleanor. The bedcovers were pulled down to her waist revealing a green hospital gown. Her one shoulder was shifted higher than the other. Her head was tilted slightly to the side. Her face was frozen in a strangely defiant expression. Louise had a terrible suspicion she might actually have struggled after the machines had been turned off, pushing back with her meagre strength against the weight of the deemed consent.

"What gave you the right," she asked Lloyd. "To take her life like this?"

Lloyd was confused.

"You did… You and the others."

The next day, when they reconvened back in the lunchroom, Louise announced her intention to resign from the Panel.

"Secretar cease!" Elliot commanded. Jackson sighed.

"This'll set us back even further."

"Are you really sure that's what you want, Louise?" Beth asked quietly.

"I don't want to be a part of this," Louise told them. "We shouldn't be speaking for these people, deciding what they want to…"

"But they're not in a position," Jackson snorted. "To decide for themselves."

"And you're all profiting from it." Louise looked accusingly around the table. "All of you."

"Of course we profit," Elliot answered. "Every one of us profits from the beneficial work of the Panel. We're profiting as a society, each and every one."

"Even you," Jackson added.

Louise was outraged.

"I haven't taken a cent from anyone!"

"Your profile." Jackson drew a deep breath. "Which we were provided prior to selection, indicates you're something of an activist. A real do-gooder - fighting world hunger, fighting climate change."

"Yeah? So?

"We thought it was admirable," Beth observed. "How much you seem to care."

"Under the regulations," Elliot agreed, "Those are the qualities we are required to look for in a humanist."

"That must be why you churn through so many of them," Louise retorted.

"But you should realize," Jackson told her. "The root cause of world hunger, climate change, of all of those ills plaguing our world, is over-population. You can get everyone to consume less energy, be more efficient, bring down carbon dioxide and methane emissions, and it works - per person. But we produce more people and the emissions keep going up. It's self-defeating. You develop agriculture to the point where there's enough food for everyone. Then you add a whole lot more people and land gets used up and suddenly some are going hungry again. It's a losing battle."

Beth leaned towards Louise

"That's why they had to institute the Balanced Population Directive."

"But there's got to be a better way," Louise objected.

"We're our own worst enemies," Jackson stated.

"The Ministry's got a mandate to control the population," Elliot added. "That's the good work we do here."

Louise felt self-righteous anger draining out of her, to be replaced with fatigue.

"Even if everything you say is true, I don't want to be a part of it."

Jackson waved his hand, as if swiping away her objection.

"You want to eat the sausage, but you don't want to help make it."

"After all," Beth observed. "You applied for a child permit."

Louise's jaw muscles contracted.

"Don't make this personal."

"But that's the thing about public policy," Elliot smiled. "It's always personal."

"Every time we eliminate someone who has no future, we open up a spot in the world for a new person, a new hope for the future." Beth paused, waiting for a response. When Louise remained silent she continued. "A future for you and your husband, Ron."

Louise glared at her.

"Our odds of being selected are still miniscule."

"Not true," Elliot responded. "If you remain a member of the Panel, your odds are excellent."

"But it's a lottery."

Jackson chuckled.

"And those who serve the public good, by assisting on Panels such as ours, are given top priority.

Louise looked at the other three seated around the table, all of whom were smiling back at her, like friends eager to help.

"So you want me…"

"To do what is necessary," Jackson finished her thought.

Louise noticed several faces peeking in from the lunchroom doorway, probably people yearning for their morning coffee but, unlike Lloyd, having the good manners not to intrude on the meeting. There would always, she thought, be those at the door looking in but not able to enter. She drew a deep breath, focussing her attention back on the others at the table.

"In that case," she exhaled slowly. "I guess we'd better get started."

Elliot, beaming, commanded. "Secretar commence!"

Louise nodded.

"After all, we've got a quota to meet."

Furry Fiona's Fun Facts

E w a n   S m i t h

Well, that wasn't so bad. I'm not going to lie, I was dreading my first kill. I mean, I've prepared for it, mentally at least. I've imagined it dozens of times since, well, you know… since. Hundreds of times, probably. But you never know how something is going to affect you until you experience it for real, do you? So, anyway, not that bad. Quite satisfying, in fact. Enjoyable even. Although there was a fair bit of screaming. More than I had anticipated.

Now for the tricky part - getting rid of the body. I mean, I'll eat most of him, obviously. Otherwise, what would be the point? You've got to eat. But there's bits of him I don't really fancy. Stringy stuff and spongy stuff and eyeballs and brains. And then there's the thorny problem of his, you know… his willie. Eating that just feels wrong, disrespectful somehow. Maybe I'll be less fussy as I get more used to this. Margaret always complained I was a picky eater. At least, she did when she wasn't complaining of all the other things about me that irritated her. And that was a long list. Especially when she'd had a few.

It's his bones, though. His bones are the real issue. I can't eat them, regardless of how unfussy I become. Maybe I should dig a hole for them? Let's face it, I've got the claws. At least, I have until the sun comes up.

If only there was a course on how to do this properly, something to get me fully up to speed. *Introduction To Lycanthropy*, maybe. That would be really handy. Actually, now I come to think, there's probably a YouTube channel dedicated to it or a podcast. Either would do. I'll have a look in the morning.

Nothing else I've ever done has even remotely prepared me for becoming a werewolf. I'm a chartered accountant for Pete's sake.

And a vegetarian.

This is what comes from dating online. I knew I'd regret it. I should never have gone for that 'nice moonlit stroll in the woods' with 'Furry Fiona' from Falkirk. But it's not like I was getting a lot of other offers.

In her messages, Fiona came across as sweet and shy. She seemed to be the complete opposite of Margaret, encouraging and supportive, rather than henpecking and bullying. Of course, I now know it was all a facade. Hindsight is 20/20, I suppose. Although my actual vision is *considerably* better than that at the moment.

It's a definite plus of this new situation: your senses get a serious upgrade. Who knew there were so many smells? Tomorrow I'll be back to needing my bifocals. Also back to my disappearing hairline. For now, lack of hair is certainly not my problem.

So, there are upsides. I don't know if they entirely offset the whole 'excruciating transformation into vicious hell beast' yet, though.

I thought I might lose myself when the wolf arrived but I'm still in here. I'm still me. It's just that I want to kill people a little bit more than I usually do. Only a little bit, though. I think I've been carrying around quite a lot of undiagnosed murderous rage.

Furry Fiona was very apologetic after the fact. She had intended to kill me outright. She'd done her homework. Found out everything she could about my life, such as it was, before luring me to a remote spot in order to tear me into pieces and eat me. She knew I wouldn't be missed. No doubt she had used the same method several times before.

However, she hadn't bargained on quite how good I was at climbing trees, a skill even I hadn't realised I possessed until that precise moment. Blindly panicking when your charming and delightful companion for the evening suddenly starts sprouting fur, talons and finger-length incisors gives you phenomenal abilities in the scaling department. And, it turns out, werewolves can't climb trees. Must be an opposable thumbs thing. Fiona only managed to get a tiny wee nip in at my ankle as I ascended a nearby silver birch at the kind of velocity seasoned lumberjacks can only dream of.

The abruptly huge, mean and *extremely* furry Fiona prowled around the base of my tree, circling, snarling and slobbering for hours. Not unlike Margaret after a night on the Bacardi Breezers. When day broke, she reverted to her regular self and, boy, was she embarrassed. Gathering up the tattered remnants of her clothes, she apologised profusely then bolted. Somewhat tragically, it was the first glimpse I'd had of a real live naked woman since my divorce. Not that I saw an awful lot of that kind of thing, even when I was married. Margaret saved all of it for her bit on the side. *Tim.* Not that I'm bitter, you understand.

Later in the day, Fiona sent me a rather sheepish email on what to expect at the next full moon. There was a kind of fact sheet attached which contained some tips for dealing with it all. Useful, but a bit basic. I'm still going to try and find a podcast. Other than that, we haven't kept in touch. She had tried to do me in and devour me, after all.

Speaking of eating, time to cut him open. I can't remember ever being this hungry before. And I had a fish supper just before I came out.

As for Fiona's advice, I'm paraphrasing here, but…

Tip 1. Be outside. You are going to grow to twice your normal size and quickly. It is likely you will experience a modicum of uncontrollable fury. Your house will need extensive redecoration, not to mention renovation if you're still inside when the wolf comes out.

Well, the tiny flat I've been reduced to since my divorce (thanks again, Margaret) could do with some remodelling. But I played it safe anyway and headed for the patch of waste ground behind the leisure centre.

Tip 2. Be naked. Or at least wear something you don't mind losing. If you do have to wear clothes for appearance's sake (say, for instance, you are on a fake date with some poor schmuck you intend to make a meal of), then have a change of clothes stashed in a waterproof bag nearby for afterwards. And a towel for the blood. Make that two towels, there's going to be a lot of blood. Actually, take three. Just to be on the safe side.

I had intended to follow this advice but mistakenly assumed there would be some warning of the impending change, giving me time to undress. But no, it comes on from nowhere. An instant, paralysing pain, like a migraine happening in every cell of your body simultaneously, while somebody douses you in burning napalm and then tries to put it out with a sledgehammer. A minute later, it's all over and you're literally seeing the world through different eyes. And from a greater height. Tonight I ruined my second favourite cardigan and a very smart pair of work slacks. I'll know better in future.

Tip 3. Choose your victim ahead of time. The wolf will need to be fed and it can't be bargained with. To avoid killing random bystanders, maybe even children, make sure you have someone specific lined up.

Well, I thought that would be the easy part. But it quickly became apparent I had an extensive list of candidates for the coveted position of 'initial victim'. There was Derek from work, for a start. And Mandy from work. Not to mention Ramesh from work. Everybody from work, basically, apart from Mel - although she's on thin ice after cooking fish in the breakroom microwave last week. Then there was everyone that bullied me at school, so more or less everyone I went to school with. Also Heavy Metal Brian from upstairs. He was a strong front-runner because he was blasting that noise he listens to at a most unneighbourly volume while I was writing my list. In the end, he felt a bit too close to home for my first time. It was a tough job but I eventually whittled the field down to a clear single contender.

Tip 3(b). Oh, by the way, do not let your victim live or they too will become werewolves.

Well, I never. Fancy that.

Urgh, I've reached his liver. I've always hated liver. My mother used to force it on me when I was little. She said it would make me big and strong, so I could finally stand up for myself. It didn't and I didn't. Until this evening, I've neither been big nor strong. Not like Margaret's fancy man *Tim*. Tim's muscles had muscles of their own.

The wolf in me really wants the liver. Hmm. It's not as bad as I remember, eating it raw would seem to be the trick. Raw and steaming in the night air. Yes, alright, I like liver now. In fact, I love it!

The wolf knows all the best bits to eat. It doesn't care so much about the meat, it wants the innards first. And the wolf gets what the wolf wants. I would have thought the big muscles of the thigh would be the good stuff - like the human equivalent of steak. And this guy had quadriceps. He is, *was*, a spin instructor, after all. That's how he and Margaret met in the first place. She was in his class at the leisure centre. Yes, it's Tim. I'm eating Tim. Please don't judge me too harshly. He deserved it.

When I really thought about it, there was one clear favourite for tonight. Tim was a cocky swine and had this coming. Back when Margaret told me the news, he was there with her. Towering over me. Smirking. Gloating. Purposefully making me feel small, weak and powerless.

Well, he was a darn sight less cocky when the wolf grabbed hold of his throat tonight. He was literally scared, please pardon my French, shitless. He went out on the most embarrassing note imaginable - sobbing and pleading, as his pants filled up. I only regret that he didn't know who took his miserable life. The wolf's vocal cords aren't really equipped to handle conversational English, but I told him what I thought of him anyway via the medium of terrifying growls. Then I ripped his head off.

I never felt so alive!

Fiona's final tip?

The next day will be very uncomfortable. Take it as a holiday if you can, cause you're going to be in a lot of pain.

Well, there's something to look forward to. But so is the next full moon. I think I'm going to enjoy this new arrangement immensely. Heavy Metal Brian from upstairs? Maybe not so much.

Oh, and P.S*. Don't stray too far from a toilet. Remember you've just eaten a whole person.*

Amoranecrosis

Christopher O'Halloran

Roy couldn't remember Isabelle looking so good. She lingered in the hall, measuring cup dangling from one delicate pinky.

"Cup of sugar, neighbor?"

Black hair hung over her shoulders like silk. Each strand seemed like cable wound from thousands of smaller fibers. Apricot shampoo danced across to Roy. Their apartment hallway had been host to countless smells: tomato soup, curry, garlic and the crowd favorite, trash. Apricot shampoo was a new one.

"Sugar?" he asked.

Isabelle blinked slowly and smiled.

Roy felt a shock. Those crooked teeth used to repulse him whenever she descended, like a horny spider, perched by the communal mailbox. He could never keep his eyes from those overlapping cuspids. Too odd to ignore. They crowded Isabelle's mouth. Flossing would be a nightmare.

Now, however, they seemed full of charm and dazzling, ivory brilliance. They mocked Hollywood's bleached, veneered snarls. Here was a diamond in the sand, a break in uniform and a breath of fresh air. Something different, something beautiful in its courage to stand out among the ranks.

"I'm making a cake." Her words were a song.

Roy had never seen this outfit. If she wore something like that before, he would have obliged her desperate attempts to bait him into asking her out. Her button-up missed a few buttons. It attracted Roy's gaze, the V of her shirt an arrow framing a cavern of smooth skin. Isabelle's nipples poked out against the blue fabric, drawn to Roy as if by biological magnetism.

He slammed the door. With fumbling hands, he shot the deadbolt and latched the chain.

"Roy?" His name was so goddamn smooth in her voice. As if she whispered it softly in his ear. One syllable somehow packed to the brim with the melody of seduction.

He dug in his pocket, tearing from it the travel-sized bottle of hand sanitizer. She hadn't touched him, thank god, but better safe than sorry.

Better breathing than pissing chunks.

Roy pressed against the peephole. Its metal made a cool ring around his eye. His hands crawled over each other like desperate lovers. They dripped with sanitizer.

The hall was empty.

Wood rasped. Isabelle rose into sight, rubbing against the door. An inch and a half of cheap pine separated him from that soft touch. Her lips pursed. She knew he was watching.

"Come on, Roy. I *want* you. I want you so *bad.* You don't have to love me forever." Her hazel eyes met his in the fishbowl lens. "Just a few hours."

His pants stirred. Roy stumbled away from the door, pinching his biceps.

"No, no, no." He shook his head back and forth, nails stinging him with every pinch. Anything to distract himself. "Stop it."

Isabelle chuckled from the hall.

"When you change your mind, you know where to find me." With a wet, kissing sound, she was gone.

Roy felt her absence in the hall, luring him out into her embrace. A vacuum sucking him into space. To his salvation.

To his doom.

Amoranecrosis.

Every news station gave the same warning. It infected with a kiss. Turned you into the object of desire for anyone unlucky enough to cross your path. A week of ecstasy. Seven days of pleasure, the likes of which would make the denizens of Sodom blush.

Then you'd spend a long twenty-four hours rotting from the inside.

Roy hyperventilated. He tore a face mask from his kitchen cupboard, ripped it from the plastic wrap and frantically placed it over his mouth, fixing the elastic straps behind his head and pinching the metal nose clip tight.

Logic admonished him, chided him for his panic. It wasn't airborne. The mask provided no safety, no inoculation.

Despite logic, it calmed him. He fell upon the couch, running hands through his hair. His bachelor's suite lost its pulse. It no longer clenched around him like a fist. He could breathe.

His thigh began to tingle.

This is it, he thought. *This is how it starts.*

Years of fucking around coming to bite him in the ass. Martin always told him he'd catch something. You don't sleep with the amount of people Roy did and come away free of afflictions requiring penicillin.

He dug at his hip pocket and pulled out his phone.

Speak of the devil. The tingling was not the infection taking hold. It was his best friend.

"Jesus Christ, Martin, she almost got me."

"What?"

Roy pulled the mask from his face and let it hang under his chin.

"My fucking neighbor," he said into the phone. "She's infected with that shit."

"Did she mention me?" Martin had been trying to get Roy to slip Isabelle his number for months now - but the blushing girl with ebony hair had eyes only for Roy. Her nose always wrinkled at the mention of Martin. The guy wasn't a hit with the ladies.

"She did not," Roy replied.

"Probably for the best. Did you hear?"

"Hear what?"

There was a rustling sound on the other end of the call. The sliding of drawers as Martin fumbled with the phone. Keys jangled.

"There's a vaccine."

Roy stood suddenly, the ratty couch slipping back with the force of his ascension.

"For this?"

"For *Amoranecrosis*!"

Roy's mouth went dry. "Bullshit."

"They're keeping it on the down low, dude. I only heard about it because my cousin, Dicky, is a pharmacist-in-training. A journeyman or something."

"Apprentice?"

"I don't know. But he said we gotta get there today. He doesn't think they'll have much in stock if we fiddle-fuck around."

"Where?"

"I don't know," Martin said. "I'm waiting for his reply. You're the first person I told."

"The only person, Martin. Make me the only person. If supply is limited, I'd rather we get the needle before spreading the word."

Martin chuckled on the other end.

"Shit man, you know me. You're the only person I know worth talking to."

"You depress me in even these dark times, buddy."

"Take it as flattery. Get here and we'll head out together. My car's out of gas."

"Your life is a mess." Roy grabbed his keys and looked through the peephole. The coast was clear. Lighted wall sconces stood sentinel for a world populated by the copulating diseased. Who knew what was happening behind those closed doors?

"My life is a mess by knowing you," Martin laughed.

"Race you to rock bottom."

Roy hung up, smiling. It had been too long since he had seen his friend. The fear of looming lust kept him inside for weeks. His hermit days were over. Medical intervention was here to save the day. It was only a matter of time. Trust in the establishment had never failed him before.

At the door, Roy made a call that received no answer. He tried again but was greeted by voicemail. He hung up before the canned greeting could finish. She never listened to his messages. Sure, they were in the grips of a modern-day plague that would have even the laziest chick checking her voicemail - but he didn't want to take the chance his sister would miss crucial information.

He shot off a quick text telling her to meet him at Martin's. Hopefully, Kristen would see it in time.

Hand on the deadbolt, Roy stopped. It would do no good to rush into the world without taking precautions. He backtracked to the fridge. There were many items to use as a repellant in case he ran into Isabelle again. Anything in the back would do.

The smell made him fasten his facemask securely over his nose again.

Roy's muscles unwound at the sight of Kristen's car in Martin's driveway. His sister had listened to him for once. Her teenage years had been a campaign of sloppy attempts to get with Roy's friends. He had lost many to her advances, breaking off friendships each time a buddy fell to her charms. He and Kristen were only a year apart but, in their younger days, that year had felt long enough to warrant his protective streak. Creeps low enough to whip it out for any young girl weren't fit to be around anyway.

The one friend she had left alone was Martin.

Martin, sweaty knight in shining cargo shorts.

Sharing a ride with him would have Kristen groaning loud enough to shake her own condo.

At least she had come. She had put aside her repulsion of the guy and rounded out their entourage. They would be safe, the three. No *Amoranecrosis.*

When he parked, Roy noticed Martin's door halfway open. Kristen never was one to follow the rules. She probably had her shoes on in there and everything.

He checked his phone. Martin had sent the address to the pharmacy close to ten minutes ago. It was already plugged into his maps app.

Don't take any chances. Get yours first, then double back for them.

He thought about it. Could he leave his best friend alone with his sister, both waiting for the team to assemble?

No. It would have been easy to ditch the geek in the past, easy to tell Kristen her lifestyle was her own business and stop worrying. But Roy wasn't that kind of guy. He *could* do the right thing, even if it wasn't easy.

Roy stepped over the threshold.

He was greeted by the sounds of skin slapping against skin.

"No..."

He rounded a corner and caught his sister bouncing on the lap of his best friend.

The plastic bag under his arm slipped and crashed on the floor. The sound caught the attention of the two deep in the throws on Martin's sectional.

Roy had helped Martin move the heavy piece of furniture. He made jokes about how many women Martin would bed on the thing, knowing all along he was a lost cause.

Kristen craned her head, moaning in pleasure.

"I got your text, bro." Her words came on little puffs of breath. Her back arched, the bare skin of her torso stretching taut as the setting sun shot lines of red across her breasts, her hips, the belly-button ring that reflected sunlight during every day of summer. Golden hair lay over her nipples. She shook it back, revealing them.

Roy licked his lips, paper mask adjusting against his cheeks.

That's your sister, dude.

Martin groaned in pleasure.

"Roy." His hand rose, covered in coarse, black hair, to paw at Kristen. Martin groped her like a wrinkled, old fortune teller, trying to see the future in her milky flesh. "It's not so bad."

"The…" Roy faltered, blinking sweat from his eyes. "The pharmacy, Marty. What happened to the pharmacy?"

"This is better." He laughed, hands falling to Kristen's hips. "Did you know I was a virgin, Roy? I know, I know. The girl in the library. The girl at the bar. All the stories I've told. All lies."

Roy knew. He had known all along. One only had to look at his best friend to know that ladies acquiesced only after receiving money in advance.

Only now, he didn't look so bad.

Sure, his gut hung lose around his waist. If Kristen wasn't holding it up, it would probably droop over his manhood. But the way he sat and received her was powerful. His hands flexed on her hips, drawing her down and thrusting up at the same time. Forearms lined with veins. Jaw tensed in concentration.

He was a fucking bear and Roy never admired him more.

He wanted desperately to join Martin and his sister. Wanted to slip in behind her, fill other vacancies or even tend to *him*. He wasn't gay but Martin was his best bud. What kind of friend wouldn't want the best for his pal?

That's your sister!

Roy didn't care. In fact, it kind of made it hotter. Made him want it more.

The door opened behind him.

"My friends," crooned Martin. "I didn't know if you'd be comfortable, taking turns on your own sister, so I called in reinforcements from next door."

Strong hands wrapped around his shoulders. Roy smelled a musky cologne and stale sex. The man was taller than him, but not by much.

His stubble brushed against Roy's jawline as arms wrapped gently around him.

The woman came from the other side. Her wedding ring glittered in the sun, much like the barbell stud pierced through Kristen's left nipple. The woman brought her plump lips to Roy's face and playfully kissed at his facemask. She sighed against it. Her breath was a bouquet of roses, freshly cut and begging to be enjoyed.

This woman and her husband begged to be enjoyed.

Roy was going to give it to them. He needed to unload. Needed it on a spiritual level. There was a madness tensing in him, ready to erupt.

The man reached around and grabbed Roy by the crotch.

Roy fell. He could not tell himself to run. To fight. All he could do was allow his legs to become loose. To get away as passively as possible. Everything in his body wanted to take all four of these people at once. Man or woman. Friend, stranger and kin alike.

He landed on the Tupperware container. Up until then he had forgotten it completely.

The woman descended, pulling at his mask.

"Come on, baby," she said, smiling like Medusa. "Let's see what you're working with. I want to feel you. I *need* to feel you…"

With a snap of elastic, the mask came away. The woman tossed it over her shoulder.

Roy spun onto his stomach and buried his head in the plastic bag. He ripped the lid off the container.

Immediately, his world of rose petals and Calvin Klein Cowboy Sweat turned to rot as compounding gasses from six-month old Fettuccine Alfredo filled his nostrils. It was mossy and sweet in all the wrong ways.

Roy took a bite of the repellant, burying his face in it like a dog. He chewed. Moldy growths burst between his teeth, gagging him, grinding against his gums like moss. Noodles slid around in his mouth, congealed Alfredo sauce turning them into elusive worms that clung to the lining of his throat. Pale white meat that used to be chicken stuck to his molars, something within the flesh throbbing, as if with a pulse.

It did the trick. His erection became a memory. He scrambled away, vomit meeting food as he violently purged all over Martin's hallway.

Sliding through puddles of the stuff, Roy hurried outside. He needed fresh air, to smell something other than that uncommon combination of every bodily fluid. Nobody chased him. Apparently a four-person orgy was as good as a five.

Roy looked back at the house, through the doorway. The man who had grabbed his crotch buried himself in Kristen's face, her hair wrapped in his clenched fist. Martin took his sister from behind now. She formed a bridge between the men, smiling around a full mouth.

Roy left them behind, speeding away from that place of disease while spitting fungal growth out an open window.

The drive was deserted. Fresh plywood had been plastered over rancher windows down the winding road. His phone's navigation prompted the car through this residential area as a detour. Apparently, there had been a major pile-up on South Fraser Way, which made traffic a nightmare.

In five-hundred meters spoke the phone. *Turn right.*

Roy glanced down at his phone and, in doing so, almost hit the man who stumbled into the road.

His heart lurched, whether from sudden decrease in speed or at the sight of the stranger. Without thinking, Roy pushed in the lighter beneath his car's radio. He had never used it but held out faith that it worked. He was out of fettuccini alfredo.

The man was wiry, clearly dehydrated and manic. Veins popped all over his body as he shuffled over to the hood of Roy's car.

"Hey," he said, working his privates with a grip that pulled the tendons in his hand taut. He was naked, his pale skin like a scarecrow's. Each vein was a blue thread, the stitching that held the man together.

Pearly chunks dripped from the eye of his penis, the opening stretched to accommodate his discharge.

In spite of this dreadful man, in the throes of disease, Roy couldn't help but feel himself stir.

Seven days of being a singular object of lust. Then... this.

Amoranecrosis turned your innards to jelly. Through some method of cellular mutation, the disease assaulted the vitals. It made you irresistible to all who laid eyes on you. The perfect way to spread: via a weeklong bender of widespread fucking.

Organs decayed within, slowly turning to fat inside your own body. This fat then leaked out wherever it could.

Pearly tears tumbled from the corner of the man's pale eyes. He drooled beige chunks of fat that might have started as his stomach, his kidneys, the lining of his esophagus. With a splat, the chunks smacked into the hood of Roy's car.

Roy leaned over and tried to open the door. He needed to fuck this guy.

The door was locked. He kept trying.

A heavy, milky torrent of what must have been the man's colon fell out of his ass. It spilled onto the ground and rolled under Roy's tire.

The lighter clicked out. Roy fumbled for it, one hand reaching towards stinging heat, the other reaching for the door lock.

A smile stretched along the man's jaundiced face. He began to pull on himself faster, never achieving erection. It was limp flesh, sliding in and out of his fist.

I want it so bad, I want it, I want YEOOOOO!

Roy's skin sizzled against the burning metal of the lighter. It wiped his brain. He could only think of the pain, striking deep into his index finger and thumb.

He screamed. His foot came down on the accelerator. Tires spun, slipping in the man's excretion.

Roy was taken down the road, away from the stranger. A part of him cried out to turn the car around but was overwhelmed by the endless string of curses loosed in his head. Pain was the ultimate distraction.

The cashier tried her best not to make eye contact with Roy. He smiled at her but it went unseen. It was a feeling he had to get used to. People avoided him. On the street, in the aisles of the grocery store, even at stoplights. They treated him with disgust, as if he was something they had stepped on, a careless leftover by a neighbor too self-important to pick up after Fido.

He shuffled the basket from his right hand to his left. His bicep ached tremendously. The pharmacist had explained that the tenderness might last a while but no longer than a week.

Or was it a month?

The pharmacist only gave sparse information. As soon as Roy had received the vaccine, the man couldn't stand to look at him. Instead, he turned from Roy, calling for the next patient while staring grim-faced at a loose stack of papers.

"Next!"

It was an unfortunate side effect of the vaccine but better than dying in the streets when your heart leaked out your asshole.

As he passed a fifty to the cashier, their hands touched. The girl's eyes squeezed shut. She turned from Roy, fist rising to her twisting mouth.

A month ago, Roy would have done his best to charm this girl into giving him her number. He would have complimented the layering of her hair, made small talk about ongoing sales and store brands of surprising quality. They'd have a great night a week later. Going out to dinner, mini-golf, downtown Maclure with all its old charm.

Instead, the girl threw up in the trash can at her feet, as she lost the battle with her disgust for Roy. Her retching echoed in the front end of the nearly empty store. There was nobody in line with whom Roy could commiserate. No other cashiers to take notice of her repulsion. Nobody to offer the poor girl aid after she had been subjected to a man who would know affection no longer. Who would become deprived of lust, of romance, friendship and companionship of any kind.

He could get a dog. Dogs had to love you, right? They wouldn't be affected by the unseen hideousness that had been injected into him.

He pocketed the fifty and left, basket and all.

It wasn't the first time Roy had received this reaction since the vaccine. It would not be the last. Whatever was in that syringe repelled Amoranecrosis.

Repelled and repulsed every single living person.

Frogman

Jan-Andrew Henderson

It was a nice night for a murder. Nothing much on TV, plus the local drugstore had a sale on stain remover.

And murder was Harlan McFarlan's business. Not that he killed people. At least, not very often.

He was, in lieu of the fact, a private dick - though his personality hadn't much to do with anything. *Smarter than the average bear* was his slogan because he had been abandoned in the forest as a baby and only survived by raiding picnic baskets.

Harlan was rummaging around in a garbage can when a short, rotund man in an overcoat strolled over. This was his associate, Fats Norbett. If crime was a fairy-tale, Harlan liked to say, Fats would be the Duke of York. Neither had any idea what that meant - but it sounded good.

"Looking for clues, buddy?" Fats asked.

"I saw someone throw a Subway foot-long meatball sandwich in here." Harlan shook his head in disbelief. "Only had a couple of bites taken out."

But I digress.

In a way, the pair got into this whole crazy mess - which I am about to describe at great length - because Fats had a birthday coming up. If he had never been born, none of it would have happened.

"Sorry," Fats apologised, forgetting I was the narrator and he wasn't supposed to know I existed.

"Not your fault," I replied. "Your parents should have thought their actions through a bit more, is all."

"Yeah? Well, you've just gone into a long-winded explanation of who we are," Fats retorted. "Me and Harlan were in the first story of this anthology, so the readers already know all that."

"People skim," I said. "Anyway, I'm being meta. It's all the rage on Netflix. Now leave me alone or I'll have you killed off."

That shut him up.

For Fats' birthday, Harlan decided to give him a surprise. This involved driving to New Jersey, which was a surprise in itself, since they lived in Australia.

As Harlan and Fats approached their destination - *Bad Boy Blobby's Sinister Clown Museum and Aquatic Trailer Park* - they saw a plethora of police cars parked outside a nearby mansion.

Looks like we may have to take a detour and do some investigating." Harlan ground to a halt.

"Thank God." Fats pulled off his blindfold. "I've been wearing this for two weeks solid."

"You're allowed to take it off when you go to the toilet, bud."

"I *am*?"

The mansion turned out to be the scene of a horrible mass killing. The police had no suspects, so they arrested the duo and tried to get them to confess. Fats confessed he was wearing his girlfriend's underwear and Harlan admitted to secretly liking Eric Roberts movies.

Eventually the police let them go but, by then, Harlan was intrigued and offered his services. After all, he pointed out, he and Fats weren't doing anything important.

The troopers relented and showed them the crime scene. Out on the highway were five unidentified bodies in fancy dress. A witness claimed they had run from the house and thrown themselves under a passing truck. Inside the mansion was the corpse of aging millionaire playboy, Bruce Payne.

"Isn't he the person everyone suspects is secretly Batman?" Fats hopped around with his hand in the air.

"That's Bruce *Wayne*," Harlan corrected. "Though I personally harbour the suspicion that Batman is Eric Roberts."

If Bruce Payne ever had a secret identity, however, it would remain a clandestine one. His head had exploded.

Behind a couch in the living room lay the body of Bruce Payne's daughter, Lois. Beside her lay a blood-stained egg whisk.

"Looks like she's been beaten to death," Fats giggled. "Get it?"

"Try to show some decorum," Harlan was helping himself to the contents of the fridge. "Ooooh. A jar of pickled eggs."

Strangest of all, in the bedroom were a pair of diving flippers, size nine. With the feet still inside.

The cops were baffled, mainly because one of them had brought along a box of Chupa Chups and they couldn't work out how to get the wrappers off. There was no sign of forced entry at the dwelling, which belonged to Lois Payne, and no clue as to what had happened.

However, after seven cheese daiquiris and a sherbet dip-dab, Harlan deduced exactly what had occurred and recounted the story to Fats. Which saves me having to do it.

"It all began this morning," Harlan stated. "In the offices of Payne Industries."

The glass of the window exploded and Bruce Payne, wearing a furry onesie, landed on top of the nearest filing cabinet. It wobbled alarmingly, so he attempted to leap onto a large executive desk. But his back gave out, forcing him to simply sit there, looking miserable and holding on for dear life.

A younger man entered, sporting an expensive suit with a DC comics tie. He glanced at the intruder and groaned loudly.

"Shall I order my secretary to fetch a ladder? Or she could bring you coffee, if you intend to sulk up there all afternoon."

"Hi Donald," the man said awkwardly.

"Hello father. Want me to help you?"

"No, I don't. I can manage."

Bruce climbed gingerly down, using the drawers as steps, hobbled behind the desk and lowered himself painfully into a leather executive chair. He fiddled with the levers and it sank several inches, until all Donald could see was the top of his head.

"It's no surprise to me that you should arrive at this precise moment," Bruce grinned. "Want to know why?"

"Not really."

"Superpowers, Donald. Your untapped abilities sensed I was in trouble and this caused you to rush to my office, exactly when I needed aid."

"This is *my* office, father. I just went to the toilet. You came through the wrong window again."

"Shut up and take my money! Nothing gets past you, eh?"

"Why are you so obsessed with the notion I have superpowers?" Donald sighed. "I'm an accountant."

"Did you say mild-mannered accountant?"

"Actually, I'm an easily irritated accountant."

"Aha! Do you fly into a rage and turn green?"

"Get to the point, please." Donald looked at his watch. "I have a goat yoga appointment at Miss Wheezy-Pop's Massage Parlour and Leaf Blower showroom in ten minutes."

"Donald," Bruce Payne said gravely. "I want to show you a very different side to my character."

"You did that at the office Christmas party."

"I'm going to finally reveal myself."

"You did *that* at the office Christmas party. I had to give the staff pay raises and make them sign a non-disclosure agreement."

"Son." Bruce took up a heroic stance and clicked his teeth together. "I am the superhero they call… Ratman!"

"I know."

"I understand, it's hard to believe but…" Bruce blinked rapidly. "What do you mean, you *know*?"

"Little things gave it away. Like the Ratmobile always being parked outside your house. On a yellow line, too."

"Alfrick was supposed to hide it."

"Alfrick retired to run an ant farm in Burrumbuttock ten years ago."

"Did he?" Bruce scratched his cheek. "I better stop talking to him, then."

"There's also the fact that you're wearing a rodent costume in the middle of a heatwave."

"Bloody fashion expert," Bruce huffed. "Since you know my true identity, you must also realise I have an obligation to protect Gothum City from crime."

"And?"

"Times have changed, son. My knees are a bit stiff and people keep emailing my website to ask if I do pest control."

"Why don't you just retire?" Donald looked at his watch again. "Gothum City won't care."

"Why not?"

"We live in New Jersey."

"Beside the point." Bruce smiled winningly. "The world will always need a Ratman, even after I've gone to the great trashcan in the sky."

"Not a chance, father."

"Donny," Bruce said cajolingly. "Donny, Donny, Donny, Donny. DonnyDonnyDonnyDonnyDonny."

"Please don't call me Donny. Especially not that many times."

"You're the obvious person to assume my mantle. You don't know it yet but, in your genes, there's a huge… thing trying to get out."

"*Excuse* me?"

"Your superpowers. Powers you inherited from me!" Bruce hesitated. "Now, if I can just remember who *I* am."

"Let's get a few things straight, shall we?" Donald sat down. "To begin with, I am not related to you in any way, shape or form. I'm merely your son-in-law. Furthermore, you do not *have* any superpowers. You've got a rodent suit filled with inane gadgets like the rat bollock shaver."

He waved his tie at the elderly man.

"*Superman* has superpowers. And I'm not related to him either, before you ask."

"Don't talk to me about that poncy, non-aging, do-gooding cock womble in tights," Bruce sulked. "He looks like Elvis with his head on backwards."

He limped round the desk and laid a furry glove on Donald's shoulder.

"Ye Gods," the man coughed. "When was the last time you had that outfit dry cleaned?"

"It's the only one I've got. Can't fight crime in my undies, can I?"

"It's probably a human rights violation but I'd still pay serious money to see it."

"Look, there's a reason Ratman must carry on a little longer," Bruce pleaded. "See, everyone thinks there are no super villains left in America. They believe Superman and I defeated them all."

"The way I heard it, Superman did that on his own."

"Oh, I must have been on *vacation* at the time!" Bruce exploded. "Then that smug git goes traipsing off into space, looking for his home planet, which the smarmy dobber never should have left in the first place. And I, who am obviously not a superhero by any *stretch* of the imagination, spend the next twenty years getting thrown off tall buildings - the kind Superman can leap in a single fucking bound - by psychopaths titting around like Marcel Marceau or dolled up circus freaks on happy pills."

"Take it easy, father." Donald held up a placating hand. "You'll have another stroke."

"Now I hear, through the rat-vine, the last group of supervillains in the world have gathered in New Jersey. But I'm no longer young enough to tackle them."

"And I'm not dumb enough."

"I suppose appearances can be deceptive," Bruce conceded. "In that case, I have another idea."

"And I have another appointment. I missed the last one, thanks to you jabbering on."

"It's a good idea," Bruce said slyly. "See this one through and I'll never ask you to become Ratman again."

"Really?"

"What's more, I'll retire and move to Florida with She-Gerbil." He blushed demurely. "We've got a bit of a thing going."

"I'm gonna regret this," Donald sighed. "But what's the plan?"

"You disguise yourself as a supervillain, infiltrate their group and find out what nefarious scheme they're planning. I'll take over from there."

"Hmmm. I can see why you didn't call yourself Mr. Intelligence."

"But you'll agree if it gets me off your back?"

"Oh, all right."

"I knew you were stupid enough!" Bruce crowed. "I've got your costume right here."

He dipped into the filing cabinet, pulled out a plastic carrier bag and handed it to his son-in-law.

"It's simple but functional. I feel it makes a real statement."

"Yeah," Donald peered inside. "It's saying *hello sucker*."

"It doesn't talk, fool. Alfrick handled all that advanced gizmo stuff. I got this from K-Mart."

Donald sighed again.

"Stick it on and let's see what you look like." Bruce rummaged some more and retrieved a cigar from the cabinet. "I'll have a Rat-puff to celebrate."

"Stop smoking my Havanas." Donald put on the outfit. "They'll be the death you. Listen to your old lungs wheezing away."

"I'm not sure that's me."

Donald was now wearing flippers, swimming goggles and a snorkel, the noise of his laboured breathing drowning out all other sounds.

"Just which super villain am I supposed to be?"

"Frogman, of course."

"Great." He took a few waddling steps. "Now I can leap onto small pavements in a single bound."

"Here's where the villains will be gathered this afternoon." Bruce handed him a piece of paper with a map drawn in yellow crayon. "They'll most likely welcome another baddy to swell their ranks."

"Are these guys dangerous?"

"I defeated all the really serious ones," Bruce assured him. "Though they do have a leader you should watch out for. Doctor Baghead."

His voice dipped conspiratorially.

"Nobody knows his true identity because he's a genius. And because he has a bag on his head."

"Well, I'm off to the Frogmobile, otherwise known as my Volvo." Donald trudged out, making slapping sounds on the floor. "Please leave through the door or I'll have the fire escape removed."

"Don't need a fire escape," Bruce chuckled, pulling a can from his pocket. "I've got my Rat Ground Repellent. Or is it shaving foam?"

He squinted at it more closely.

"Can't be fake snow, can it?"

As Donald sped towards destiny, his vehicle quickly converted to look like a pond, the villains were gathering.

Swedish Hairdresser and Big Nipple carried a table into the middle of their meeting room on the top floor of Madame Benbecula's House of Fluff.

"This hasn't been wiped down properly." Big Nipple squirted some milk onto the surface and polished it with his sleeve. "Last time I steal from *that* restaurant."

He plonked down his end.

"Did you bring a bottle? It was stipulated on Doctor Baghead's invite."

"Yah. Conditioner vit Henna."

In trooped The Rifter and Voiceover Man. They grabbed plastic chairs from the corner and sat.

"A gathering of villains," Voiceover Man rasped in a deep baritone. "Each eying the other suspiciously. Waiting for their leader to arrive. What will be the outcome?"

"That's gonna get old, real fast," Big Nipple moaned.

"And one of them already marked for death." Voiceover man growled, glaring at him.

There was a knock on the door and Donald shuffled in. The others stared at him.

"Hi, fellow reprobates," he panted, hopping over to them. Before anyone could object, the opposite door opened and a suited man with a briefcase strode in. He placed his case on the table and opened it.

"I am Doctor Baghead's lawyer, Mr Kimkardashian." He took out a paper bag with eyeholes and put it over his hand. "Doctor Baghead regrets he cannot attend, for he has another important engagement."

"Someone vit his head is the shopping doing?" Swedish Hairdresser guffawed.

"Highly amusing." Kimkardashian appeared unruffled. "As I was saying, Doctor Baghead has instructed me to inform you why you are all gathered here."

"He wants an aircut, a pint o gold top an some swimmin lessons," The Rifter cackled. He was a sweaty sort who looked like a used car salesman from Albania.

"But that was not Baghead's plan," Voiceover man corrected. "Instead, he wanted his preposterous team to take over the world."

"Precisely. Doctor Baghead has a foolproof plan for global domination. Carry it out and you'll be rich beyond your wildest dreams."

"In me wildest dreams I'm floating down the Ganges on a giant avocado, being chased by Dame Judi Dench." The Rifter shrugged. "I eat a lot o cheese."

"How do I know this lot won't cramp my style?" Big Nipple glanced at Swedish Hairdreser Man. "The personal grooming freak sounds like Muppet Yoda on acid."

"An I usually work alone," The Rifter added.

"That's cause you smell like a builder's jockstrap that's spent a week under a Bangkok tuk-tuk driver's armpit."

"Oh yeah? Well, check *this* out, mate."

The Rifter let loose an almighty parp that seemed to go on forever. Big Nipple was catapulted over the table by the sheer force and turned an alarming shade of blue. Donald clasped a hand over the top of his snorkel. Swedish Hairdresser pulled out a gigantic hair dryer and deflected the smell towards Voiceover Man.

"The stench of Rifter's fluffy was so overpowering he could not help himself," Voiceover Man gasped, throwing up on Swedish Hairdresser.

"Projectile spew, his superpower is," the villain screamed, trying to scrape it off his face with a straight razor.

"Let me assist." Big Nipple squeezed the huge teat on his forehead and squirted milk into his companion's eye. "Sorry. I've got a terrible sense of direction."

"Stone the bleedin crows," Rifter gagged. "That is truly disgustin!"

"Enough!" Kimkardashian shouted. "There will be plenty of time for fisticuffs later."

"Ere!" The Rifter goggled. "Ow come *you* weren't blown away by me epic pump?"

"I'm a lawyer. It's hard to move me." The suited man pointed at Donald. "What about you, newbie? Got a special talent?"

Donald sank down below the table. When he rose again, he had tousled his hair and wore a fake plastic nose and moustache.

"Not another damned shapeshifter," Big Nipple complained. "You guys are ten-a-penny."

"It works for me, yah? I'm tinking, perhaps, you would like a little tache wax?"

"All right." The lawyer clapped his hands. "Take a seat."

The villains did so.

"I mean, sit *down*." He shuffled some papers. "Turns out there is one obstacle in your path to world domination."

They looked at him expectantly

"Everyone else in the world."

"Say *what* now?"

"That was a joke," the lawyer giggled. "People just don't get my sense of humour. The obstacle, of course, is Ratman. He might be a bit long in his exceedingly buck teeth, but he's the last superhero left."

"Technically, he isn't *really* a superhero." Donald raised his hand, then glanced around at the hostile faces.

"I'll shut up."

"So, Ratman ve vill be killing dead as last year's mullet. No problem."

"Yes, problem," the lawyer corrected. "You see, Doctor Baghead has heard a nasty rumour."

"That's just a rash I get from these tights." Big Nipple went red.

"No. Word on the street is that Ratman's son has superpowers too."

"Ratman hasn't got a son!" Donald tried again. "He has a daughter and a son-in-law. Both perfectly ordinary."

"Son, daughter. Whatever." Kimkardashian sniffed. "To be on the safe side, kill the whole family."

"The rest nodded in agreement," Voiceover man intoned. "It seemed like the perfect plan. Almost *too* perfect."

Donald rolled his eyes.

"Ratman lives near his daughter Lois and her husband, out in Stone Harbor." The lawyer continued. "Go to Lois' house and bump them off. Ratman too, if he's there."

"And if he's not?"

"He's always coming over to bug them. Just hang around. Order a takeaway. Watch the Disney Channel." He stuffed the papers and bag into his briefcase. "Doctor Baghead will contact you with instructions once the deed is done."

Donald sped ahead of the other villains, who had stopped to beat up a mime. He parked out of sight and rushed into his house.

"Lois? Lois!!!"

His wife entered, smoothing down her skirt and patting her hair into place.

"Hello, honey," she stammered. "You're… eh… home early."

She gave a double take.

"Have you been swimming?"

"Pack your bags right now!" Donald commanded. "We have to leave."

"I get it," Lois smiled. "We're going to the beach."

"No. We're going to die." Donald grabbed her arm. "There are four completely insane men on their way to murder us. I really think we should blow this joint."

"Oh, you!" Lois laughed. "Don't you realise what's going on?"

"I'm wearing a mask and snorkel. Do I fucking look like I realise what's going on?"

"This is one of Daddy's tricks. He's trying to force out your hidden superpowers again."

"Of course!" Donald slapped his head. "He pretends to be Doctor Baghead and hires a bunch of no-hopers to spur me into action. That's why he didn't turn up at the meeting. Even with his face covered, I'd have recognised his voice."

"Dad's nothing if not persistent," Lois agreed.

"He's always pulling shit like this. You know what I caught him doing last week? Putting gunpowder into my cigars. Said the shock would bring my abilities to the surface."

"So, it's all sorted, silly."

"It's not sorted," Donald groaned. "I don't *have* superpowers, as you well know. At school, even the kindergarten kids next door picked on me. When I went to the beach, I was so insignificant I had to kick sand in my own face."

"Point taken. I'll call daddy." Lois grabbed her mobile and dialled.

"Hi, pops. Apparently, I'm about to be killed by a bunch of deluded villains intent on taking over the world by nefarious means. Well, yes, they might be Trump supporters but that's not the point… Yes, I know you voted for him… Look, just get over here and save us, all right!"

She looked around.

"Darling? Where have you gone?"

Donald rushed back in, leading The Big Nipple, Swedish Hairdresser, Voiceover Man and The Rifter. He pointed to his wife.

"That's Ratman's daughter, boys. Found her for you."

"Donny! What are you doing?"

"Frogman's the name, babe. Baddest of the bad." He shrugged. "You can shoot her now. And Ratman, when he gets here."

"Wait a minute!" Fats interrupted. "Are you sure this is what went down?"

"Think, Fats," Harlan said. "What happens if Ratman dies?"

"He goes to heaven?"

"Less literally. Lois inherits Bruce Payne's millions."

"Oh, yeah." Fats thought. "But if Lois dies too…"

"All the cash goes to her husband, Donald." Harlan patted his companion's head. "So, you see why he'd want her gone. Besides, she's really annoying."

"That's why Doctor Baghead couldn't be at the meeting. Doctor Baghead is really Donald!"

"Brilliant deduction, Fats." Harlan winked. "But totally wrong."

"Oh." Fats looked crestfallen. "Carry on then."

The villains halted in the middle of the living room, looking uncertain.

"Go on, kill her," Donald repeated. "What's got into you?"

"They won't do it, honey." Lois gave a sinister grin. "They secretly work for me."

"I don't understand."

"I always suspected you married me to get your hands on daddy's money. So, I put together this little ruse." She pouted. "And you failed the test."

"I got it!" Fats' breathed. "Lois is Doctor Baghead! That's why she couldn't be at the meeting."

"Yup. Wrong again."

"Huh?" Fats tugged at his hair. "I'm utterly bamplussed."

"That's not a word," Harlan snapped. "Will you let me finish?"

"I've been working *with* Doctor Baghead," Lois said. "He was the one who convinced me how dishonest you were."

"So, Baghead *is* Bruce Payne! I knew he never liked me!" Donald tore off his mask. "Mind you, nobody does."

"Of course not, sweety. We're going to kill daddy too." Lois blew on her nails. "Then I can spend his money on buff gardeners and hairdos."

"A vonderful beehive I can be giving you," Swedish Hairdresser offered.

"I accept. Dispatch my husband, please."

The villains circled Donald.

"You won't take me without a fight." He took up a boxing stance. "You bunch of dirty rats!"

His assailants stopped. Then they crouched, hands in front of them, making squeaking noises and bouncing up and down.

"What are they doing?" Donald gasped.

"They think they're rats," Lois wailed. "You told them they were rats and now they believe it!"

"I've got a superpower!" Donald looked at his hands in amazement. "OMFG."

"Great," Lois replied sarcastically. "Maybe you can open a pet store."

"I don't think a mere mortal like you should criticize." He turned to the villains. "You're all a bunch of..."

He glanced at Lois.

"What do you call those animals that destroy themselves in huge numbers?"

"Republicans?"

"Lemmings! That's it." He pointed. "You're all a bunch of lemmings."

The villains kept hopping around, staring at him vacantly.

"Not that different from rats, lemmings," Donald observed. "Go on, then. Do what you do best."

The gang turned and scampered out of the front door. There was a sound of squealing tyres and several loud thumps.

Donald turned back to Lois, who backed slowly away.

"Now it's your turn, you snake in the grass."

Lois paused, tongue slipping from between her lips

"Ssssnkakes eat frogs," she hissed.

"Eh? Wait a minute."

"Come into the dining room, froggy." Lois shot out a hand and clamped it over her husband's mouth.

"And that," Harlan said. "Was the end of Donald and the supervillains."

"Lois ate him?" Fats wrinkled his nose. "Gross."

"All except the feet."

"So what happened next?"

Bruce Payne burst in through the window, clutching an egg whisk.

"I'm here to save you, baby," he cried. "Didn't even stop to put my rat suit on. I would have gotten here sooner but I forgot the address."

He glanced around.

"Don't muck about, Lois." He began searching the living room. "I've got a rat-souffle in the oven and I don't want it to go flat."

He was peering over the back of the couch when Lois ran in from the dining room.

"Ssssnkakes eat rats!" She launched herself at him and they disappeared over the couch

"Aaaaargh!" Bruce yelled, raising the egg whisk. "You've dislodged my contact lenses. Take that.. and that… and that."

Finally, he emerged, breathing heavily.

"I didn't know Lois had a python. Especially not one with arms and legs." He crawled into the centre of the room. "I'm getting too old for this shit."

His hand landed by Donald's cigar box, sitting on top of the coffee table. He grabbed one and lit it.

"Well done me, though," he puffed happily. "Still got what it takes. Now where the hell is everyone?"

He coughed violently and shook his head.

"Really must make this my last."

There was a loud boom.

"That's how it transpired, Fats," Harlan said. "Case solved."

"Not really, buddy. We still don't know who Doctor Baghead was."

"I do." Harlan looked smug. "I just pondered to myself, who would inherit the millions if *all* the Paynes died?"

"Who? Who?"

"Alfrick, of course."

"You mean the butler did it?" Fats looked puzzled. "I thought he retired to Burrumbuttock?"

"Came back a few days ago. Claimed he got an anonymous email asking him to attend a surprise birthday party for his long-lost nephew."

"A likely story!" Fats scoffed.

"Of course. I tipped off the cops and they've just arrested him. End of story."

"What a tragic tale of greed and destruction." Fats shook his head. "What will happen to the money now?"

"It goes to Alfrick's only living relative. His long-lost nephew, Fats Norbett."

"What a coincidink. That's my name too."

"It *is* you, Fats. You're a rich man." Harlan looked sincere. "Sorry it ended with your only remaining kin getting locked away."

"It wasn't your fault, Harlan."

"I know. Go start the car."

Fats turned to leave, then stopped.

"If Alfrick was Doctor Baghead, why didn't he turn up at the meeting? Donald wouldn't have recognised his voice after all those years."

"Beats me. Maybe he had a dentist appointment this morning."

"Another coincidink! *You* had a dentist appointment this morning."

"Life is full of them, old friend."

"Poor uncle Alfrick," Fats sighed. "I guess you're my only family now. If *I* died, I'd leave everything to you."

"I was hoping you'd say that. Now let's proceed to the Sinister Clown Museum as planned. I booked you on the Pennywise Sewer Ride of Almost Certain Death."

"I can't *wait*!"

"Me neither, buddy."

"Listen." Fats stopped. "You don't have to wait until I cark it to get rich. I'm perfectly happy to share the dosh with my best mate right now."

He winked at Harlan and skipped towards the car.

"Oh." Harlan went red and hung his head. "You always know how to say the wrong thing at the right time, bud. Guess you live to fight another day."

He pulled a paper bag from his pocket, crumpled it up and threw it behind the nearest bush.

About the Authors

The Friendship Machine

Jan-Andrew Henderson is a Scottish author of 38 childrens, teen, YA and adult fiction and non-fiction books. His novels have been shortlisted for 15 literary awards and he is the winner of the Royal Mail Award, Aurealis Award and Doncaster Book Prize. He lives in Edinburgh and Brisbane and runs the Green Light Literary Rescue Service, offering advice and editing services to writers.

www.janandrewhenderson.com

March of the Monsters

Cliff McNish is a best-selling children's and YA author, winner of The Salford Book Award, The Calderdale Book Award, The Hillingdon Award and the Virginia Readers' Choice Award. His fantasy *Doomspell Trilogy* was translated into 26 languages and sold several hundred thousand copies worldwide.

His novel *Breathe* was voted by The Schools Network of British Librarians as one of the top adult and children's novels of all time. His adult horror has appeared in the *2nd Spectral Book of Horror*, Hellbound Books and Nightjar Press.

www.cliffmcnish.com

The Queer

Graham J. Darling of Metro, Ottawa designs molecules such as the Universe has never seen and demonstrates medieval science and technology to school kids and passers-by. His singular hybrids of diamond-hard science fiction, mythopoeic fantasy and unearthly horror have escaped through *Dark Matter Magazine*, *Pulp Literature* and *Brain Games: Stories to Astonish.*

He also snarfed second prize in the National Fantasy Fan Federation Short Story Contest. Residents are advised to lock their doors and windows, then tune in for survival tips at

https://fiction.grahamjdarling.com

Vampires On Vacation

Mandy Chandler has been working with words for the best part of twenty years as a freelance editor and writer. She has an upcoming running memoir *Worst Parade Ever* and *Join the Worst Parade Ever* and is working on her first novel, a historical fiction based on her grandfather's life - entitled *Nine Lives.*

Find out more info at LinkedIn.com/in/mandychandler or www.facebook.com/mandychandlerauthor

Yes, Prime Minister

Karen Lieversz is a writer of women's fiction and has been a finalist in several Romance Writers of Australia competitions, including the Valerie Parv Award. Her short stories can be found in anthologies published by RWA, Stringybark, and the Hunter Writers Centre..

Karen lives in Sydney with the Australian bush at her doorstep. www.karenlieversz.com and www.Instagram.com/karenlieversz

Clink!

Ishbelle Bee is a writer of poetry, comedy horror and dark fantasy. Her novels *The Singular and Extraordinary Tale of Mirror and Goliath* and *The Contrary Tale of the Butterfly Girl* were published by Angry Robot and she was shortlisted for the Funny Women Writing Awards with her radio play series about a psychotic Victorian butler.

She hopes, one day, someone will be daft enough to produce it. www.ishbellebee.com

Miss Nonny is a C*nt

Brad Cobb is the winner of the Inscape Editor's Prize and his works have appeared in *The Arkansas Review, Fear: A Modern Anthology of Horror and Terror, Relief, Louisiana Review, China Grove, Tulane Review, Blue Crow Magazine, Sobotka Literary Magazine, Bayou Magazine, Dark Gothic Resurrected, Dust Jacket Short Story Journal, Gone Lawn* and *Blue Mountain Review*.

Email him at poma19622000@yahoo.com

Very Well

Nathan Cromwell teaches kung fu in the San Francisco Bay Area and, with fellow members of the Horror Writer's Association's local chapter, gets up to all sorts of adventures (only some involving margaritas). His work has appeared in *Stupefying Stories, Another Realm*, and *Strangely Funny III*. As Ken Hueler, he appeared in *Space & Time, Weirdbook, Weekly Mystery Magazine* and the charity anthology *Tales for the Camp Fire*.

https://kenhueler.wordpress.com

Dances With Scissors (But Slowly)

Edward Palumbo is a graduate of the University of Rhode Island. His fiction, poems, shorts and journalism have appeared in numerous periodicals, journals, e-journals and anthologies, including *Rough Places Plain, Flush Fiction* and *Mystery Weekly*. Ed is a prize-winning poet and playwright. (Poet's Page's Poetry Contest). Ed's literary credo is: if you fall off the horse, get right back on the bicycle. Ed is a disabled writer, suffering depressive psychosis, among other mental and physical afflictions - but he is happy to report that none of the foregoing diminish his love for writing.

Giant Midgets from Neptune

Kyle Owens lives in the Appalachian Highlands and his stories have appeared in *The Bear Creek Gazette, Ahoy Comics, Eastern Iowa*

Review and *Liguorian*, among others. His novel, *A Mountain Christmas Wedding*, was published by Books To Go Now. His cartoon collection, *The New Yorker Hates My Cartoons* is published by Clash Books.

Temporary Cavity

Jodi Stone decided that the pandemic would be a perfect time to get into nursing. She was so wrong. She is in her final year of a four-year nursing degree, where she has been emersed in neurosurgical and intensive care units.

In her spare time, she sits silent in her backyard, watching idly as woodland creatures destroy her deck. Her work has been published by Random House Canada, *Geist*, *Broken Pencil*, *Kiss Machine* and *dANDelion Magazine*.

https://www.instagram.com/stone.rox

That Old Time Religion

Gary Battershell is a writer of speculative fiction, much of it with a humorous slant, who lives in the Ozark Mountains of Arkansas. He retired from teaching college history in 2017 and now writes when he feels like it, which is fairly often. His most recent work can be found in *The Society of Misfit Stories*, *The Fifth Di...* and *Sci Fi Lampoon*.

He receives both support and inspiration from two cats, a dog, a chinchilla, and his long-suffering wife, Emily (not necessarily in that order).

A Helpful Guide to The Men's Bathrooms of R.J. Fortune University

Anthony Neil Smith is the author of numerous crime novels, including *Yellow Medicine*, *Slow Bear* and *The Butcher's Prayer*, as well as many short stories in several genres. He is a professor at Southwest Minnesota State University. You can find more information at

www.anthonyneilsmith.com

What's in a Name?

Marc Shapiro is a Canadian *New York Times* and *Los Angeles Times* bestselling author, poet, short story and comic book writer. He has written and published over 90 unauthorized celebrity biographies. Recent books include *Keanu Reeves Excellent Adventure* and *Beatle Wives: The Women Who Fell In Love With The Men We Fell In Love With* and his debut collection of poetry, *Existential Jibber Jabber*.

He actually makes a living doing this. Don't tell the authorities.

Behind the Blue Door

Dale Sproule has published more than 50 stories including two collections, *Psychedelia Gothique* and *Psychedelia Noir* and two novels *The Human Template* and *Escape from the Carnivorous Forest*.

https://www.dalelsproule.com

Catfish

Geneve Flynn is an award-winning editor and author. She co-edited *Black Cranes: Tales of Unquiet Women* (with Lee Murray) - winner of the Bram Stoker and Shirley Jackson awards and finalist for the British Fantasy, Aurealis, and Australian Shadows awards.

Her short stories have appeared in various markets, including Flame Tree Publishing, Things in the Well, PseudoPod, Crystal Lake Publishing and Black Spot Books. Her poetry appears in the Bram Stoker award-winning collection *Tortured Willows: Bent, Bowed, Unbroken*.

www.geneveflynn.com.au

Prince Charming Finds His Sleeping Beauty

Ann Wuehler is the author of five novels. *Oregon Gothic, House on Clark Boulevard, Aftermath: Boise, Idaho, The Remarkable Women of Brokenheart Lane* and *The Adventures of Grumpy Odin and Sexy Jesus*. She has had short stories published in *Sun Magazine, Ghastling's 10, Ghastling's 13, Litmag, Agony Opera, The Bosphorus Review, Gore,*

World of Myth, Toilet Zone 3, Annus Horribilis and *Musings of the Muses* - among others.

Her plays are in the *Santa Ana River Review* and have been performed at the Stockton Civic Theatre.

Deemed Consent

Robin Pond is a Canadian writer of plays and prose fiction, as well as the mystery novel *Last Voyage*. His works have received hundreds of performances and appeared in numerous anthologies.

Fury Fiona's Fun Facts

Ewan Smith lives in a wee red town in Scotland. Having singularly failed at achieving his initial childhood ambition of growing up to be a cheetah, he is now trying his hand at becoming a writer. This is his first published short story. Or, indeed, his first published anything.

Amoranecrosis

Christopher O Halloran is a milk-slinging, Canadian actor-turned-author, with work published or forthcoming from Hell Bound Books, *Tales to Terrify*, *The Dread Machine* and others. His novelettes can be found in anthologies *Howls from Hell* and *Bloodlines: Four Tales of Familial Fear*.

Fans of stories about vein-removal and Phoenix-women against the patriarchy can visit www.coauthor.ca for stories, reviews, and updates on his upcoming novel, *Pushing Daisy*.

Frogman

What? It's Jan-Andrew Henderson again. He gets to put in another story because it has the same characters as first entry. And because he's the editor.

www.janandrewhenderson@gmail.com

ABOUT THE EDITOR

Jan-Andrew Henderson is a professional member of the Institute of Professional Editors, an industry assessor/mentor for the Queensland Writers Centre, an ambassador for Australia Reads, a peer assessor for the Australian Council for The Arts and a convenor for the Aurealis Awards. He runs the Green Light Literary Rescue Service, offering advice and editing to writers.

He has been published in the UK, USA, Australia, Canada and Europe by Oxford University Press, Collins, Hardcourt Press, Amberley Books, Oetinger Publishing, Mainstream Books, Black and White Publishers, Mlada Fontana, Black Hart and Floris Books.

www.janandrewhenderson.com
www.greenlightliteraryrescueservice.com